SCOUNDRELS
Tales of Greed, Murder and Financial Crimes

EDITED BY
GARY PHILLIPS

Down and Out Books, LLC
3959 Van Dyke Rd, Ste. 265
Lutz, FL 33558
www.DownAndOutBooks.com

The characters and events in this book are fictitious. Any similarity to real persons, living or dead, is coincidental and not intended by the author.

Cover design by JT Lindroos

ISBN-10: 1-937495-22-1
ISBN-13: 978-1-937495-22-0

CONTENTS

Foreword
Scott Phillips
1

What the Creature Hath Built
David Corbett
3

We Shall Overthug
Tyler Dilts
23

The Movement
Travis Richardson
35

The Prophet
Reed Farrel Coleman
59

Arbitraging the Blood Brain Barrier
Eric Stone
73

Occupy This!
SJ Rozan
85

Digital Dingus Four-Point-0
Bob Truluck
95

Easy Money
Pamela Samuels Young
117

The Biggest Fish in Texas
Darrell James
133

Sentence of a Lifetime
Brendan DuBois
147

Leverage
Lono Waiwaiole
151

Eight Ballers
Gary Phillips
165

The $3,300 Loser
Seth Harwood
181

Survivor
Kelli Stanley
193

Contributors
213

Foreword
Scott Phillips

"The business of America is white-collar crime."
    —Calvin Coolidge

"Any man's death diminishes me, because I am involved in mankind. Except for that assclown Ken Lay; fuck him."
    —John Donne

"CHECK THE COFFIN!"
    —Page one of the New York Post on the death of Kenneth Lay

What other group of human beings inspires such a level of hatred and disgust in us as the white collar crook? Lesser thieves don't get the level of hatred and contempt that these high-flying kleptomaniacs generate. Why does a Bernie Madoff or a Kenneth "Kenny Boy" Lay inspire nearly as much opprobrium from the rest of us as a serial killer, a genocidal dictator or a child molester?

Because they're essentially quite similar to the latter two groups. Der Spiegel reported in September of 2011 that the University of St. Gallen in Switzerland measured the egotism and cooperative skills of 28 professional stock traders and compared the results with those of diagnosed psychopaths. The traders outdid the psychopaths in tests measuring selfishness and risk-taking. According to a recent article by journalist Sherree DeCovny in *CFA Magazine*, the rate of clinical pysychopathy among Wall Street suits may be as high as ten per cent. They lack empathy, take risks with other peoples' lives and, having quite casually ruined them, feel no remorse apart from self-pity. Remember those reports of Enron traders laughing and high-fiving at reports of elderly Californians dying from the heat during the blackout of June, 2000, artificially created by Enron's manipulations of the energy markets?

And then there's the self-pity. My hometown produced one of the most horrifying serial killers of the previous century, Dennis "Bind,

Torture, Kill" Rader, who whined in one of his first interviews after being arrested that people didn't appreciate the fact that, now that he was in custody, things were rough for him, too; he'd never go out for pizza again, or walk his dog. Compare that to this gem from Dennis Kozlowski, the former CEO of Tyco who notoriously threw a $2,000,000 birthday party for his wife in Sardinia with a replica of Michelangelo's David carved in ice and urinating Stolichnaya. He said in a 2008 prison interview with writer Peter Hossli, "If I could at least have people stop and think a little bit about how I had been railroading in this process and how unfair and unjust and untrue the process has been toward me..."

All of this is a roundabout way of saying that corporate America is a fitting and rich subject for a book of crime stories. In *Scoundrels: Tales of Greed, Murder and Financial Crime*, Gary Phillips has put together a collection that will enrage, charm and titillate the reader. Some of it will make you laugh, and some of it will make you want to go out and get a nice sharp pike, the kind onto which a freshly guillotined head sticks so nicely; read it and release your inner Jacobin!

What the Creature Hath Built
David Corbett

He wasn't sure how long he'd driven or exactly why he'd stopped. The sign read *Scully's*: wood-shake roof and faux stone cladding, glass-brick windows, almost more a bunker than a bar. Even here, the smell of cinders.

He'd slalomed down the hills in a fury—curving parkways with overgrown medians, sawgrass, wooly sage, towering eucalyptus—glancing again and again in his rearview, watching the sky turn a plummy shade of brown. He'd finally hit traffic near the bottom, joining the stop-and-go, others fleeing. Act normal, he'd told himself, and carried that thought with him now as he pulled on the heavy studded door.

The deep room blurred. Hazy late-day sun behind, murk and glow within.

His eyes adjusted and he spotted two men at the bar, turning toward the doorway to stare. Beyond them, a TV flickered high in the corner, sound muted, the channel set to news of the fire.

"In or out, cap'n," one of them said.

The thick door whispered shut behind him.

A chaos of filthy, half-filled glasses cluttered the length of the bar, each one bearing the filmy remains of some concoction, grown watery from melting ice. A party, Bernardo thought, or its aftermath, wondering if it was just the pair of them here now, left behind.

The nearer of the two had bristly, straw-colored hair and a hefty build, with a sunburn that stopped midway up his face like a soot line. The eyes were small and lifeless, despite the welcoming smile. He wore painter pants and a white *guayabera* with embroidered tracery down the front.

The other was knobby and tall with a backdraft of nutmeg hair curling away from his brow. He too wore a billowing shirt, adorned with hula girls and pineapples.

Taken together they looked like refugees from a redneck cruise. That or a Baja wedding.

"Bartender around?" Bernardo pulled back a stool, tried to arrange himself on it with conviction.

"You mean Henry," the thin one said. A smoker's voice, like a wasp in a jar.

"I suppose I do." Despite himself, Bernardo glanced up at the TV, an unbeliever beholding a vision. An aerial shot, houses engulfed in flame. Boiling smoke. "Or Scully. Whoever."

"Scully's just the name on the sign." Sunburn offered that same blank smile. "Place been through a couple hands since Ol' Scully left the scene. New owner tends bar himself sometimes, name is Henry."

Bernardo surveyed the derelict glassware. "Whoever he is, looks like he's been busy."

"Hell, Henry's got nothing to do with this. Had to run, square away the homefront, told us to help ourselves. We took him kinda literal. You heard about the fires."

"Yeah." Bernardo was trembling. The surface of the bar felt sticky with grit. "Sure."

"In Henry's regrettable absence, Eddie here is pouring." Sunburn clapped his hands. "Eduardo, where's your manners?"

The rangy one jumped up and bit back a grin as he scuttled around to the other side of the bar. The state of things back there was worse yet—ravaged lemons, eggshells cradling unused yolks, maraschino cherries bleeding into the sink. Bernardo guessed the two characters had been here alone for a while.

"Name's Glendon." The sunburned one stuck out his hand.

Bernardo took it, felt the intimate leathery calluses. "Mike."

Glendon, still in Bernardo's grip, thumbed his lighter's flint wheel with the other hand, caught a flame, lit his cigarette. Taking a deep drag, he smiled through his exhale. "Welcome to Scully's, Mike."

"Name your poison." Eddie leaned forward, fingering a cigarette from Glendon's pack. Smoking prohibitions clearly had no truck here. "Happy hour's never been happier."

The two men laughed. Bernardo could not remember ever feeling so tired.

Glendon added, "Least not since we got rid of Bitchy Miss High Hat."

Eddie chuckled, lit up. "Tell him the story."

"Oh, he don't want to hear—"

"C'mon, tell him the damn story."

Glendon tapped some ash onto the floor. "About fifteen minutes before you got here, Mike, there was this woman sitting right where you are. Kinda full of herself, if you know what I mean. Had an attitude."

"Thought she was tits and turmoil," Eddie said.

"We're all just sitting here watching the news," Glendon continued, "and there was talk about this and that and finally some damn thing about *trauma*—you know, the people who stand to lose everything up there, oh boo hoo. Anyways, this woman, she apparently thinks 'trauma' is some kinda cue. Like we'd just been sitting around waiting to hear all about her sad and screwed-up life."

"Says, 'Oh, I know about that,'" Eddie chimed in. "'I know about trauma,' like it's someplace with a tour. Graceland. The Alamo."

"Anyway, off she goes. Tells us some guy busted into her house one night, held her at knifepoint for two hours—so she said, God only knows if it's true—but giving her the benefit of the goddamn doubt and assuming, yes, some nitwit snuck into her house, put a blade to her throat, she just—now these is her words, not mine—'did what she always does.'"

"Always," Eddie noted, "meaning with damn near every man she meets."

"That was kinda the gist," Glendon agreed. "Like the guy's having a knife wasn't the issue. The fact he was male and standing there was the damn issue."

"Not the most charming woman on the planet," Eddie said.

"Be that as it may," Glendon said, "the story goes on and the meaning of 'what she always does' becomes a little clearer. She didn't fight. She didn't just lie there and let him get it over with. She whined and wheedled and basically just nagged the poor bastard out of the house."

"Got so sick of the sound of her voice," Eddie said, "just turned around and left."

"And Eddie and me, we're sitting here listening to this, wondering why the hell any sane woman would admit to such, at which point suave Eduardo here—"

Eddie grinned. "Sometimes I don't know when to bite my tongue."

"He looks this ogress dead in the eye and says, 'You mean to tell me, the point of the goddamn story is not even a rapist would fuck ya?'"

They broke into a helpless spate of laughter, Glendon slapping the bar and spewing smoke, Eddie shivering with the giggles. Bernardo worked up a go-along smile.

Glendon wiped away a tear. "Where's our manners? Seriously, Mike, have a drink. Eddie here's quite the mixologist. Tequila gimlet, rum alexander, sloe gin rickey—if he don't know how to slap it together, he'll look it up in the *Mr. Boston*. Or just improvise." Another laugh, low and chesty. "He does like to improvise."

Bernardo surveyed the glowing shelves behind the bar, noticed the conspicuous absences—Courvoisier, Bushmills, Boodles, Pernod—the distinctive bottles plucked from their spots and abandoned elsewhere. The gaps in the backlit array conjured a strange feeling of lonesomeness, like he was looking at the future.

He spotted his brand finally. "Crown Royal," he said, "double, neat. Water back. If you don't mind."

A kind of nervous attention rose in Glendon's face, like a blush beneath the sunburn, stopping at the eyes. "Mind? Eddie, you mind?"

Eddie stared. "I can mix you a first-rate cocktail." The scratchy voice low, not inviting. "Don't mind the glassware, plenty more in back. Nothing *but* fucking glasses in back."

They both eyed Bernardo. He was spoiling the party. The hair on his neck bristled, he knew what came next—a flinch, a reckless grin, a swing. Leave, he thought, too weary to move. "Sure. Sorry." He glanced back and forth, one man, the other. "How about an old fashioned."

Like that, Eddie clicked back to affable. "Now you're talking." He rapped the top of the bar. "Crown Royal your brand, I take it. Top shelf Canadian, nice rye. Should work well."

Drunks and their mood swings, Bernardo thought. He felt like he was looking up from underwater. "If you would."

Eddie chafed his hands and went to it. Bernardo glanced up at the TV again. Same image, different angle, the view from a hovering chopper. Flame and smoke and devastation.

"So what line of work you in, Mike?" Glendon lifted a nearby glass, thought better of it, nudged it aside and chose another.

Bernardo lowered his gaze from the TV. "Real estate," he said, the lie bubbling up from nowhere he could name. He almost laughed, the irony.

Eddie and Glendon exchanged another glance.

"Huh," Glendon said. "Seriously."

"Yeah. Seriously. That a problem?"

Glendon studied him, as though taking his measure. "I dunno, Mike. Build like yours?" He gestured to suggest the arms, the chest. "I woulda figured you for a cop. Firefighter maybe."

Eddie mulled an orange slice and cherry in the bottom of a glass, tossed in a sugar cube, dashed in bitters. "But if he was a firefighter, Glendon, he'd be up there on the hill, you know, fighting the goddamn fire. Cops no doubt are all up there too."

The ensuing silence lingered. Glendon lifted the plastic sword from his nameless cocktail, plucked the cherry off it with his teeth. "Touché, Eddie. Looks can deceive. Am I right, Mike?"

* * *

Six months earlier, Leeanne had buzzed his cell mid-shift at the station house, telling him they had to meet. "Rickshaw, booth near the back. I'm here now. Please."

Eight years they'd been married, he'd never heard that voice.

He begged off a civilian volunteer seminar on triage and hoofed over to the restaurant in his blues, six blocks away. Sinewy and freckled, cornsilk blond, Leeanne was already working on her third Tanq & T as he sat down. "Hey," she whispered, finger-brushing her bangs.

The tiny smiling waitress appeared. Her nameplate read May but Bernardo, a regular, knew her as Meifeng. Beautiful wind. She took his order—coffee, black, two sugars—then scooted out of earshot.

"You may want something stiffer," Leeanne said.

She was the scrappiest, sunniest woman he knew, poster girl for the ongoing experiment known to the world as California, but in that moment he saw thunderheads behind her eyes.

"What's this about?"

Things had taken a turn between them a little over two years before, when she teamed up with Coughlin and his mortgage operation. She began having grand ideas, all anchored to money. Bernardo felt all but certain she and Coughlin were catting around, the only thing keeping her in the marriage being a half million in shared equity on the house in Montclair and his healthcare package through the IAFF. But that was okay; he was hardly a saint himself.

"How much cash," she said, "can you put your hands on right now?"

"That's an answer?"

The coffee arrived. They smiled grimly and asked for more time with the menus. Beautiful Wind rushed away.

"You know those properties I told you about up in Black Diamond?"

What he'd known, up to that moment, was that she and Coughlin had 'invested' in a half dozen languishing McMiniMansions on a cul de sac in the toniest new enclave up near the Mt. Diablo foothills. Called Black Diamond Estates, the development sat backed up against a protected wilderness, which, to men of his profession, meant fire country. She'd promised him they'd insured wisely.

But what he learned that day, his stomach shrinking to peach-pit dimensions as she explained, was that they'd used straw buyers on title—creative paperwork, fake occupations and incomes plucked from thin air—no money down, teaser-rate monthlies. She said everyone had done it, only a fool wouldn't. Join the stampede or get trampled. "Besides," she said, "high-end demand is inelastic." Geniuses and their jargon.

The goal was to let the straw buyers enjoy the extravagant houses, pay the monthlies on the underlying notes as rent, while Leeanne and Coughlin worked to flip the properties before the balloon payments hit. Once the houses rolled over, everyone would earn points on the windfall.

That all seemed a cruel joke now. The economy hadn't just hit a ditch, it was cratering. Four of the six bogus owners were jobless or chasing ghost commissions. They couldn't make the monthly nut and were threatening mutiny.

"I don't get it," he said. "They've got no stake. Why not just walk away, hand the damn things back to the bank?"

"It'll tank their credit. Seven years in financial purgatory's a lot to ask."

"Work a short sale."

"Same deal, Mike. You think we haven't thought this through?"

"Honestly?"

"State passed a new law this year—bank agrees to a short sale, they can't go after the difference between the sale price and the amount of the note. That's frozen things up. Lenders are hanging tough."

"Then I'm unclear on what 'mutiny' means."

She downed the rest of her gin and tonic, shook the ice, went after the dregs. "Ever hear of the Financial Fraud Enforcement Task Force?"

Bernardo took a quick glance outside the booth, making sure no one was listening in. "That's FBI. You mean these *prestanombres* of yours would rather wear a snitch jacket than botch their credit? Where did you find these toads?"

"Coughlin's golfing buddies. One sells Chris Craft. Another, I dunno, has a car lot out in Turlock I think. The others are in the biz."

"Played by your own kind."

"Don't start, Mike, okay? Besides, you're kinda in the biz yourself, yeah?"

One of the perks about life as a firefighter, especially in Contra Costa, was the time and means it gave you to pursue a second career. Given his rank and seniority, Bernardo's salary topped two hundred grand, at a job that amounted to working out, eating well, and tagging along on the pumper truck to watch paramedics deal with accident victims. With all the innovations in construction, house fires were almost history; if the crews fought a blaze, it was almost always in the grassy hills out in the tractless boonies.

He worked on the side renovating fixer-uppers, and thus had the same flip mentality she did, except he aimed somewhat lower: neglected Craftsman bungalows in west county, Martinez and San Pablo and Richmond. He liked the work, the physicality of it, the demands it placed on your concentration; tearing out the old knob-and-tube, running new wire through the walls, stripping the roof, taking a crowbar and hammer to the ancient cabinets, slamming in new sinks and shower stalls, bolting the foundation, sanding, caulking, painting. End of the day, you felt like something had happened.

"How much are we talking?"

She was staring at her placemat, the Chinese zodiac. Year of the Rabbit, a time for peace and prosperity. "One point two-five."

A needle-like numbness tinged his skin. "A hundred twenty-five grand?" He did a quick mental tally, working it out. Six loans, all top of market. "That per month or..."

She fiddled with her glass then leaned out of the booth, scoured the room for May the waitress, gestured for a refill.

"Leeanne—"

She looked ready to get hit. He felt ready to oblige her.

"One point two-five mil."

The floor buckled. "How many fucking months—"

"Don't be an ass, Mike. Keep it down."

"How stupid could you two—"

"The loan desks are crazy, all the repos and walkbacks and REOs, we figured we had time."

"No way I can put my hands—"

"I'm not asking for it all, just—"

"Even if I did, you'd just be caught up. What about next month, the month after—"

"Don't lecture me."

"Don't come begging."

He got up to leave. She latched onto his wrist. "Mike, don't. You can't." She swallowed hard. "One of the houses is in my name."

He cocked his head like an Airedale, wondering if he'd heard right. She just stared, her eyes locked on his, and for some reason he flashed on the last time they'd gone at it, down in the den, watching *The Naked Kiss* on IFC, a mid-flick urge, both of them half in the bag, pink sweats yanked down from her hips, one knee on the sofa, one foot on the floor, him pounding away from behind as she glanced over her shoulder, tucking her hair behind her ear, waiting for him to finish. For better or for worse, till death.

The waitress delivered the Tanq & T, took the empty away, no pretense of ordering lunch anymore.

"You were gonna tell me this when?" California was a community property state. He was on the hook right with her.

She shrugged, scraped at her bangs, drank.

"We'll call a lawyer."

"There's no bankruptcy protection for fraud, Mike."

Now he really, truly wanted to pop her.

"I'm not gonna waste time saying I'm sorry, because time's what we haven't got. But money buys time. I mean it, I don't need the whole amount. But I need something. We do."

Nice touch, he thought, hating her. "No way I can pony up even a fraction of that kinda money."

She gazed into her glass like it was a tunnel, a way out. "Then I need to hear some ideas, hon. Like, now."

* * *

"What's this?"

The cocktail was in a bucket glass, bits of salvaged orange and cherry floating in shaved ice. Smell of whiskey but something else, something medicinal.

Eddie beamed, leaning forward. "I call it a Dirty Rotten Secret." He looked like the kid at the birthday party everybody's scared of.

"I thought you were making a Crown Royal old-fashioned."

"I did. More or less. Just added a Benedictine floater, plus some of this stuff." He held up a bottle of something called Aperol.

Glendon wagged a finger. "I told you he liked to improvise."

"Made from a blend of rhubarb, cinchona, genziana," Eddie recited, reading from the label, "and a secret combination of herbs."

Bernardo stirred the cocktail so the weird liqueurs blended a bit better with the whiskey. He needed something, his nerves were a mess. If this was it, bottom's up. "Thanks," he said, and drank. It tasted like something worked up by his little league buddies after a raid of the parental liquor cabinet. He tried not to wince.

"I'm still working on the right proportions," Eddie admitted.

"It's fine." Bernardo resisted an urge to spit. "Might think about easing back a touch on the rhubarb."

"Work in progress," Eddie said.

"Isn't everything."

* * *

Looking back, he would wonder at how even bad love reasserts itself, insinuates itself into the gentler regions of memory, sweet-talks your conscience, reminding two people that despite all the resentment, the unanswered want, the squandered hope, they're still bound together. All it takes is a threat from outside—the messy, cruel, indifferent world—to re-knot the ropes, lash you together tighter than ever. No love was perfect, nor needed to be. What family he had was her. You could talk it through with anyone you wanted—lawyer, shrink, priest, the ER nurse you met at a fundraiser who dragged you back to her place—it was all just that, talk. Better to stand pat with the unhappy past than stagger blind into the shapeless future.

And once he agreed to help, Leeanne did soften a bit.

He was assistant treasurer for his local, and as such served as the hands-on man. They were gearing up for elections across the county— mayor and council races in five key cities, all trying to arm-twist concessions in pensions, benefits, wages, staffing—and the war chests were flush. They had five PACs, two held jointly with the police union, one with the IBEW, and were constantly shuffling money around to fund this candidate or that, and make the money trail hard to figure. The state lacked the manpower to audit, and the self-reporting was farcical. Thousands routinely tumbled out of one fund, suddenly materialized in another, the amounts rarely if ever squaring. If that ever became a problem they'd hang their heads and admit to being sloppy. Hey, they were heroes, not abacus jockeys.

But the PAC accounts afforded at best seventy grand, and that had to be plucked from several different places after a lot of sleight-of-hand, phantom transfers of varying amounts, a head-scratching smokescreen.

If he pilfered any more than that it'd stand out as a fistful of missing change even to a bunch of lunks.

That meant he had to turn to the operating accounts—non-interest bearing money funds for day-to-day operations held by various local banks. He mocked up work orders for station-house repairs and renovations, shoved them in a file he buried in a cabinet, buying in to Leeanne's theory that all they needed was time.

The thing about thievery, he discovered, is that once you make a few moves and don't get caught, you get a bit more bold, which is to say clever, otherwise known as reckless. He managed to scratch up just shy of three-hundred-fifty grand, more than he'd ever thought he could realistically bring to the table. Leeanne seemed pleased, and showed it with a bit more wag in her tail.

But if the money bought them time, that was all it bought. A developer Coughlin knew supposedly hoped to muscle the lenders into a package deal for a majority share of the enclave, but if such a maneuver was ever real it quickly turned to myth. After that, isolated buyers appeared and vanished like trick-or-treaters, and what money they offered was always a joke. Not even the hard money boys were stepping up; they knew all they had to do was wait.

Meanwhile, a citizens group was crowing for accountability in the union PAC funds and out of the blue the assistant chief asked for a work-up on a new roof for Station House 5, including funds on hand. And the FBI, of course, lurked in the wings.

I need to hear some ideas. Which was how Fireman Mike came up with Plan B.

* * *

"Real estate," Glendon said, like it was the name of a despised aunt. He sat with his arms twined across his paunch. "Not to beat a dead horse, Mike, but I gotta tell ya, you just don't fit my picture."

Bernardo took another sip of Eddie's concoction. God help me, he thought, getting used to the taste. "Not sure I can do much about that, Glendon." Sensing that this might seem snide, he added, "I like to work out."

"Real estate mucks I know," Glendon said, "how should I put this. Fat boys and fairies."

Eddie, looking up at the TV, nodded. "Not to put too fine a point on it."

The crawl at the bottom of the screen reported that the entire Black Diamond enclave had been evacuated. Every property on the perimeter was now involved, total losses. Bernardo knew he should feel relieved, but instead the weariness just burrowed deeper.

"A cleansing fire." It was Glendon, arms still wrapped across his belly, eyes glued to the TV screen.

Eddie said, "That'd be the Bible?"

"The Bible, or something like it." Glendon tapped out another cigarette, lipped it, struck a flame from his lighter. "And God shall come as a cleansing fire, not to consume the creature, but what the creature hath built—of wood, of hay and chaff."

"Damn straight." Eddie set his chin on his arms, still peering at the screen.

"Everything you need to know about property," Glendon said, pointing at the TV with his cigarette, "you can learn from watching that right there."

Bernardo reached for his cocktail but couldn't quite bring himself to drink.

"People who work in real estate," Glendon went on, "they don't make nothing, they don't fix nothing, they just keep selling the same chunk of dirt and wood over and over so they can take a bigger cut. They don't add value, just add cost. And who ends up having to pay for that? Not them. Never them. Biggest racket there is. People need a place to live, a home for themselves and their families, but what they get, day after day after goddamn day, is cheated."

"Brought down the whole damn economy," Eddie said, "bankers and real estate people. Politicians in their pocket."

Bernardo, now regretting his lie, considered telling them what he really did for the bulk of his money, but he wasn't sure at this point what difference it would make. He felt like he'd walked in on an argument that had started long before he'd arrived, and would continue long after he'd left, if he was given that chance. A quick glance for weapons discovered only the paring knife behind the bar—no truncheon near the cash register, no pistol or shotgun that he could see. He told himself to relax.

"Like I say, don't mean nothing personal, Mike. But people are angry. Right, left, middle, they're pissed. They know the treasure is gone. And they know who took it."

Bernardo realized silence was no longer an option, but neither was ass-kissing. "Look," he began, "the economy's not simple. It's like the weather. More factors than you can think of, so many unknowns. The tiniest thing can have the strangest consequences." He felt his heart ticking inside his chest, his hands felt hot. "Know how many supercomputers the National Weather Service uses? Any idea how massive the system of differential equations is they need to predict whether it's sunshine tomorrow or rain? The answer they come up with, it's just an approximation, it's guesswork. But that doesn't make it random. Any more than the wind is random. There's answers, is what I mean, even if we don't always like what they are."

Stop talking, he told himself. Say thanks for the drink, put down some money if they ask for it, get up and walk out. Something inside him, though, cautioned that a little more defraying of the tension might be wise before he made a move for the door.

The two men studied him, their faces blank. Smoke from Glendon's cigarette curled upward.

"You guys ever hear of the Diablo winds?"

* * *

He'd explained it to Coughlin and Leeanne, when it became clear only a disaster could save them. The Diablos, northern California cousins of the Santa Anas, came every spring and fall, the latter season particularly dangerous because of so much buildup through the drought months of fire-ready vegetation—flashy fuel, it was called. The winds developed from high pressure systems to the east, off the sunbaked Great Basin, the air squashed by storms over Nevada and Idaho, with low pressure systems squatting off the coast, pulling like gravity, dragging the winds west through the Sierra canyons, down the arid foothills and across the scalding central valley—perfect fire weather. Case in point: the Oakland hills disaster.

And the Black Diamond layout was particularly ripe: high parched grass in steep ravines just beyond the enclave, with dense pockets of non-native eucalyptus, ornamental clumps of wooly sage, sawgrass. The place was landscaped in tinder.

They met to talk through the final details at Leeanne's property, a sprawling four-thousand-foot monument to misbegotten greed: long granite counters and towering cherry cabinets, beveled glasswork and Florizel parquetry with its churchy accents and eerie 3D feel. More to the point, it sat in precisely the right place, at the cul de sac's tip, right at the mouth of a deep arroyo winnowing east. Stand out there on the patio, the furnace-like wind almost knocked you down.

Coughlin looked like he'd stepped off the back nine, moussed and tan, with hints of work around the eyes, that sandblasted squint. Leeanne wore white—sundress and sandals, a billowing hat—an outfit Bernardo remembered from a garden party at a Livermore vineyard years before. Despite the incongruity, she looked good. She looked happy.

"I've been tracking the weather service," he said. "It's this week or never. Today's likely best."

"Unless I'm missing something," Coughlin said, a bloated voice honed on cold calls, "you're leaving a lot up to random chance."

"Wind's not random," Bernardo said, "neither are fires. I don't believe in luck. There's planning, and then there's ignorance and miscalculation. Been plenty of that already, by my reckoning."

Coughlin started to fire back but Leeanne cut him short with a look. They'd already decided it was Bernardo's show, no point sniping. He needed to slip money back into the operating fund and PAC accounts, and fast. Leeanne and Coughlin needed to be able to walk-away with everyone's credit intact and nothing to trigger audits on the underlying loans. The houses were insured at replacement value, including contents, and they'd mocked up invoices for furnishings far in excess of what was there. That would be their cushion, their walk-away money. And that meant whatever happened, it had to be a total loss—no salvage, no rebuilding, no sifting through the wreckage by bean counters, arson wonks. It had to be a holocaust. Leeanne and her seven dwarves would slip away, collect a measly couple hundred grand for some made-up finery while the banks and insurance companies squared off over the big money. Let the lawyers hammer away. Can't foreclose on an ash heap.

Because arson was easier to allege than prove, Bernardo felt certain he could rig things, not perfectly, no such thing, but create enough of a nightmare any foot-dragging would look cruel and venal, justifying a claim of bad faith. The insurers would waive off the bother. To get there he needed to create both interior and exterior points of origin without making it look too obvious what had happened. An accident triggered by a catastrophe—who couldn't comprehend that? Coughlin assured him the rest of the dunces had signed on. But Bernardo also knew, if things went south, he'd be the one left to hang.

The solution, he decided, was linseed oil, mixed with nitrocellulose, the touchy stuff film stock used to be made of, back in the days of projector room fires. The oil and oxidizer combined to make an unparalleled varnish, but the mix was also insidiously flammable. The

One Meridian Plaza fire, caused by spontaneous combustion of rags left piled at the worksite, killed three Philadelphia firefighters. And that risk of fatality, given how hot and fast the fire would spread, would push the engine crews toward containment—they'd let the houses already involved burn out.

"You can't have the fire start inside the house, not with the loan in arrears the way it is. But if the fire starts outside, moves close, and triggers secondary combustion in here—that's the way to go." Bernardo fingered the smooth, elaborate carvings in the cabinetry, an interlocking design with deep relief, a pattern called Portland Scroll—nothing like what he was used to in the houses he rebuilt. "Bad enough we haven't got time to strip every house, just this one. But if it burns the way it should, the rest are close enough along the cul de sac, all nestled in this little pocket, they should all go up pretty quick."

The three got to work, donning coveralls, sanding off the old finish in three of the rooms, not worrying about completion, just making it look like they'd made a good start. Now and then they practiced aloud the story they'd tell the insurers: Leeanne had decided to upgrade, hoping the improvements would help move the property quicker—high-end demand being, after all, inelastic. When she saw the grass fires barreling toward her from the hills, she'd had no time to store the rags properly, needing to get out while she could. Keep it simple, Bernardo told her. A mistake, especially in the face of danger, doesn't equal motive. Hold that thought.

Three hours passed. Coughlin was the first to bag. "I'll leave it to you two to wrap this up." He combed his hair in the doorway, and Bernardo doubted he'd ever hated him more.

Eventually Leeanne stepped out of her coveralls as Bernardo arranged the rags. This part was critical—piled too close, they'd lack the air needed to ignite, too loose and they wouldn't generate sufficient heat. He dragged the containers with the rest of the mixture near, so once the flames hit there'd be no doubt the stuff would catch. The fire outside would follow its natural path, the ravine like a funnel of boiling wind, plus all the sun-shriveled grass and bark and leafage. Once flame reached the house, with the pile of oil-soaked rags inside, it would go up quick, take the neighboring houses with it, and after them the rest of the cul de sac. As for all the other houses up here—well, that was up to the wind. The wind and the fact that, strapped for funds, the county had closed the two nearest firehouses.

He was still in his coveralls finishing up when he felt Leeanne's hand settle gently on his arm. "Mike, I know I've been short in the sorry department, but that's not because I'm ungrateful." She straightened the sundress, shouldered her handbag. The broad-rimmed hat rested like a giant lily on a nearby table. "I know this is all on me. Without your help, we'd be screwed. I don't know how to thank you."

She eased up on tiptoe, left hand on his shoulder, lips pursed. Despite the stinging oily scent of the varnish, the worry knotted up in his midriff, he readied himself for her kiss. They'd regained a little juice the past few weeks, the old slap and tickle. And yet something felt off. Maybe it was the fact her eyes stayed open, maybe it was the fact she'd only balanced herself with the left hand, the right hand free, but when the knife came out of her purse Bernardo had her wrist locked tight almost instantly. He twisted outward, her face contorted in pain. The knife dropped.

She grimaced. "You're hurting me."

He let her go, leaned down to pick up the knife, and she was on him with a fury he'd never seen. Hammering with her fists, raging against the sheer injustice of her lousy life. Of course he had to die—the weak link, last man in, the one who didn't understand that the point was to be free and that meant money. Fireman Mike, Mister Fixer-Upper. The fists turned to fingernails, she clawed at his eyes, a mewling growl in her throat that came from some part of her he didn't know and at last he felt afraid.

The knife went in easily, and he wasn't even sure at first where his hand was or what he'd done. But she winced as though from a punch, buckled, backed away, holding her side. The blood came quick, bubbling between her fingers—he'd cut an artery—a giant smear on the sundress where she pressed her hand.

He remembered that very first night: dinner at Enoteca, champagne with appetizers, a velvety Barolo with the entrees, Armagnac with espresso and dessert, then speeding in her Beamer ragtop to the condo in Lafayette, her unbuckling and unzipping him, stroking him as she drove, gripping him, that distinctly feminine brand of ownership, then almost stumbling up the walkway to her door, his pants slipping to mid-hip, a couple of teenagers whisper-giggling around the pool—he pressed her against the door as she worked the key, then the two of them tumbled inside, he lifted her off her feet in the entry, her legs locked tight around his waist as he entered her, a good hard hello, a shot across the bow of love, pushing, pushing as she whispered—*yeah, come on, yeah, Mike, yeah, give it to me*—and he exploded within her then as the knife did now, for he'd stepped in close to stab, stab again.

She did not fight or even cry out. Call it what remained of their marriage, he supposed, that silence. The blame was hers, after all. Except, of course, it wasn't. Not hers alone. She'd made sure of that.

She clutched his arm as she fell, no strength in the grip, dropping raggedly to the floor. She bled out—legs tangled, breaths quick and shallow, mouth open, eyes like glass. His rage dissolved, leaving behind a regret he felt in his body like a need to lie down. And from somewhere in the back of his mind, a flicker of dread, like lightning spotted through trees.

After a moment he sensed it, someone there, and glanced up. Coughlin stood in the coved entrance to the room, staring. At her. His protégé, his accomplice, his squeeze. He too held a knife, had come back as part of the plan, finish it, except he'd come too late—cowardice or second thoughts or who knew what? Finally his gaze rose, their eyes met and he dropped the knife, got halfway to the door. Bernardo would feel a little embarrassed by how hard and deep he ripped the blade across the man's throat, damn near severing his head. And as Bernardo crouched against the wall, eyeing what he'd done, his mind clicked like a machine, trying to remember what fire would destroy and what it wouldn't.

* * *

"Glendon, fetch me some ice from the walk-in, will ya?"

The larger man belched, glanced at the welter of glassware atop the bar, and slid off his stool. "Make me something normal while I'm gone, Eduardo. Early Times, rocks, with a splash. See if that's artistic enough for your newfound sensibilities."

Once Glendon was gone Eddie leaned forward, rested his elbows on the bar. "Don't make nothing out of all his guff about real estate," Eddie said quietly. "He's just kinda bitter."

Bernardo, from manners as much as thirst, sipped his drink. The flavor was evolving. "About what?"

Eddie had gone off somewhere in his mind. He looked like he was struggling with a calculation—carry the seven, divide by five. Snapping back: "Excuse me?"

"Bitter about what?"

"Oh him and me, we used to work at the shipyard over in Richmond. Pipefitters, the both of us. Good work, union wage, but that's all gone. This country ain't got use for the workingman no more. Not less he's Mexican. Anyhoot, we been scraping by, doing a little this, a little that, and we stumbled on this thing called Cash for Keys—you heard about this?"

Now it was Bernardo's turn to wander off. He was back up the hill, outside the house, following through on the plan, figuring even with two bodies to incinerate the surest path to a big mistake would be to change things up. Clutching a bag of M-80s and cherry bombs, he trotted out toward the parched hills rising up behind the property. The knee-high grass, dry as straw, rustled and hissed in the westerly gusts keening through the ravine, the wind blasting hot and dry against his skin. He glanced around, here and there a scrub oak but mostly eucalyptus, God's gift to fire.

"It's this program through the banks," Eddie said, "Cash for Keys, all these empty houses, the foreclosure mess. Well, you leave them untended, you're just asking for trouble. Damn gangs move in, set up grow houses or meth labs, jerry rig the electric—I seen jumper cables trailing down from a high tension wire and hooked up to a junction box, I'm not making that up. Juice for all the lights you need, grow marijuana." He pronounced it *merry wanna*. "But there's some folks, they just need a place to stay, you know? Glendon and me, we had some rough luck lately, we're just looking for a roof over our heads as we settle up accounts, you know, ride out this damn economy. And once we got good and comfortable in this one place—"

"Squatters," Bernardo said, regretting it instantly.

"That's a damn unpleasant word." Eddie seemed genuinely offended.

"Sorry, I didn't mean it that way. I just..." He shrugged, lifted his cocktail, Dirty Rotten Secret, rattled the ice in appreciation. "I'm sorry."

He knew the problem too well. You bought a house on spec, property underwater, previous owners walked away, and you're hoping for an easy rehab and then a quick flip. But you head on over to the address and find there's someone living there, people no one's ever talked to or heard of. Whole clans—kids, cousins, grandparents, goats.

"We weren't taking advantage. We kept the place up—repaired the plumbing in the kitchen, the brass pipes were all corroded. Rewired the living room, there was an outlet that'd shorted out, faceplate all black. Picked the apples off the ground so they don't attract rats, put out poison for the snails, must've killed a gazillion spiders. Bagged up the garbage, touch of paint here and there. Bank saw what we were doing, they were grateful. Woman comes over, V-P of something, got her card in my wallet, introduces herself, says we keep the place up the way we're doing, we'll get a thousand crisp ones a month."

Hidden in a stand of eucalyptus, he began lighting cherry bomb fuses—major cause of wildfires, fireworks set off in tinder-dry conditions. Sure enough—*boom*—and a patch of grass caught, the flames licked up the nearest tree, the ratty bark glowing into ember then a pop, a spark, ignition. He tossed the remaining firecrackers around and headed back, hearing the staccato explosions behind him like gunfire as he ran.

"And okay," Eddie continued, "so we saw an opportunity, put down roots in more than one house. What's the crime in that? We was looking after each place, we deserved every god damn check. Oh but the neighbors, they start bitching about property values. They start moaning about strangers with no investment in the community and how we're, like, scamming the system. And they get this local real estate agent, Mister Plumpfuck from Pussyville, got several houses up for sale in that neighborhood, and he decides he's gonna ride to the rescue—gathers signatures on a petition, goes on TV, identifies the houses and the banks, figuring, 'Hey, this here's cheap publicity for me, I'll score big with the locals, get me a dozen new clients.' Next thing you know, me and Glendon, we get the heave. Sheriff telling us we got thirty minutes to quit the premises, camera crews on hand, details at eleven. So there we are, on the street, no roof over our heads, nothing."

Back inside the house, he tried not to look at Leeanne or Coughlin as he peeled off the coveralls and set them beside the stack of rags, soaked in linseed oil. The rags were already beginning to smolder, a thin acrid plume of smoke rising from the pile. Looking out the patio door, he saw the hillside flames gaining ground, the fire creating its own weather—fire whirls, hairpin vortices, forward bursts—gathering speed, windswept cinders or whole tree branches blazing away, exploding, rocketing into the parched yard, onto the roof, hurled by the fire's own force. Given the contour of the hillside, the strength and direction of the wind channeling through the arroyos, its dryness and heat, the pressure differential between inland hills and coastal plain, the tonnage of fuel load provided by the eucalyptus and scrub oak, the sawgrass and wooly sage, the ratio of surface area to volume for every desiccated twig, the flash point of all that withered vegetation—flashy fuel—in conjunction with the blistering heat, the severity of the drought conditions and the rate of acceleration for the downhill flames, the topography of the rags, the chemistry of the oil and nitrocellulose, its auto-ignition temperature, the abundance of interior wood, the precise moment of the first 9-1-1 call, the response time required for an engine crew to make it up the switchback parkways from a firehouse thirty-five miles away, the tactical on-scene decisions made, primacy of evacuation, containment versus combat, what structures if any to save, which to surrender. It wasn't luck, it wasn't random. It was the inscrutable calculus of complexity, a world beyond our knowing. It was the wind.

"So that's why Glendon's got a hair up his hind parts about real estate agents. Me too, truth be told. But like he said, don't take it personal. We're not on some kinda rampage."

Good for you, Bernardo thought, remembering the arrangement of the bodies as he'd placed one knife near Leeanne, the other near Coughlin, making it look like they'd gone at each other. He stepped toward the entrance and opened the door, creating a cross-draft of oven-like air. The rags ignited, a sudden bright flash filling the room like a vengeful djinn. And he'd felt tired. A weariness like poison in his blood. It hadn't lifted.

* * *

"Hey, Eddie, Mike!" It was Glendon, bellowing from the walk-in. "Come on back here, will ya? You're not gonna believe this."

Eddie shot Mike a glance and a shrug, then the two of them filed back through the storage room, past shelving piled high with glassware, napkins, swizzle sticks, olives and cherries, sour mix, Snappy Tom, heading toward the open door of the cavernous fridge.

Glendon stood inside, near the back. The overhead light was off, burned out maybe. On second glance, though, Bernardo realized the bulb was shattered. Glass shards littered two lumpy forms heaped beneath a tarp on the cold damp floor. Amid the frigid mildewy odor of the space, a faint scent like firecrackers—or was he imagining that?

Glendon raised his voice to be heard over the condenser's rattle and hum. "Guess me and Eddie here got a confession to make, Mike." All things considered, he sounded contrite. His breath formed a misty cloud as he gestured to the motionless forms on the floor.

"This here's Henry. And the woman we told you about, Ol' Tits and Turmoil, never did get her name. But Henry, he owns this bar, owns a couple others in Oakley and Clayton, even a strip mall, if you can call it that, out on Bethel Island. But given your professional inclinations, you may also know him as Henry Ireton, Ireton Realty, LLC."

So that's what this is about, Bernardo thought. "I lied," he said, realizing it was too late for the truth. "I should've told you earlier. You were right, I'm no realtor. I'm a firefighter."

Glendon and Eddie looked at each other, like that was just the damnedest thing.

"Don't quite know what to make of that information, Mike."

"If you're a fireman," Eddie said, "how come…"

The rest of the question drifted off, which apparently was answer enough. Bernardo couldn't take his eyes off the tarp. The biting cold of the walk-in created a burning sensation on his skin, a kind of hallucinatory recompense for the scalding, charring heat inflicted on the other two bodies he'd left behind, one of them his bride. He felt an eerie sense of déjà vu, as though the dead had somehow followed him here.

"All we was after," Eddie said, "was a place to stay. This damn economy. But Henry here, he couldn't have that. Had to play hero, kick us out."

"Some have, some don't," Glendon said. "And those that have, more times than not, they got more than their honest share. No logic to it. Just luck."

"Like you walking in here when you did," Eddie said. "Lousy god damn luck. Sorry."

Bernardo felt the tip of the gun barrel pressed against the base of his skull, Eddie behind him with the weapon. I don't believe in luck, he wanted to say, wondering if he'd already mentioned that.

We Shall Overthug
Tyler Dilts

The World Trade Center never fell.

At least not the crapstatic, wanna-be imitation version in Long Beach. It's thirty stories of ugly planted right down on Ocean Boulevard.[1] It had only been a month or so since I had driven past a group of about fifty stalwart souls[2] who held a little candlelight vigil downstairs to commemorate the tenth anniversary of 9/11. I honestly didn't know whether to laugh or to cry.

I was up on the twenty-sixth floor waiting. Herman Reed had a very nice office. It was so big his furniture was grouped by purpose. A desk and work area by the floor-to-ceiling window, what appeared to be a leather living room set close to the inside wall, and a modest[3] conference table closer to the door to the reception area. I was behind his large cherry desk poking around his computer files and Googling[4] random search terms like "Long Beach World Trade Center." I knew a good amount about Herman before I ever came upstairs, but I was learning even more with my present explorations. He had, for instance, a brother with a famous namesake, Lou[5]. I took the time to be sure of the coincidence. Surely I would still have done what needed to be done, but it would have been infinitely more interesting if I would have been doing it to the brother of the new guy from Metallica.

At any rate, Herman had been at a dinner meeting at L'Opera[6] and I expected him to return presently. His driver, who had chauffeured him the two blocks or so to the fancy-pants restaurant in the back of a

---

[1] According to http://www.emporis.com/building/one-world-trade-center-long-beach-ca-usa, the LB WTC is a postmodern skyscraper with a concrete structure and a black, blue, and a dark orange glass-granite façade over a curtain wall façade system. With a helipad on the highest roof in Long Beach. Woo hoo.

[2] Who, in hindsight, turned out to be a rather intriguing prefiguring of the civic-minded individuals who would soon make up the Occupy Long Beach movement.

[3] Only eight seats!

[4] He had a remarkably fast internet connection and a very impressive twenty-seven-inch iMac.

[5] "Holly came from Miami, FLA," the lyrics went.

[6] A well-known high-end Long Beach Italian eatery with reputed underworld ties.

custom Lincoln Navigator proved to be surprisingly susceptible to reason[7] had tipped me that he would be heading back up to the office, alone, after dinner.

This was, of course, to be my first meeting with Herman.[8] I had thought seriously about how to approach my proposition for him. Most of the persons with whom I do business on any given day are victims of either greed or stupidity[9] and while Herman was of a different social strata[10] than most of the consumers of my rather unique services, I harbored little doubt that he too would be possessed of the twin qualities that provide my usual employer[11] with the means and opportunity to ply his trade. This is to say that while I harbored some small degree of hopefulness as to Herman's reasonability and rationality[12], I certainly did not expect said qualities to be a significant factor in our immediate dealings, nor was I, alas, preparing myself for a disposition of my business with Herman predicated on their presence.

No. I fully expected that the circumstances at hand would require me to use the means of negotiation and compromise I normally employed[13] during the swift completion of my appointed rounds[14].

---

[7] It would not be until some days later that I would learn that Melvin, the driver, had personal reasons other than the ten one-hundred-dollar bills that somehow slipped from my hand into his. His cousin, too, it turned out, was a victim of Herman's malfeasance.

[8] And with a bit of clear headedness and sound critical thinking on Herman's part, it would also be my last.

[9] And in many cases, both.

[10] According to Chip, the forensic accountant with whom I had contracted to consult on some of the unique aspects of the situation at hand, Herman was a bona fide one percenter!

[11] My business with Herman was, it should be noted, not a part of my usual remunerated bailiwick, it was rather a matter of significant personal import. I presently endeavor to do a fair amount of, oh, let's call it pro bono work, and these efforts and endeavors are of increasing importance to me. They enable me to experience a feeling of a certain generosity of spirit, an assured liberality, a comforting humanity, even, if you will, a heart-warming sensation of benevolence thoughtfully bestowed. I should state at the outset, though, that I harbor few illusions. This magnanimousness, this munificence, which I believe, at least in my case, truly serves a greater good, comes, though, at least in part, from what is essentially a place of self-interest, a sort of, as it were, selfishness.

[12] See Note 8, above.

[13] I had with me a custom-crafted leather valise containing tools of my trade, including, but not limited to, a pair of Fiskars 7685 Ratchet Anvil Pruners, a Leatherman Charge ALX multi-tool, two Craftsman Ball Peen Hammers (one sixteen ounce model 38465, and one thirty-two ounce model 38467), one pair of Irwin Vise Grip Fast Release™ Curved Jaw Locking Pliers, a Dremel 8200 12V Max Lithium-ion Cordless rotary tool w/ a full set of attachments, one roll of Kimberly-Clark 75040 Shop Towels, and a one-pint bottle of generic rubbing alcohol. Interestingly, in the interim between my first visit

I would, though, as always, endeavor with the utmost earnestness to convince Herman not to force my hand and require me to resort to some of the more persuasive means at my disposal. I can, after all, be a very convincing fellow[15].

The elevator opened in the hall with a ding so nearly inaudible I surely would have missed it had I not been awaiting it and actively listening for its occurrence. Following my predetermined course of action, I took a position to the left of the door and waited. I heard the soft squeal resulting from the alarm's termination code being punched in by Herman's pudgy index finger and knew he was on his way. A few seconds later, the door swung open, separating me from his troll-like[16] physicality. When he was three steps in front of me, I strode forward and with timing that would have been the envy of many a sixth-grade boy, I swept his right foot inward at the apex of its rearward travel causing it to catch behind the heel of his left, effectively tripping him. He fell forward with considerable force and the momentum drove his face into the ecru Berber carpet with sufficient energy to break his nose[17].

He muffled a groan as he began to realize how much discomfort he was experiencing. Rolling over, and apparently attempting to discern what had caused his unfortunate fall, he discovered me towering above him. An expression of considerable shock and fear complicated his already pained countenance.

---

with Herman and the conclusion of our business, I saw a news report on Pete Seeger's visit to the Occupy Wall Street encampment and was reminded of his banjo, famously emblazoned with the phrase "This machine surrounds hate and forces it to surrender" (itself inspired by Woody Guthrie's guitar that read, "This machine kills fascists"), which led me to briefly consider engraving the stout hickory handle of my larger hammer with a similar inspirational motto.

[14] Which should not be confused with those of the USPS. See http://en.wikipedia.org/wiki/United_ States_ Postal_ Service_creed.

[15] I stand six-foot and weigh 282 pounds. I also suffer from a rather pronounced case of alopecia areata, which renders me virtually hairless. While I am loathe to exploit this or any other disability, it would be disingenuous to suggest that it does not have some expeditious effects on my work. (For more information on alopecia areata, visit the National Alopecia Areata Foundation's website at www.alopeciaeareata.com).

[16] Which description I base of course not on any actual personal knowledge of mythical beings, but rather on multiple suppositions and observations rooted in my youthful exuberance for fictions fantastical in genre.

[17] Which, in fact, was an unanticipated consequence. I would, much later, come to question whether or not this first injury experienced by Herman in my presence had a deleterious effect on our subsequent negotiations. This is, like so many other nuances of my professional experience, simply unknowable.

"Motherfucker!"[18]

"Hello, Herman."

He struggled to a semi-upright position. I stepped around and behind him, slid my left hand into the back of his collar, and dragged him over to the black leather sofa. When his shoulders made contact with the front edge of the cushions, I yanked upward and deposited him ass first into a very comfortable[19] seat.

While Herman moaned and rubbed his face, I crossed behind his desk and took three ice cubes from the small freezer section of his mini-fridge. I wrapped them in the dark gray silk handkerchief I removed from his suit coat pocket and said, "Hold this on the bridge of your nose and put your head between your legs."

He did what I told him to[20].

For nearly two minutes he was content to groan and nurse his wound. I waited. Patience has always been chief among my virtues. I knew, though, that his pain would not long distract him from the fact that there was a very large and imposing stranger in his office who may or may not have just caused him a great deal of pain.

When he finally eased his guttural whimpering and looked at me again, I said, "I'm sure you're wondering who I am and what I'm doing in your office."

He nodded dully.

"It's not really important who I am."

A drop of blood escaped from the edge of his silk compress and ran down the corner of his mouth and onto his chin.

"But several other things are."

My words didn't seem to be registering fully.

"Important, I should say. Several other things are important. Do you understand?"

He nodded.

"Good," I said. "The first important thing for you to understand is that I didn't mean to hurt you just now[21]. Do you understand that?"

---

[18] It is, I think, safe to assume this is what he did in fact shout, although his mouth and sinuses were too filled with blood and phlegm to allow anything resembling clear enunciation.

[19] While waiting for Herman to return to his office, I had tried out each position on the sofa, and each of the various chairs in the office. Best practices call for such a practical knowledge of any and all work environments.

[20] A promising sign at that early stage of our intercourse.

[21] It was absolutely true that I had no intention of hurting him as I did when he entered the room. I was not, in fact, until minutes later after a substantial portion of our discussion had been concluded, that I intended to hurt him.

He nodded again.

"Good. Now I need you to listen to me very carefully. Can you do that?"

Another nod.

I spoke to him for several minutes, relaying the narrative of a former neighbor of mine, Gloria [22], who had, due almost exclusively to the malfeasance of Herman and a gaggle of his underlings and cronies, fallen victim to predatory lending practices that resulted in the loss of her home[23], the institutionalization of her developmentally disabled adult daughter, and, ultimately, Gloria's death from hypothermia caused by her resultant homelessness.

"She was sleeping in her car, Herman, and she froze to death."

He looked at me with a mounting concern that furrowed his brow and narrowed his eyes.

"Do you know how many nights it was cold enough to freeze to death in a car in Long Beach last year?"

"No," he said, his voice thick with nasal drainage.

"Turns out it was probably just the one."

He looked confused.

"She was in her car on the coldest night of the year because you stole her home."

"I didn't do anything of the short[24]."

"Yes, you did, Herman. I could explain exactly how you're responsible[25]. I don't ever enter into a business relationship unprepared."

"Then do it," he slurred.

I flicked his nose with the tip of my middle finger. It was neither particularly forceful nor particularly fast, but it was more than sufficient to make Herman squeal in pain and begin gurgling again[26]. I looked closely at his expression to be sure he was able to breathe well

---

[22] A pseudonym.

[23] Which had been inherited from her own parents, and was in fact, owned fully free and clear before Herman's minions had their way with her.

[24] He was trying to say "sort," but proper pronunciation was something of an impossibility with the aforementioned nasal discharge interfering with his speech.

[25] As Chip explained it to me over the course of three hours, it is a long, complex, and convoluted tale involving predatory subprime lending, fraudulent underwriting practices, over-leveraging, credit default swaps, etc. which ultimately resulted in the foreclosure of Gloria's home.

[26] While it might have given me some small bit of satisfaction to see Herman choke to death on his own nasal discharge (which is, perhaps surprisingly, a not unheard of manner of fatality) I had a more immediate and pressing matter to "discuss" with him.

enough to provide sufficient oxygen to his brain. I was still hopeful he might capable of some small degree of reason.

"You need to understand something, Herman. I realize you're used to situations in which you are free to exercise a significant degree of agency, and perhaps even power, and that you're accustomed to being able to assert your authority and bring your will to bear upon others across a broad spectrum of individual circumstances."

It was clear from the expression behind his swollen and purpling eyes that I was correct. Herman was quite used to being the man on the top.[27] I was quite sincerely hoping that his ego would allow him to listen to what I had to say him and to fully comprehend my seriousness of purpose. If it didn't, well, Herman was unlikely to be satisfied with the outcome of our dealings.

"What I hope you can grasp is that, in your current situation, you are without power and without influence. Utterly and completely without them. Do you understand this?"

He garbled a phrase that I believe was "Do you have any idea who you're dealing with?" As he sputtered out his indignation, he raised his left hand and spread his fingers, showing me his palm as if in a symbolic attempt to hold me back.

I paid him the courtesy of not laughing.

Instead, I reached out and yanked his hand and arm into a wristlock[28] that afforded me a measure of control over him and allowed me to drive his face into the Berber carpet a second time. I manipulated his arm into a relatively standard arm bar that forced him quickly and without ordeal into submission. When it seemed that Herman had calmed down[29], I rolled him onto his back, and asked him in a calm and soothing tone if he was finished.

"Finished!?" he said[30]. "Finished with what!?"

---

[27] Not only was his workplace on the upper floors of the tallest buildings in Long Beach, so too was his home. Herman lived in a sprawling luxury penthouse suite a few blocks east on Ocean Boulevard.

[28] The lock itself was a variation of *kotegaeshi*, a foundational technique of the non-violent martial art Aikido, which, in other circumstances, can be used to throw, pin, or even break the wrist of an attacker.

[29] This phrase is, of course, being used here in a strictly relative sense, in that what I would consider "calm" in this particular context would be rather different than it would in other times and/or places and/or situations.

[30] Do understand that as strict matter of usage and style, I am not fond of phonetic spellings. It is my belief that they interfere with the clarity of a writer's prose and often break the flow of the narrative for readers. So I've chosen to largely refrain from the technique in reporting Herman's dialogue. As we move forward, please imagine

It was clear that he wasn't, so once again I took his hand and quickly and cleanly broke his thumb[31].

The pain was becoming something of a constant for him at this point. So his yelp was rather unenthusiastic. He did curl up his left hand and pull it into his chest with his right.

My valise was on the coffee table. I opened it, reached inside, and brought out my Fiskars pruning shears. They have a very comfortable ergonomic orange rubber grip. I held them up in front of Herman's face. When he began to cry, it was clear he was finally achieving the proper perspective.

"You don't need to say anything now, Herman. You only need to nod. Do you understand?"

Herman nodded.

"Good. I need you to listen carefully and think about what I say to you. Is that clear?"

I was still holding the shears in front of his face. He looked at them while he nodded again.

"If you don't do that, I'm going to cut off your thumbs. Do you understand?"

He did.

"Do you believe that I will indeed cut off your thumbs?

His eyes left the Fiskars and met mine. What he saw there convinced him and he nodded yet again.

"Good."

"I don't expect you to believe me about Gloria. That's perfectly all right. I'm going to allow the opportunity to investigate her case. When you do, you'll see that I'm right. When you cut out all of the bullshit and rationalization and ass covering, you'll come to the same conclusion I did. Do you understand?"

---

throughout this scene that all of Herman's words sound as if they're being pronounced by someone with a mouthful of peanut butter and ball bearings.

[31] Since I first began to chronicle certain of my professional exploits, the proper technique for a clean thumb break has come under considerable discussion and scrutiny. I still maintain, based on a considerable body of experiential evidence, that the ideal method is as follows: grasp the thumb at its base, as close as is possible to the hand itself, wrapping your own thumb and forefinger around the joint. Repeat the process at the upper joint. The idea is to support each of the joints to the greatest extent possible. Once this has been accomplished, snap the thumb sharply sideways, perpendicular to the direction of the thumb's own movement. You should, in most cases, feel the bone snap in your hands. Imagine breaking a pencil wrapped in several slices of bologna for some idea of the sensation.

He did.

"I'm certain that won't agree that you should be held accountable, but you will most certainly not be able to refute the case against you. You are responsible for Gloria's foreclosure and everything that followed from it. I'm not going to ask you to nod here."

I let in sink in for a moment.

"But there is good news, Herman. I'm not here for revenge or retribution."

I could see that he wanted to ask me what I was then in fact there for.

"I'm here for a settlement."

He raised his eyebrows in unison.

"Gloria's daughter is in a serious predicament. She requires, without her mother's care, a permanent place in an assisted living facility."

He looked puzzled.

"She requires four million two hundred sixty eight thousand four hundred dollars[32]."

"What?" Herman said.

"I wrote it down for you. It's on your desk. You have three days to research Gloria's situation and another seven to make arrangements for the cash."

"What?" he said once more.

"Be careful, Herman."

I could sense him beginning to question our power dynamic again. "No," I said with a firmness of tone I might deploy with a generally well-mannered but ever-so-slightly misbehaving dog. [33]

Rather than saying anything else, I began removing the tools from my valise. He'd already seen the pruners, so I started with them. For some reason, the ball peen hammers always seem to raise an eyebrow or two among those I work with. Herman was no exception. He got the message fairly early in the progression.

"I'm going to ask you one more question, Herman."

He looked up at me.

"Can I trust you?"

---

[32] I arrived at that number by consulting actuarial tables to determine the girl's probable life span (and added fifteen years to cover any health-related good fortune that might befall her), translating that number of years into months, and multiplying that result by the monthly amount currently required to provide her care (adding in a five-percent-per-annum increase to cover cost-of-living and inflationary price increases).

[33] Have I ever told you about my experience several years ago at Torrance, California's Wilson Park with a wonderfully spirited but nevertheless tragically fated Pomeranian?

This befuddled him.

"What I am asking is, if I can indeed count on you to fulfill your responsibility in this matter?"

He still didn't know what to say.

"I've broken your thumb as reminder and as a warning. I find that sometimes it's more effective to actually remove the thumb altogether. Do I need to remove your thumb, Herman?"

When I saw the dark circle spreading beneath him on the sofa and the wetness blackening his crotch, I knew I didn't need his wild bobbing head to answer my question. I could trust Herman. He would hate it, and he would scheme and plot and try to wiggle out of his responsibility, but ultimately the same fear that had just led him to piss himself would also compel him to comply with the requirements of our arrangement. I had the utmost confidence in him.

"I have the utmost confidence in you, Herman."

He said nothing, but there was a weary resignation in his posture that I found rather rewarding.[34]

"I'll see you soon, Herman. You should get cleaned up, then get to work. You've got a story to check and some cash to gather."

He began to speak.

"Don't worry," I told him. "I'll know when you're ready and I'll find you to make the pick-up. Have a lovely evening."

I took his dread and trepidation with me out into the brisk fall evening air and welcomed the munificent warmth they brought me.

* * *

A week later, Herman had yet to assemble the required funds. He received a package[35] via the United States Postal Service and within forty-eight hours after his receipt of said parcel, four million two hundred sixty eight thousand four hundred dollars were packed into a large leather rolling duffle bag[36] in his bedroom.

---

[34] Once, a very long time ago, when I was early in the apprentice stage of my present profession, a mentor of mine had told me that the secret to true contentment in professional life was not in doing what you love, no, it was in loving what you do. I took his words to heart and honestly believe that endeavoring to follow that simple mantra has made a significant difference in my life. It is the fortunate man who enjoys his work.

[35] Containing two severed human thumbs.

[36] Upon subsequent inspection, the bag would prove to be an Orvis Large Leather Weekender Rolling Duffle from their very luxurious Bullhide Collection line. Deciding

* * *

It was increasingly common for utterances such as "usury" and "shark" and "predatory" and myriad other terms more commonly associated with the lower strata of the financial industry to be applied to Herman and his ilk.But my own particular professional experience had taught me something of vital importance in this discussion. Those I most often work for operate in a manner in which full and complete disclosure of their business practices is an imperative element of any successful transaction[37]. This is, I believe, the vital distinction between individuals like my employers and those like Herman. There is honesty and openness in all of our concerns. I am loath to operate in any other manner.

I found Herman on one of the balconies of his penthouse on the top floor of the 1900 Ocean building. This was but one of his several homes and its appraised three-and-a-half million-dollar value placed it among the more modest dwellings.

There was a leather sofa very similar to the one in his office positioned ideally to take advantage of the fireplace, the wall mounted sixty-inch plasma screen TV, and the impressive view. At the moment the sun was setting in the west on the far side of the harbor, its dying orange light silhouetting the multitudinous waterfront industrial structures into a skeletal and apocalyptic relief. The Orvis bag had been relocated to the center cushion of the sofa, its top unzipped to reveal the bundles of hundred dollar bills waiting inside.

Herman stood on the balcony, watching, waiting, as I counted the bundles to make sure they were all there[38]. When I found they were, I took a few steps toward Herman to assure him that our business was now concluded and he would not likely be seeing me again.

But.

---

whether my personal ethical boundaries would allow me to retain the bag, which I quite admired, for my personal use proved something of a quandary.

[37] The gentleman, for example, whose opposable digits were now in Herman's possession, exhibited a broad range of emotions as we concluded our dealings, but surprise was not among them.

[38] This was not, as you might guess, the first time I had handled such a large sum of money. Before I began counting, the size, shape, and weight of the bag led me to assume that Herman was not, in fact, short-changing me. I was more than a little satisfied to find my assumption proven correct.

Herman's sense of self, his alpha-male authority, indeed, his very identity, would not, unfortunately, allow him any semblance of graciousness or cordiality. Herman, alas, felt the need to speak.

"Choke on it, you bald fuck."

I am, it is fair to note, a very even-keeled fellow. I pride myself on my magnanimous collegiality and my almost preternaturally high degree of unflappability.

And it was, I think, subsequent to some not inconsiderable after-the-fact deliberation on my part, this very imperturbable composure, that caused the look of confusion on Herman's face as I closed the distance between us[39]. It was not, I believe, until after I had lifted him off of his feet and drove him toward the railing that he suspected the intent of my actions. It was, by then, too late for Herman to change the course of events and it seemed he was nearly halfway to the pedestrian concourse many floors below us before it occurred to him to scream.

I didn't look over the railing, but rather went back inside, set the wheels of the Orvis on the floor, and locked the door of Herman's luxury penthouse behind me. As I rode the elevator down into the bowels of the parking garage below the building, I thought again of the Occupy Long Beach assembly I had witnessed on the way to conduct my business with Herman, and I thought too of Herman's resentment and anger at having been held accountable for, what was in actuality, only a very small way for his actions. I had, I realized only then, been, as it seems I am often wont to be, overly optimistic. In my naïveté, I thought Herman capable of understanding, even perhaps of growing in his ability to take some small measure of responsibility for the effects his actions had on others. But that was, unfortunately for both Herman and for me, a virtual impossibility.

I wanted to think that my own actions were just and fair, and that I was seeking a sort of moral reckoning in which Herman had the ability to understand his wrongs and redress them. But Herman's lack of vision did not allow him to understand a simple and fundamental truth.

No matter how divided we are, no matter how unbalanced the percentages into which we separate ourselves, the one inextricable reality we all ultimately face[40] is that when life barges into our luxury

---

[39] I had no way of actually observing the expression on my face as I approached him, but I imagine it held a fairly high degree of self-possession and perhaps even a touch of gentility.

[40] And perhaps this is the real space between us. Do we face this reality knowingly or unknowingly, and this most of all—do we have any choice?

penthouse and hurls us into the void, when we plummet through our own great fall, when we thud into the adamant ground, when our blood and viscera run thick and red on the unyielding concrete, then are we faced with the one, and perhaps the only, truth that we can carry with us: that we are the one hundred percent.

The Movement
Travis Richardson

The white-blue moonlight sinks behind the jagged silhouettes of redwoods that surround your hidden campsite. The sun won't rise for a couple more hours. Though the damp air is chilly, you don't notice. You know today is the day. You feel it in your bones. He will come. Even though his options are unlimited, you've obsessed over that prick long enough to predict his behavior. This journey you've been on, full of miscalculations, staggering heights, and ocean bottom lows, will end today.

You're a wanted man. In a matter of weeks, you went from darling of the downtrodden to public enemy number one. It wasn't your first fall from grace either. Although you know this might be the final day of your life, you're okay with that. In your 37 years, you've had more experiences than most people will have in a hundred.

However, thoughts of public perception and your legacy have been gnawing at you and keeping you awake. Nobody knows your true story: the reasons why and the unfiltered truth of it all. You've already published a few books, casting yourself as the whistleblower of the corrupt elite. But that is your alter ego, Jack Hamilton, the man who created The Movement and fought the corrupt powers. People should know the real you, Randall Waters, the one-time ambitious, misguided boy who metamorphosed into several incarnations before ending up as you are, a fugitive avenger.

All night you have been feverishly writing a memoir while staking out his compound. Eighty pages written in this composition notebook hold everything about you. Written on the front and back pages are your life, your thoughts, your history. You flex your cramped fingers, dropping the roller-ball pen on the redwood-needled carpet. Only one page left. You stare at the vast blankness of white. What will be your final words?

Reputations can change in an instant; that is why, if you die today, this manuscript must survive. You've been demonized and praised. Now you've given the reasons for your actions, documenting the why so people will understand. You just hope the manuscript will be revered like Julius Caesar's campaign notes and not reviled and dismissed like John Wilkes Booth's diary.

* * *

My Life as a Scoundrel and a Savior
By Randall Waters aka Jack Hamilton

I was born Randall Eugene Waters in Goldspar, Arizona. My father worked as a maintenance man for the school district while my mother raised seven children. I was second to last. My brothers and sisters fit perfectly with the school and the town. The boys devolved from jocks to blue-collar, beer-bellied couch jockeys. The girls transformed from cheerleaders to baby machines. I had nieces and nephews who were only a couple of years younger than me. I knew early that I didn't belong. I was the runt with brains, and I wanted out of that squalid backwards town.

My grades and test scores were good enough for any of the Ivy League schools. I even got scholarships, but my parents, who didn't have a dime of savings and never gave a positive thought to education, couldn't afford to send me east. I had to settle on a state school where I became the big fish, even with thirty thousand students. President's Honor Roll, Phi Beta Kappa, and all the awards in between without breaking a sweat. I majored in finance because it dealt with the one thing I never had: money.

The first time I met Jeffrey Donahue IV was during our internship at World Trust Bank. That was my only shot to get the future job I wanted, and we were forty of America's brightest college juniors vying for two positions the following year. I scraped by on the less than minimum wage salary eating the meager snacks in the lounge, often working close to sixteen hours so that nobody could even come close to the volume of work I generated.

Jeffrey, this tall, blond and blue-eyed Aryan's wet dream, seemed to do no work at all. He walked around the offices like he owned the place--joking with men and flirting with women. Soon they were gloating about the bars and parties from the previous night. I ignored it all and crunched numbers, knowing there was no way in hell Jeffrey would make it.

Yet, the next summer the two of us, fresh graduates, entered the executive program. I wore the same suit as the year before, but Jeffrey didn't. And every day following it seemed like he wore a different tailor-made suit for three weeks solid. I couldn't understand how he, of all people, made the cut. Jeffrey had done the least amount of work of any intern. True, he went to Princeton and his grandfather or somebody had been Treasurer in the Eisenhower administration, but I doubted if he could even carry a remainder on a simple N648 form.

I hated his very existence and as before, wanting to differentiate myself, I immediately dove into work, creating extra analysis and reports on trends that weren't required. My hard work was always praised, but Jeffrey, the social butterfly, kept joking with the execs, and went to parties even veteran employees were never invited to. I kept my distance from him, but he approached me one day.

"Hey, Randy."

"Randall." I remember him rolling his eyes.

"Sure. I realize we've been working here for the same amount of time, and I don't know you. We should get a drink tonight."

"No, too busy. I promised Mr. Wynn a report on..."

"Don't worry about Max. He can wait. Seriously, tonight at six I'm taking you out of here. They don't pay you enough to see the janitors."

He slapped me on the shoulder causing me to pitch forward as he gave off his goddamn winning smile. Though I tried to resist his charm, the rich prick won me over. Max...Mr. Wynn's report could wait.

Over a few rounds of scotch, Jeffrey outlined banking and finance in a way I'd never heard before. "We don't need people in banking, they need us," he said. I tried to argue how asinine that statement was, but he held up a hand. I still remember his speech, delivered with utter confidence and contempt.

"People make lousy livings doing shitty jobs. They choose to do that, right? This is America, you can choose what you want to be, so if you choose to be a poor schmuck and be stupid with your money, then fuck you. I'll take your savings, and if don't have any, I'll lend you money as long as you keep on paying it back to me with interest, biatch. Banking is a numbers game. If you have all wealthy clients, you'll get rich, but they'll count every goddamned penny that comes and goes. Not the masses though. They have stuff like Friends, NFL playoffs, and PTAs to worry about. Take a little here and there, they'll never notice. Of course we need numbers, a lot of them since we'd only take a quarter of a cent to the dollar, but it'll work. They'll never notice."

I was astounded, ripping off the working class, people like my family, and insulting them on top of it. But he had said something even more important to the hyper-ambitious person I was then. "You said we?"

He threw his arm around me, embedding a cufflink into my shoulder. "I've got the plan, and you've got the number crunching skills. What do you say?"

"We'll do this at Greater American?"

"No, we start our own bank. I can get the capital, but you come up with the business model. We'll stay here for a few more years, building up connections, and then strike out on our own. I'll be the president, you'll be the CEO. Are you in?"

Perhaps it was the three glasses of Scotch burning through my body, but I said yes. A CEO before thirty, how could I not?

* * *

"The skunk has landed," crackles over the walkie-talkie by your knee.

Your pulse quickens. Skunk: the code word for Jeffrey. The man you planted at the Santa Rosa airport two years ago has finally paid off.

"Ready on positions," you speak softly into the wireless. The message travels out to the remnants of your crew, the last fragments of The Movement.

Oren is at the back of the property. An Iraq veteran demolition expert who lost his house and eventually his wife and kids, he is full of anger with nothing to lose. You've given him direction to tunnel that aggression.

Greg is at the bottom of the hill behind a large coyote brush shrub, watching the massive steel gate at the front of the compound fifty yards away. A sweet country-boy looking for a family, he found you, and you accepted him. Of everybody remaining, you feel the most responsible for him, wishing he had deserted you like others had.

Cam, your right hand and lieutenant, is east of the hill with a view of Russian River Road. You see yourself in him, the same energy and ambition. You feel like you know him thoroughly. If it weren't for him, you'd be dead, and this final strike wouldn't be possible. His loyalty is unmatched.

Inside the compound is a security guard named Murray. You've never met him, but Cam says he's solid. He's in on the plan. If he were a snitch, you'd be caught by now.

You stand, stretching your taut muscles and trying to relieve the ache of hunching over a notebook on hard ground all night. Walking to the edge of the hill you check the chamber of your Berretta and blow into it making sure nothing is lodged inside. The sky is gray, the stars fading away like mist. Looking down across the road, you see lights from the compound below. You taste the bitterness of disgust from the back of your throat as memories flood through your body, recalling your first visit there.

***

Jeffrey's family has owned a northern California estate for a couple of generations. Known as a retreat from the eyes of the world, powerbrokers traveled there to relax and plan the fate of the world. For many of the exclusive guests, it was the stop before or after the drunken orgy at the Bohemian Grove. Mostly finance executives and congressmen on important committees made annual visits to the compound where brandy and red wine flowed freely.

I was summoned there to meet Jeffrey's father and a few of his cronies almost a year after that drink with him. I had slaved away at my home computer creating the master document for a new mega bank, generating dozens of models that yielded the highest growth and accumulation of assets in the shortest amount of time. I had marked all the policies and regulations that might hinder progress and then provided workaround solutions, noting that legal advice should be sought first. This was my magnum opus, 800 pages detailing a truly streamlined, powerful bank that could grow exponentially and create wealth faster than any other financial institution ever had.

A week after I finished the manifesto, they flew me out on a private jet from New York to Santa Rosa's tiny airport. A limo escorted me to the compound. Back then there was only a small remote-controlled gate at the entrance. The limo motored up a paved road to an enormous house that looked more like a university library. Redwoods surrounded the massive house, but the three-story marble columns in front seemed almost as large. A quote from Adam Smith was etched in wood above heavy lacquered doors: "All money is a matter of belief."

The interior was even more ostentatious. Antique furniture and enormous oil paintings of European hunters on horseback littered a cavernous entry.

"In here!" a voice shouted from a room on the left.

I walked into a room covered from floor to ceiling in dark wood panel. Tree-sized logs burned in a fireplace as large as a compact car. Mica lamps added to the sinister orange glow on the faces of white haired men sitting on leather couches, holding brandy snifters, looking at me in flickering shadows.

"Randall, the man of the hour," Jeffrey said jumping up from a couch, his perfectly aligned teeth set in a wide smile. He threw an arm around me. "I want you to meet the board."

I had never been in a fraternity. Either because of my financial background or less than pedigreed looks, I had been declined in two rushes. In front of me sat men of consequential power that any one of those frat hacks at my state school would have given a testicle to meet. They smiled at me, approving. My body shook with nervous and excited energy. If I could impress these powerbroking geezers, I would reap the vast amounts of money I had dreamed of.

Three days of intense debate, study, brandy laced coffees, and Cuban cigars later, I was nominated and accepted the position of Vice President of the Home Equity Division of the yet to be formed Statesmen Bank and Trust. A few of the old coots would sit on the board and Jeffrey's father would be the CEO, with Jeffrey as the Chief Operations Officer.

"Honestly, Randall," Jeffery Donahue III said. "You are a nobody. Financial genius, yes. A known player in banking, no. We need to build trust from investors over the next few years. If you bring in the money and assets that you say you can in the housing loan area, you will be in line for CFO and then CEO after that."

The group infused close to $80 million. Like the Silicon Valley tech companies, we were a startup bank. For the first time in my life, I was on the cutting edge.

Jeffrey had spent some time with me while I worked like crazy on the proposal. Small stuff like having food delivered to my apartment or taking me out for a drink when I finished a section. But after the powerbrokers approved Statesmen Bank, we had dinner almost every night. He took me out shopping to improve my look and confidence. He taught me how to tie the Windsor knot, how to match variations of beige, the fine difference between a good and an excellent tailor. He also taught me how to talk to women with a confidence bordering on arrogance and condescension, and then leave coldly in the morning so there are no mixed messages. For once in my lonely life, I felt like I had a real friend.

My division, home loans and equity, pulled in the most money. The variable interest rate locked customers into a forever-changing percentage that I controlled. If they defaulted, Statesmen would own the asset, able to foreclose and resell the property. It worked very well for the bank's portfolio, and I heard chatter from the board that I might leapfrog to the CEO job when Jeffrey III stepped down.

I met Katrina, a blonde, surgically-enhanced woman who did things I didn't know were physically possible. I spent a fortune on her needs. Like Jeffrey, I had a month's worth of Italian tailored suits. I bought a penthouse condo in Manhattan and a beach house in Cape Cod. I felt like Superman, totally invincible. It seemed nothing could stop me.

Then there was a sudden downturn in the housing market, and all of those houses Statesmen bank owned lost their value almost overnight. It wasn't a snowball, but an avalanche of bad and worse news. Suddenly the majority of customers defaulted on their loans within a couple of months, and I was stuck with a glut of unsellable McMansions in shitty areas of the country. The board put pressure on me to stop the bleeding, as the bank had lent millions to customers who were abandoning their houses. I changed the variable rates to lower fixed ones, but they still couldn't make the payments. When I kicked the defaulters out, the homes were trashed with the appliances and copper piping torn out. Planned neighborhoods became ghost towns with squatters taking up residence and weeds growing waist high in the yard.

It was around that time that Jeffrey stopped coming into the office. He gave half-hearted excuses at first and then nothing. He didn't return calls or email. The board also fell suspiciously quiet. It was unnerving.

I remember heading to work on a Monday with a massive hangover. I had split up with Katrina after a vicious argument on Friday night and then spent the weekend on a bender. It wasn't because of her I drank myself stupid. There were several banks in trouble and the entire country was swirling down the crapper. The sense of doom was overwhelming.

When I arrived to the office, it was eerily empty. Just the receptionist and a handful of assistants. We wondered aloud if we missed a holiday. I sat at my computer and found that I was locked out. Before I could make a call to Jeffrey or the IT department, SEC and FBI agents swarmed into the offices. They led me out in handcuffs, reading the Miranda.

* * *

"Skunk is coming from the east," Cam says over the air.

The gray sky melts into hints of blue. Holding up your binoculars, you watch the shadowy outline of the road. It seems like it takes hours, but seconds later a pair of headlights punctures the darkness below. The outline seems to be a Lincoln limousine. It is Jeffrey. You're sure of it. You shiver, feeling excitement. Revenge, no, justice, can finally be exacted. The car turns at the gate, stops for a brief moment while it opens, and then rolls up to the estate. Three men get out. One has Jeffrey's shape, and the other two are built like linebackers. You know it is Jeffrey. It has to be, but the distance is too far and it's too dark to be certain.

You can't be wrong. The FBI and most Americans think you are in Mexico. You gave your cell phone and a credit card to a follower with a similar build. He is supposed to use one or the other every couple of days in different towns. It seems to be working. A thought crosses your mind. Maybe Jeffrey has a body double. You stifle a laugh, but acknowledge a little paranoia is prudent.

"Are we ready?" Greg asks over the radio. His voice has a nervous quiver.

"Hold your positions," you say softly. "We need confirmation from inside. We can only blow our wad once."

* * *

I remember sitting in the courtroom as a parade of wealthy liars and a few impoverished souls testified against me. I had done bad things, I admit that now, but I did not act alone. The board members lined up one by one to say that they were shocked and horrified when they 'found out' what I was doing. These were the same bastards that praised me and, like starving dogs, begged for more money. Even my secretary testified against me, making me look like a lecherous ogre by twisting our causal daily banter into harassment.

The deepest cut came from Jeffrey. Immaculately dressed, he put his hand on the Bible with an expression of absolute solemnity. The holy book should have seared his hand, but he held it there, vowed to tell the truth, and then stared at me, squinting his eyes with intense reproach. I realized then that I did not have a single friend in the world, and I felt the ground sink from under me. Reversing the facts of our first meeting, he said I pushed him to use his family connections to start up a new lending organization. I was flabbergasted. A brazen lie, told so coolly and confidently. I lost it. My body shook, and I saw only red. I remember shouting and running toward that son of a bitch, and then the world went black.

The next thing I remembered was waking up in a hospital handcuffed to a bed, my head throbbing. My attorney, Clive, was there. Nobody else. He told me I was tased by a deputy and then fell forward, hitting my head against the bench. Clive wanted to settle immediately. I didn't. I wanted to tell my side. The truth of what really happened. He shook his head like I was a child.

"Too late. You look like a crazed lunatic to the jury. Maybe on appeal."

I was furious. I settled for ten years in federal prison. I hated everyone and everything, but I hated Jeffrey the most.

*　*　*

An unfamiliar voice murmurs, "Skunk." It must be Murray's. Jeffrey is indeed inside. Wrapping the memoir in plastic, you shove it behind your bulletproof vest. You check the Berretta on your side and the pistol on your ankle holster. They're both there. You reach into your supply bag and take out a grenade and a smoke bomb, stuffing them into your jacket pockets.

"Move to position B," you call out on the walkie-talkie.

Using the contours of the land, you run from bush to tree to boulder. The weight of heavy boots and equipment, plus the ache of bones and joints, do not bother you. You are at the end. A clear light shines at the end of a tunnel.

You sidle next to Greg. He smiles warmly, but his eyes are bulging in excitement. He looks like he is fifteen.

"We're really going to do this, aren't we?"

You nod and want to tell him he can stay behind. But you both hear crunching undergrowth and turn to the gully a few yards away. Cam, in full camo, crawls over to you. Twigs and bits of leaves hang from his curly hair. He smells rancid, probably as bad as you do.

"Oren has the explosives in place, sir."

You never like it when he calls you sir, but he was in the army. Habits can be hard to break. You know he'll be a cornerstone once you rebuild The Movement, which will be even stronger with today's victory.

"Great," you say. "When the gate opens, we'll get into the second location, then we'll detonate and breach."

Cam nods. He has an uneasy smile.

"It'll be all right," you whisper with a light slap on his shoulder. "This will be over in a few minutes. I know this place."

*　*　*

My first year in the federal penitentiary was the worst. It's not as horrific as movies make it look...maybe for violent offenders, but I wouldn't know. I was with mostly white-collar criminals and a few bank robbers. In those initial weeks I felt I could have torn the head off of any convict there. Not that I had much physical clout, but intense anger seethed through my body. It was centered on Jeffrey Donahue.

To me, he was the sole reason I was locked up, but I was willing to take it out on anybody who upset me. Oscar, my under-sized ex-bank robbing cellmate, took a lot of abuse. It got to the point that the fifty-year-old flinched anytime I moved.

Around my second year, I decided to channel all of that anger into a tell-all book about the Statesmen Bank. I worked on it for over thirteen months, fact checked as much as I could from the prison library, and finally composed a detailed, seven hundred page account. I was shocked to find that nobody wanted it. Only three years into my imprisonment, and the scandal was old news.

When a small press asked to buy it, I was more than happy to sign over all my rights and give the fact checkers my entire research. I found out later it had all been a ruse. The publisher had been purchased by Statesmen, and the contract I signed prohibited me from writing anything else about the bank.

I cannot explain the fury and impotence I felt. I had been totally outflanked for the second time by these bastards. To add more insult to injury Jeffrey oversaw the publishing house operations. That slimy, blue-blooded weasel. I vowed to do many horrific and painful things to him when I got out, but I still had over six years to go. Then, I found Jesus...and Mohammad too.

What I really found was the power of faith and devotion. I watched different charismatic leaders in the prison chapel and on TV preaching from a single book with devoted disciples following every word to fortify themselves with inner strength, satisfaction, and hope. There was a lot of repetition, and evidence of God came from the gut. Verifiable proof was not necessary...or even possible. The emotion of faith, however, made God real. There were very few, if any grays. Every decision in life seemed to be either black or white, you either made the righteous choice or you committed sin. And evil had a leader, the ultimate boogey man, Satan. He was the one who caused humanity's misfortunes. Like talk-radio jockeys who blast liberals for every problem happening in the world, I knew I could crush Jeffrey and the Statesmen Bank with these tactics.

I found a role model in Saul of Tarsus. A tireless persecutor of early Christians, he later became the biggest evangelist for their cause. He just changed his name to Paul and said Jesus spoke to him.

The name change was easy. I hated the name Randall Waters. I took Jack Hamilton as a handle, the masculine name I never had. To transform like the Apostle Paul, I needed to be blinded by Jesus. That would be difficult. Then it hit me. Reform. That's what every prisoner is supposed to do in the clink, right? I didn't need to go to Antioch. I could have a spiritual epiphany behind the bars.

The first person I needed to win over was my cellmate. We hadn't spoken in years. I remember our conversation vividly.

"Don't you think it's wrong..." I started one night in my bunk.

"You talkin' to me?" he said.

"Who else is in here?"

"I don't want to hear it. Especially if it's from you."

"Is that so? You just enjoying sitting in this cell here, biding your time...decaying into dust."

"What kind of dumbshit question is that, stupid bank man?"

I knew that if I could win over Oscar, I would convert others. I jumped down from the bunk. He flinched.

"Why did you call me a bank man?" I asked.

"Say what?"

"A bank man. Do I look like I'm working in a bank?"

"You're nuts, man."

"I used to work at a bank. I used to sell reverse mortgages and variable interest loans intended to skyrocket. I used to, but no longer. I'm in prison, and I'm reformed."

"Yeah, we all are in here. You ain't so special."

"I'm only special in that I've seen the light. The light of change. The light that says not only do I need to change my ways, but I must expose those who do as I once did."

I gazed at Oscar, wide-eyed...crazy like I meant it. Oscar tried to hold my stare but finally dropped his head.

"Whatever you say, man."

I knew I had him. It might take a few weeks of ~~harassment~~ indoctrination, but he was listening. So I gave him the hard sell.

"What I'm trying to say is that you put in the time for the crime and yet there are so many people out there that haven't. They are CEOs running banks. They don't lift wallets; they steal millions of dollars of hard earned money from thousands of honest people. They enjoy the good life and have political protection. Doesn't that get you mad?"

Oscar looked up, eyes blazing. "Of course it does. But there ain't a damn thing we can do about it. You know that. So shut the hell up."

I shook my head. "No, there is. We need to expose those motherfuckers, and take back what they've taken from the people."

"And how do you plan to do that?"

"We're going to start a movement."

"We?"

I slapped Oscar on the shoulder and jumped to the top bunk.

"Sleep tight, partner."

I kept after Oscar two weeks until we started discussing inequities and the best ways to bring awareness to the masses. By the end of the month he was my first believer. I started going around the prison yard asking other prisoners the same questions. "Have you served your time to society?" "What do you think about the white-collar criminals who make millions illegally and are untouchable?" "Isn't it time to do something about it?" They gave me skeptical looks and shook their heads, but I could tell they were listening. I kept at it. Soon they were talking back to me, saying they were powerless. I countered. They weren't powerless as a whole, only as individuals. Even prison guards leaned in closer, and I noticed barely perceptible nods.

Organized meetings came next. Oscar arranged them, and each one was larger than the next. Locations varied around the prison yard and the convicts would break whenever a guard walked by. But then I talked to the guards and they had been screwed too by the banking fiasco. Eventually they allowed me to preach to the prisoners unabated and often stood around the periphery to listen in. Every word I said was a black and white statement with absolute confidence. "People should rule, not the privileged few." In the winter I moved into the recreation room, but it was not large enough. The warden allowed for morning, afternoon, and evening services as long as the guards monitored me.

Prisoners told their relatives on the outside. There was no official name for what I'd organized, just The Movement. Since I didn't have computer access, I wrote daily memos that were taken outside and posted on a blog. I wrote under my new identity, Jack Hamilton. The blog went from a couple of dozen views to hundreds and then hundreds of thousands.

I also contacted those whose lives I had ruined. I started with the toughest one of all, Mrs. Stella January. Her testimony was damning.

She and her retired husband had mortgaged their paid-off house for a loan at a variable rate. The interest rate shot up a few months later, and the Januarys burned through their life savings and refinanced again, only to default and hand the house over to Statesmen. Mr. January put a bullet in his head, and his wife lived out of a car. I remember feeling the sharp arrows from the jurors' eyes.

It took seven letters before she responded, telling me to stop writing and rot in hell. I kept writing her, giving her a journal of my transformation, telling her my need to make amends and to avenge against "those who have cheated the poor and have not paid the justice they owe."

Eventually she wrote back, forgiving me and encouraging me to expose "those just like you." I wrote other victims from my banking days, and soon dozens of victims who had lined up to prosecute me asked how they could join my movement.

***

"In ten," Murray's voice comes over the walkie-talkie, and ten seconds later the gate opens.

You, Greg, and Cam haul ass, sprinting across the road through the gate. It is about fifty yards up the road to the compound, but you don't need to get that far. There is a giant rose garden to the left of the mansion, planted by Jeffrey's grandmother or somebody. You just need to get there without anybody seeing you. You were out of breath several steps ago; your lungs cry out in pain.

"Oh shit. Somebody's coming out," Greg says from behind you.

You look at the enormous front door pushing open. You're less than twenty feet away from cover. A bodyguard steps out. He looks like a steroid-using ultimate fighter. You slide on the wet grass into the cover of the rose bushes. Cam and Greg fall beside you.

Anemic orange rays glimmer in the distance, but gray is still dominant. Peering through the bushes, you see the guard look your way, but then he scans the property in the other direction and walks to the car. He grabs a duffel bag from the driver's seat and strides back inside the house.

You finally breathe.

"That was close," Greg says.

Both you and Cam nod. Any minute Murray will walk out with the bodyguards. That will be the signal. Absolutely no return. You remember your memoir. You feel panicked. You might not make it out alive; it needs to be found. You pull out the plastic encased notebook from your vest and stare at it. Between those black and white marbled covers you're leaving the world an explanation for your actions, ridding incorrect speculations. Is it enough? You remember the last blank page, take out your pen and start writing.

"What's that?" Greg whispers.

"It's my memoir," you say trying to figure a tone between reverence and hokiness. You write a few more sentences but grow frustrated because you can't seem to find the words for what you want to say. Murray is going to step out any minute, and you're blanking under the pressure cooker of time. You dash a couple more lines and sign your name at the bottom. You rewrap the notebook, place it under a white rose bush, and cover it with dirt. You turn to your brothers in arms.

"If I don't make it out of here alive, I want one of you to take the notebook and put my words online."

"You're not going to die..." Greg starts.

"I'll grab it, sir," Cam says. Cam's eyes are directly on you, looking wholeheartedly sincere.

"Thanks," you say. "We'll see if we're dead or alive in just a few minutes."

* * *

When a major publishing house asked me to write a book based on my blog, I was skeptical. I wasn't going to get fooled again. So I asked an Oakland press known for more radical and controversial texts if they would be interested. They were and they sold my first book, Scoundrels, and then the call-to-arms follow up, When Scoundrels Attack: How to Stop and Defeat Those Greedy Bastards, by the boatloads.

I knew I had made a national impact with The Movement, but nothing prepared me for the day I stepped out of prison. There were hundreds, maybe a thousand people waiting for me. The banners, the cheers, it was overwhelming. It is one thing to write letters of support, but to show up in person to fucking Nowhere, Kansas. Wow. I knew I had created something powerful that could crush Jeffrey and his ilk.

In my first months with Internet access, I worked furiously to expose all of those who exploited the masses. I listed the home addresses of CEOs from most banks and every credit card company. I used social media to organize protests in New York outside of the Stock Exchange and various banking headquarters, in DC outside of the Capitol and the Treasury, and a few in northern California outside of the Bohemian

Club and the Donahue compound. I kept blogging and uploaded YouTube videos every few days. I was offered TV shows but declined. I wasn't going to have anybody dictate what I could do.

I quickly found my success created problems, not only with the elite powers who threw lawsuits at me daily, but also with my followers. Using royalties from my books, I rented a spacious Spanish colonial in Pasadena, California where I could absorb three hundred days of the sunshine that I been denied in prison. Not long after moving in, followers began showing up on my doorstep. Like the Joads, they had lost everything and had packed their cars with their remaining possessions. They wanted me to provide a solution. I was their last hope.

I employed the first few families with jobs like research and organizing rallies. But as more arrived in campers and jalopies, my well-heeled neighbors used the city council and police to fine and pressure me. I had a moment of deep reflection.

Being a leader of the poor is not easy, and I questioned why I had traveled this path. The Movement provided an outlet for my vengeance. It was personal for me, but it was also personal for all of the members of The Movement too. I went to jail, but they had lost a lot more and were slaves to credit cards with high compounding interest. We had all been screwed, but they needed my voice. I felt I couldn't let them down, but I didn't have a quick solution to provide for my supporters. Then it came from an unlikely source.

Mrs. Victoria Winston was the widow of the late billionaire Harold Winston who had manipulated California's energy crisis in the nineties, causing record high electricity bills, bankrupting thousands, and even causing death. I cited that deceased scoundrel in both of my books and condemned his family for living luxuriously off of ill-gotten gains. Guilt-ridden by my prose, when she heard of my housing dilemma--exploited by the media--she gave me a thousand acres of land along with a ranch house in west Texas. Although I was apprehensive about moving to the Longhorn State, it was the only option.

Once on that flat and dusty land, even more flocked to me. The ranch turned into a commune. I kept the newcomers busy tending cattle and planting acres of crops. The older ones had cafeteria or infirmary jobs. If they didn't work, they were kicked out. I wasn't giving handouts, I was building a self-sufficient organization.

I continued to write and send out weekly videos--but this time in front of an audience. As The Movement kept growing, we accepted donations and obtained nonprofit status.

Since leaving prison, I kept tabs on Jeffrey. He sat on several banking boards, but was not the head of anything: powerful and never public. His wealth had accumulated tremendously. I had him watched day and night.

I developed a circle of capable men and women. The guilt-ridden corporate types were sent back to financial institutions as spies, while those with military and law enforcement training were given surveillance and security duties. Like the National Guard, the latter group held a one weekend a month paramilitary training on a remote part of the property. I wasn't looking to start any violence, but since I had provoked the powerful, I wanted to be ready if shit "something" happened.

A chain of command was developed to take care of all the operations. A young man named Cameron "Cam" Jennings stood out, and became my Chief Operations Officer. He was an ambitious ex-army man with a business management degree. He always looked to expand and strengthen The Movement.

When Oscar, my former cellmate, was released, I hired him as my personal secretary. He had kept The Movement thriving in the prison after I left. He transitioned quickly to the commune after twenty-seven years in lock up and kept me organized.

From the beginning, Cam and Oscar didn't get along. Oscar didn't trust Cam and Cam thought the ex-con was too old and had institutional syndrome. I thought a little disagreement was healthy, like the way Washington had Jefferson and Hamilton bickering on the same cabinet. Cam pushed for expansion, while Oscar always voiced caution. Sometimes the atmosphere was tense, but I believed it made us stronger.

Things ran smoothly for a couple of years until the infamous Bloody Monday. I decided to commemorate the anniversary of the start of the Great Depression by holding a rally on the last Monday of October in the morning and then marching over to the New York Stock Exchange in the afternoon. We had permits for Union Park, but the march was held under wraps.

Busloads of the discontented came from far and wide. More than I had imagined, at least a couple hundred thousand. Populists and musicians took the stage and belted out their sentiments about the capitalist crooks. I finished the mid-afternoon with graphs of inequities displayed on a thirty-foot screen, along with pictures of the ultra-wealthy who made capital by exploitation. The crowd was whipped into an angry frenzy. I mentioned that Wall Street was a few miles away. "What should we do? How about we go there before the closing bell and let the goons of greed know we, the people, are watching them? Does this sound like a good idea?" The shouts of approval were tremendous.

But before the crowd made the two-mile hike down Broadway, thousands of NYPD and the National Guard had cut off several square blocks leading to the Exchange. There were too many assembled in an hour. Somebody in my organization had tipped somebody off. I had no idea who.

Tens of thousands of my supporters marched up to the blocked streets from all directions, unable to meet in front of the Stock Exchange as planned. The scene was chaotic. The police waved batons and shotguns shouting at us to disperse immediately. My people, pressed shoulder-to-shoulder and packed dozens of bodies deep, were infuriated at being denied their first amendment right of assembly. Then, all at once, ~~assholes~~ troublemakers that weren't with us tore through the crowd, taunting the authorities by throwing bottles and trash at them. Although they wore anarchy circled As and covered their faces with black bandanas, they seemed wrong, inauthentic. (I've always had zero tolerance for anarchists, having them thrown out at events.) These guys were too clean, looking bathed and their uniforms were creased as if unpacked an hour earlier.

More and more people kept arriving, compounding the insanity of the situation. I remember yelling at the top of my voice, trying to keep order, when somebody called my name, my given one, Randall. I turned, and Oscar leapt in front of me. There were gunshots and Oscar slumped.

I caught him before he fell. Around me was mayhem—screaming and shoving. A middle-aged man wearing a faded American flag T-shirt with some cable pundit's slogan pointed a revolver at me, glaring with all the hate in the world. Suddenly, Cam grabbed the man from behind and threw him head first into the pavement. Blood oozed from the man's unconscious face. There were more gunshots, and hundreds of panicked people stampeded.

I pulled Oscar along with the crowd. He was bleeding horribly, his torso covered in warm sticky crimson. I needed to get my friend to the hospital, but I was caught in a current of staggering bodies and swinging elbows. I kept dragging Oscar, pushed by the mass of bodies away from Wall Street.

Finally I found refuge in an alley. I tried to stop the bleeding, but it was too late. Oscar dying in my arms said that The Movement was worth dying for and warned me to watch my back. I sobbed mightily.

The police arrested me and another six hundred. They charged me with inciting a riot and were trying to make a homicide case too. Thirteen had died, including an officer, and thousands were injured. Windows of buildings in a three-mile radius had been smashed, and cars had been overturned and razed. The media ramped up a smear campaign against me.

I never found out who killed Oscar and attempted to assassinate me. Cam, who had also been arrested, said the man had been trampled seconds after he hit the ground. There were so many who would love to see me dead. Many powerful people wanted the populace to be sedate again. The shooter looked like a disciple of the airwave sleaze, but maybe they wanted me to think that.

There was another problem. I had traitors in The Movement, but who? The entire riot had been a set up. The police had been aware of the protest the entire time and kept quiet, never contacting us. The hooligans weren't mine either. When thinking of powerful people who could manipulate a peaceful demonstration into a riot, I thought of the board.

After making bail, I returned to Texas knowing I needed to retaliate, fast and hard. I was definitively going to serve jail time again and expected the FBI to shutdown the commune within a week. The powers that had Oscar killed, were trying to eliminate me and discredit The Movement. It was payback time.

I had prepared for violent responses since the beginning of The Movement, but only as a last resort. I wrote up a hit list and sent out a message to all of the operators to take out the trash. Five days later, in a single night, seven national execs and in one unfortunate case an entire family were terminated. Most were taken out with bombs, but bullets were used. Many more properties and buildings were destroyed, including all of Jeffrey's real estate, except for the compound which had been fortified after the first protests years earlier. Every Statesmen board member was executed, besides Jeffrey...because I wanted it that way.

A dozen of my elite staff escaped the compound before the FBI raid. We expected it and were gone hours after "The Night of Justified Vengeance." ~~I didn't feel~~ I felt bad leaving my followers behind to fend off the Feds, but time was of the essence. I had to finish this before I got caught. I had to get Jeffrey Donahue.

My staff rendezvoused in a small town in New Mexico four days later. We came up with a plan and split up. One group went to Mexico as a decoy, and another to Michigan to talk to the militias. My group composed of

Greg, Oren, and Cam headed west. Only Cam knows my true plan. He understands that Jeffrey was the cause of all of this bloodshed and nonsense.

* * *

Murray walks out the door with the other guards. He lights a cigarette, that's the sign. Cam radios Oren on the other side of the property.

"Showtime."

A moment later Oren's voice says over the wireless, "In five,"

Four. Three. Two. One. Boom! The ground shakes like an earthquake. Murray points behind the mansion, where smoke billows into the rising orange sun. He yells to the muscleheads who run to the back of the property. You sprint to the front door, Cam and Greg behind you. Murray waits.

"Skunk's in the poolroom," he says as you pass him.

You know this room, having played snooker with some of this century's great financial scoundrels. Men whose names the public never sees, because they want it that way, and yet their impact is global. Many of their names appeared in obituaries two weeks ago.

Cam and Greg follow you through an elaborate hallway and down the stairs. You feel excitement. The end is now. Jeffrey is your obligation. You could have had him assassinated, but you preached personal responsibility. You're walking the talk. You smile, thinking about the life drifting out of those cornflower blue eyes.

You hear your men's footsteps on the basement stairs behind you and stop. The poolroom door is shut, but light floods around the bottom of the door. This is where Jeffrey is—this is where generations of financial malfeasance will end, where you will be avenged.

When you kick open the door, you notice the missing pool tables. It doesn't make sense. You run across the empty expanse to the smoking room—renowned for its walk-in humidor—Berretta raised. Greg hustles to your side, and Cam is behind you. You inhale the slightest scent of cigar smoke, but reaching for the door you find it locked. Bam! A deafening blast.

The door, the adjacent wall, your hands, and your face are covered in warm, red gunk and grayish matter...Greg's brains. You watch your loyal comrade slide from the wall to the floor, the front of his young face missing. Immediately, from the base of your stomach nausea shoots upward. You know you've been set up...again. Is it Murray?

Gripping the Beretta, you swivel and duck, aiming at the entry door. You're going to die, but not before squeezing off a few rounds. You fire into an empty doorway until your gun clicks empty. It is only then that you notice Cam is standing over Greg's body and pointing his gun at you. Smoke wafts from its barrel.

You meet his cold eyes, and the gun in Cam's hand jumps with a blinding flame. You are pounded backwards into the ground. There is an echo of the blast and the stench of gunpowder. Pain is everything and crimson fluid is everywhere. The world fades to black.

* * *

I don't regret the actions I have taken. The Movement, for all of its faults, has created some transparency of the mass corruption happening in world finance, and a better understanding of how it affects all of our lives. I hope I have given power back to the people once again and sincerely hope that they will not squander it. Though my obsession with Jeffrey Donahue has been personal, I hope you, the public, will understand that it is also universal. We are all toyed with by people like him. Without Jeffrey, I would have been an exec at some bank, working sixty hours a week taking money from hard working people for the silver spoon community like him. His greed and contempt for the working class first led me into being an exploiter of the worst order, but then a savior to the people.

The violence that has happened is the result of Bloody Monday. They started it. Today I plan on finishing it, at least my beef with Jeffrey. It is me or him. If I don't make it, please keep ~~my story~~ The Movement alive and watch, always watch, those with money. They have a disease and they will destroy others so that their own pile of ill-gotten gains will continue to grow. Stay strong. Stay skeptical. Stay vigilant.

Sincerely,
Randall Waters (aka Jack Hamilton)

* * *

Light seeps back into your eyes, and you realize you can't move your right arm. Breaths of air are excruciating. Cam shot you between the front of your shoulder and the vest at a downward angle. With your left arm, you reach for the back-up pistol in your ankle holster, but Cam, the traitorous bastard, steps on your hand and kicks the gun free.

"Clear," Cam yells.

The cigar room door opens and Jeffrey walks out. He looks older, but still has the boyish, mischievous look, even with gray hairs and crow's feet. He is wearing a Kevlar vest under his Polo shirt and still has the air of a man owning the world. You cough up blood, feeling it building in your lungs. It's punctured.

"Is he going to die on me?" Jeffrey asks Cam.

"Not before you get a shot off first, sir."

Looking at Cam, you feel an odd moment of pride. Of course he betrayed you. He had all the characteristics that you had as a young man, which meant getting ahead by any means necessary. The younger you would have betrayed anybody to the next guy with more influence. What were you expecting? All you had to offer Cam was the elimination of powerful men and a life of hiding.

"Anything else I should know, Cameron?"

"Oren is out in the woods and should have been caught by now."

Jeffrey shakes his head. "Such a small pathetic team. I'd be embarrassed to have such a group of worthless third string players. But that's Randall for you, scraping the basement."

"Jack also left a diary behind," Cam says quickly.

Jeffrey's eyes light up. "Is that so?"

You try not to show hurt or outrage. Keep a stone poker face. Show nothing. Just don't let him know how important that memoir is. But something on your face betrays you, and Jeffrey catches it. He bends down, his blue eyes glowing to your dimming pair. His pupils are small, and the white of the retinas are bloodshot. He's definitely cranked up on something.

"More flattering stories about me, huh?"

You bite your lip and say nothing.

He stands, his back to you. "I think you need to come clean and admit it, Randy." Jeffrey spins and points at you like he's in a video from the eighties. "You've got a crush on me."

He howls with laughter, and Cam chuckles.

"Where is this great piece of Shakespearian horse-shit, Cammie-boy?"

"Out by the rose garden, sir. Buried in the front," Cam says.

You know you can't let Jeffrey find your memoir. If he does, he'll destroy it and The Movement. Everything you've built will be for nothing.

"I can't wait to read it...if I have insomnia. I'm sure it will put me to sleep like your other books did."

Jeffrey laughs again and so does Cam. It's pathetic to see Cam in the slimy role of sycophant, but it's an opening.

"You're still not funny, Jeffrey," you manage to croak out. "Cam's just a toady. He'll sell you out to the next asshole."

"Is that so?"

"No, sir," Cam says looking stern.

"Give me your gun. I want to finish this business myself," Jeffrey says with mischief brimming on his face.

Cam steps off your hand and hands his pistol over. You flex your fingers, readying them for use.

"Safety off?"

"Yes, sir."

Boom! Smoke fills the room, and Cam falls to his knees, clutching his chest. His eyes are wide in disbelief as his face turns to an ashen, unnatural gray.

"You did your job very well, but you're too much like Randall. You can't be trusted."

It hurts to see him die like this, but you feel some satisfaction. A traitor, he'll burn in hell with everybody else, hopefully closer to the flames.

"Don't feel bad about that jerkoff dying," Jeffrey says. "Remember when that guy killed your little friend...what was his name. Otis? Oscar? That's it, Oscar. Cam let him through. Of course, the bullets were meant for you. Cam should have let him keep shooting, but he felt it was a botched job and had to play fake hero. Oh well. We finally took you down." Jeffrey turns away with a gleeful smile.

With your free arm, you reach inside your jacket and find what you want. Fuck Jeffrey, Cam's corpse, and this world—you're ready to die.

"You know, Randy," Jeffrey says as he starts pacing. Here comes some convoluted self-aggrandizing speech put together months ago just for this occasion. "You and Cam are alike, poor trash thinking you can rise to my level by trying to impress people like me. Let me tell you why that's not possible."

See? So predictable. You're ready to finish this. You pull the pin on the grenade with your thumb and hold the safety lever, ignoring the blowhard's speech, waiting for him to step closer. You focus on your life and the insanity of it all. You had ambitious dreams, dreams that didn't include people, only you. What a waste. Maybe The Movement will continue after your death. The people will stand up, refusing to give their hard earned money to the wealthy. Maybe people will see the mistakes you made and still value The Movement, making it stronger.

Regardless, even if it is all a failure and things remain the same, at least your life will end in a blast.

You giggle, coughing up the blood you're drowning in, but you can't help yourself. Life is so absurd.

Jeffrey pauses and leans over you.

The last words you ever hear are, "What's so fucking funny?"

The Prophet
Reed Farrel Coleman

Rubes, boobs, marks, suckers, saps, and stooges...Rubes, boobs, marks, suckers, saps, and stooges...Rubes, boobs, marks, suckers, saps, and stooges...
The words went round and round in Barney Peter's head like one of those carnival rides he had spent his youth setting up and breaking down. His father was a carnie spieler, his mom a cooch dancer. Barney had about as much use for them as they for him: none. But the carnie circuit was his schooling and it was where he'd met his second father and mentor, Willis Mansard, or, as he was known in the world of geeks, grafters, and grifters, the Cruelty Man. Why the name? Because it was said of Willis Mansard that he lacked both heart and conscience. His reputation was that he would scam his own grandmother on her deathbed if it suited his purposes. In his world, damnations of that nature were grace notes of admiration and respect. The Cruelty Man wore his moniker proudly until the day a profoundly annoyed congregation of Baptists spiked him to a cross of creosote soaked railroad ties before putting him to the flame. How was Cruelty to have known, after all, that the majority of the male congregants in that part of southern Indiana were comprised of Klan members? Ah, the blessed Klan, whose notion of turning the other cheek gave newfound meaning to the concept of Christian forgiveness.

Rubes, boobs, marks, suckers, saps, and stooges...Rubes, boobs, marks, suckers, saps, and stooges...Rubes, boobs, marks, suckers, saps, and stooges...
The words went round and round to the rhythm of the rails. *Ka-ching ka-ching...ka-ching ka-ching... ka-ching ka-ching...*And so it went, Barney staring at the star-poisoned sky through a two foot hole in the boxcar roof. He wasn't alone in the boxcar neither. A man was never alone with nothing more than his own thoughts nowadays, not with the world gone into the crapper. There were five 'bos sharing the dirty straw bedding with him, the boxcar reeking of the cattle that had been herded out into the pens at Chicago to await their slaughter. While the steers themselves were gone, the earthy, gut-turning ammonia

stink of their piss and manure clung to the straw like a baby monkey to its mama's titty. His companions were dead asleep as much from the need to escape the stench as from the cheap hooch they'd passed around. Barney hadn't slept in four days. He was determined never to sleep again, not after what he'd seen in Goshen. He didn't even want to close his eyes.

It wasn't as if he hadn't run the Godwallop Con or, as some favored, the Rapture Play before. The Cruelty Man had taught it to him in its myriad incarnations early on in their partnership. At first, Barney had played the kid. Then as he grew, he acted most often as the shill. He'd made the play with Cruelty any number of times and after Cruelty's demise, Barney'd run versions of the swindle himself with a bunch of interchangeable partners and all sorts of kids. The kids were always the trickiest part of the grift. After Barney had grown too old to play the innocent, it would sometimes take Cruelty and him weeks to scout out a kid who could carry it off. But since the Crash in '29, there had been an explosion of fresh talent from which to choose. Poverty and desperation put a lot of boys out on the road to fend for themselves. Those same factors also made the God-fearing boobs even more susceptible to the con. The Godwallop always worked like a charm...until Goshen.

Cruelty used to say, "Religion is the greatest con of all. I can't testify as to whether Jesus was the King of the Jews, but I am here to tell you he was the King of the Grifters and Lazarus was nothing but a shill. Believers are the biggest suckers of them all. They are as near as asking to be taken as a spinster aunt on a whiskey and opium bender. You ever been to tent revival, boy?" Cruelty never waited for Barney to answer. "It's nothing but second-rate flim flam dressed up in a lot of hokum and hallelujahs. I played the cripple in them shows more times than a man has fingers and toes to count on. Say enough amens and praise the Lords and you'll have them in your hip pocket."

He was right of course. There were a hundred gaffes you could run on the bible bangers that you wouldn't dare run on anyone else for fear of getting your liver cut out and fed to you while you were dying. There was the Splinter of the Cross play, where you claimed to have in your possession a piece of the cross upon which Jesus had been crucified. The papists fell for that one in a big way. Them and their fetish for sacred objects was a grifter's goldmine. There were ten variations of that con alone, but since the Cruelty Man had gotten his on a fiery cross, Barney hadn't had the heart to run it. That was the thing that distinguished him from his mentor: Barney was cursed with a conscience of sorts, at least the remnants of one. Whereas Cruelty could step on a mark's throat until he choked out every penny from the rube's pockets, Barney would let a mark up for air.

"That will be your undoing, boy," Cruelty warned. "Once you've taken them, they are not going to see leaving them some crumbs as an act of kindness. You might as well bleed them dry once you've opened up the vein. Their judgment will be equally harsh regardless of how much blood you leave behind."

Barney knew Cruelty was right. Cut off three of a man's limbs, he ain't going to thank you for not relieving him of the fourth. Cruelty had also advised his protégé that the further outside the city you went, the easier it was to prey on the believers.

"The more straw in their teeth and shit on their shoes, the easier the score," he used to say.

Cruelty was right about that too. The boonies, that's where Barney had made his living since Willis Mansard's death. And Goshen was as far away from a city as you could get while staying within the confines of the contiguous United States. It was a pretty well-to-do little farming community. Well-to-do meaning three notches above dirt poor at most times, but flush these days. Goshen was founded by a group of like-minded Christian zealots in the years after the War of Northern Aggression. They were the kind of good Christians who quoted liberally from Hebrews while despising Jews as usurious Christ-killers; the kind of good Christians who claimed to love all brother and sister Christians while hating Catholics more than the Jews; the kind of good Christians who considered the colored races less than subhuman yet used them to pick their crops and sometimes raise up their children. They treated women like slaves. Didn't drink, didn't smoke, didn't dance, didn't sing anything but the psalms, didn't spare the rod. To say they were severe was to be unkind to severe. In other words, they were perfect stooges.

It was all perfect. That should have been the first sign to Barney that he should queer the Goshen play himself and take it to Missouri or Arkansas. Cruelty had warned him a hundred times about perfection.

"When it all goes right, it's all wrong, boy. You best throw in your cards and take the game out of state."

Barney couldn't bring himself to fold the play. For once he had the funds to do it right, to run the gaffe with style. This was not to say that Cruelty and him hadn't showed their high strutting stuff, but they were always having to compromise, to make do. All Barney'd ever hear from

Willis Mansard was how he had run big stock scams in KC and St. Loo.

"That was the cream on the top of the cream at the top of the bottle. Big money in, bigger money out. That was living, boy. Fancy suits, fancier dames, champagne and fish eggs on crackers. We wore spats on our feet, not shitkickers. Problem with them plays, though, is once you run 'em in a town, you're burned. Word spreads in the city and from city to city faster than you could set up shop. No, son, your best shot is to stay out here with the hayseeds and haystacks."

Barney knew it was dumb to try and prove a point to a dead man, but he'd done dumber things. He was sure Cruelty would be so proud of him. Everything was aces. He'd found a pure red heifer at a dairy farm ten miles outside Goshen. The farmer either didn't care a lick for bible prophecy or cared more about the fifty dollars—half now, half later—Barney had paid him for the beast and to continue to shelter and feed it until show time. Pure red heifers weren't easy to come by when you needed them. Even now, even after Goshen, Barney laughed to himself about some of the stunts he and Cruelty had pulled to get around that part of the prophecy. They'd once even used ladies hair dye mixed with shoe polish to cover a spotted brown cow. Takes a lot of hair dye and shoe polish to cover a cow head to hoof. Barney had been scared to death they would get found out.

"Now don't you worry none, boy," Willis told him. "These country folk got some strange notions about what the Good Book says and even stranger ideas of what it means. Most of them can't read and those that can usually just twist it up to suit their needs. You and me, we got nothing on these yokel preachers and prophets."

The good fortune Barney had stumbling across the red heifer was nothing compared to the luck he'd had with the kid. The rest of it was nothing if the kid couldn't pull off the play. And the kid Barney found was worth ten red heifers. He was born to the part. Near twelve years old, but looking small and young for his years. Had the kind of blond hair that was closer to white than yellow and when the wind wasn't blowing it this way or that, it fell in a long limp sheet to the nape of his neck. Had them cold blue eyes looked like they were made out of river ice. He was milk white complected. With his full face and soft jawline, the boy might've been an angel, but his gnarled mouth put the kibosh on that angel stuff. There were cottontails had prettier upper lips than this kid. Even with his mouth clamped up tight, you could see the hint of his teeth. Your child prophet always needed an affliction or deformity. That's what sold the hustle. When Barney'd done his child prophesying for Cruelty, he'd done it with a stammer.

"… and the peo—peo—people of the p—p—pri—prince who is to c—c—come will de—de—de—destroy the city and the sanctuary. From Da—Da—Daniel, n—n—nine:twenty-sss-sss-six. "

Worked, but it sure did get on folks' nerves. Cruelty used to joke that they gave up their worldly goods just so's they wouldn't have to listen to the child prophet struggle so with his preaching. Cruelty told his protégé he was really happy when he'd grown out of the part.

"No wonder to me why Pharaoh let go his grip on the Hebrews. Forget the angel of death. Probably couldn't take Moses and all that stuttering and stammering and such. Boy, I don't suppose I could take much more of it neither. If I had to sit through it one more time, I might've started praying for the End Days my own self."

With the night sky passing overhead, Barney was thinking back to the Monday when the kid wandered into Goshen as if out of the wilderness. He remembered saying to himself that even if he was having second thoughts about the Second Coming, the time for him to crumb the play had since passed. For weeks he had greased the gears of the yahoo grapevine with whispers and innuendoes of a boy preacher carrying the true gospel. With the world in the outhouse and with believers looking to the Lord for answers, it hadn't taken much for the whispers to become shouts, for the shouts to echo across the valleys, for the echoes to become a fever. It had also seemed to Barney that the Almighty grifter himself had taken a hand in setting up the con. For soon after Barney's whisperings had taken root, Goshen and the surrounding area was beset by a plague of traveling preachers, tent revivals, and bible salesmen. Barnabas Bixby the Bible Man was the guise under which Barney had taken up temporary residence in town. It was against this backdrop of false prophets and profiteers that the barefoot, harelipped boy—carrying nothing but a beaten, leather-bound bible—strode into town to feed the fevered souls of Goshen tales of the four horsemen.

Barney or, more accurately, Barnabas Bixby, had done such a good job of priming the apocalypse pump that the kid's arrival alone seemed itself a fulfillment of biblical prophecy. When he walked down Main Street, cars and tractors, horses pulling carts, swung to the curb. People on the dusty street stood staring, their maws hanging open with a mixture of fear, hope, and awe. An old woman fainted dead away. Another sobbed. One shrieked, "We are delivered." But it was only when an old man pointed and called out, "It's him! It's the Prophet!

The Boy," that Barney knew this would be something special. When the men bought into the con even before you got it going, you had them. But the set up, as good as it was, as perfect the timing, they were nothing compared to what happened next.

The kid stopped in the middle of the street in front of the general store on one side and Bock's Boarding House across the way. Bowing his head and raising up his arms up so that his silhouette looked like the letter Y in the afternoon sun, he held himself perfectly still and waited...and waited...and waited. He waited for the murmur to die down, for all engine noise to stop, for pin-drop silence. It didn't take but a moment for him to get it neither. Barney, watching through his open window at the boarding house had never seen anything like it. Then, when the kid had the silence he had seemed to want, he lifted his head, lowered his arms, and turned to look at Josephus Waring, owner of the general store. He did not speak in words, but Waring understood. The bespeckled, apron-clad Waring picked up a wooden fruit crate, carried it to the center of the street, and laid it at the feet of the boy prophet. He turned it upside down.

"Thank you, sir," said the Boy in a hush that everyone on the street could hear. Even Barney, perched up on the second floor.

That was one of the things that made the kid so good. Harelipped as he was, he spoke as clear as polished glass and never seemed to have the need to shout. It was that uncanny calmness that had drawn Barney to him in the first place, that and his perfect affliction of course.

"A storm is coming," the Boy spoke in that hushed voice. "A storm that will sweep all of us away in one form or another. In spite of what you may have heard, that storm, brothers and sisters, is not years away but nearly upon us."

And Barney would be goddamned if an icy gust of wind didn't just then blow down Main Street, kicking up dust into the faces of the crowd gathering around the Boy. The Boy himself did not blink or turn away even as the yokels grabbed their collars, pulling them tight to their necks and shielding their eyes with their hands. They all moved closer and closer to the Boy. Soon it seemed everyone for miles around was at the Boy's feet. Barney didn't hear the blare of Gabriel's horn for the din of cash registers ringing in his head.

"You have been told there are signs and omens, trials and tribulations to come before the End Times. And so there are, and so there shall be, but as in all ways of the Lord, there is mystery too. The signs are there for us to read, but we are blind. We have been blinded by the devil himself. Over the next few days, the people of Goshen will see again, for the Lord has sent me to peel the blackness from your eyes. For the next six days I will be right here at this same hour, in this very spot, on this very crate, and I will deliver sight unto you. Come if you will or come not. Attending me won't win you the Lord's favor and save you nor will the opposite be true. Being raised up or left behind is your own doing; not mine, not the Lord's, your own. Come and behold or come not at all, but be saved." The kid stepped off the fruit crate, turned, and walked out of town the way he walked in.

Barney lifted his eyes to the ceiling of his spare, little room and whispered, "Willis, are you seeing this? Are you hearing this?"

* * *

Barnabas Bixby the Bible Man didn't begin his part in the con until day four of the boy prophet's preaching on Main Street. No, for those first three days he was content to watch from his box seat on the second story of the boarding house. As Cruelty had taught him, you had to be patient, you had to let a thing build a momentum all its own.

"Listen up good, son. You cannot pick a crop before its time. Corn, for instance. You pick corn too green and all it's ever gonna be is green corn. The best scams are the ones you just set in motion and let roll down the mountain of their own accord. Let the thing breathe like wine. You'll know when to pour it."

So it was with the Godwallop. You had to let it breathe. And man oh man was this Rapture Play breathing. Each day, the crowd had doubled until Main Street was crawling with rubes, boobs, marks, saps, suckers, and stooges from near and far. On that Tuesday, the Boy eased into things with stuff the people of Goshen had no doubt already heard from every itinerant preacher who had passed through the area for the last decade and a half. He spoke on how many of the warning signs had already shown themselves, on how the Dust Bowl, the Great War were all a part of biblical prophecy. Except when the Boy said those things, it was different from when them other preachers said them. When they would have shouted, he whispered. When they would have pounded their fists into their palms with rage, he stood stone still, calm and serene.

"The apocalypse is not a time for fear or anger for those of us who have accepted the Lord Jesus Christ as our savior and master," he told the crowd in his signature hush. "It is a time for peace and reflection, for forgiveness of those who would not be taken up. We should not revile them, but pity them."

On Wednesday, the Boy explained how others had misinterpreted the Good Book. That, in fact, the Jews had already returned to Zion. That they had never really left.

"The Hebrews are God's chosen people and they are a shrewd and stubborn people. They have never fully abandoned the land the Lord gave to them as their birthright. For years they have worked secretly to rebuild the temple. The foundation is already in place. And soon, when they take back all of Israel and their language is restored, the first stone walls shall rise."

The lines—written by Cruelty over thirty years earlier—worked beautifully with the assembled crowd. It appealed to their bone-deep anti-Semitism. No one in attendance had trouble believing that the Jews had plotted secretly and were clever enough to fool the A-rabs or them Brit sons of bitches. Barney and the Boy didn't need the Almighty's help with this part of the con. They had another, almost as powerful ally in this: Henry Ford. His railings against the Jews were as a good as gospel with the good people of Goshen. Yet here again, the boy took the words from Cruelty's script and made them his own. And good god damn if the kid didn't almost have the crowd crying for the poor Jews who would make the Second Coming possible, but who would not reap its benefits.

On Thursday, it was Barnabas Bixby's time to shine. Of course by then, none of the yahoos and yokels would remember that it was Barnabas Bixby who had whispered in their ears about the boy preacher. That was the thing. It didn't take much whispering to get this play rolling down the metaphorical mountain that Cruelty had talked about. And when he whispered in those ears, Barnabas Bixby had made sure to couch his words in ambiguity so that if anyone did recall his identity, they could not say he was a liar.

The Boy had stepped up his game some. He wasn't screaming exactly. He never had to scream, but he was speaking more rapidly, more excitedly so that his deformity was very pronounced. It gave him a snarling, feral look that belied his usually calm demeanor. That day he was speaking of the mongrel hordes, of the secret pact between the Bolsheviks, the yellow-skinned Chinese, and the brown-skinned Indians. How their armies were already two hundred million strong and growing and how they would overrun the world like a tidal wave. And just when he got them thoroughly whipped up and near breathless at the thought of these mud people ruining the world, the Boy returned to his usually hushed tones.

"But none of this, my brothers and sisters, no army of any kind will inflict the damage to the world that this upheaval of the earth itself will do. We will see this in the earthquakes that will—"

"False prophet!" someone cried out from the crowd—Barnabas Bixby, pointing a bible directly at the Boy. "You are a false prophet. Let me quote to all of you from Matthew, words most of you know by heart. 'For many will come in my name, saying I am Christ, and will mislead many. And many false prophets will arise and mislead many.' And don't give us any of your mumbo jumbo talk about how clever the Hebrews are and mysteries we don't understand."

"You know your Matthew, sir," the Boy bowed his head in respect. The bow wasn't in the script nor was what followed. "Let me quote some Matthew to you. 'And in various places there will be famines and earthquakes.'"

Barney wasn't concerned at the kid's playing it off the cuff. He had done masterfully so far and didn't see how a little variation from the script could hurt. Besides, Barney had run this so many times that he felt he could get the play back on track if the kid strayed too far.

"Very good, prophet." Barnabas applauded by thumping the bible. "Well, when will these earthquakes—"

Just then, a chorus of barking and howling dogs rose up in the distance. The horses that some of the farmers used to haul their goods reared up, neighing wildly. Cows that had been brought into town for sale and that had stayed placid in their corals bolted, creating a small stampede. Pigs in their holding pens shrieked and squealed as if being slaughtered. There was a moment of utter stillness and then the ground rumbled and shook. People scattered, running to and fro. The stores swayed, some bricks falling from the boarding house façade. And then just as suddenly...nothing. Stillness once again. In that moment, Barney realized he was no longer in control of the hustle, but that the hustle was in control of him. Yet, he'd been at this too long to turn and run.

"Do you still name me a false prophet, sir?" the Boy called to him, but with no anger or belligerence in his quiet voice.

"Trickster! Huckster!" Barney cried out. "Everyone gets lucky now and again."

"That is true," the Boy agreed. "So tomorrow let us see. Let the good people of Goshen bear witness tomorrow on this very street."

"To what, another one of your tricks?"

"Let us all see what tomorrow brings, sir. What do you good people of Goshen say," the Boy asked, his arms extended, palms up, to the crowd. "If tomorrow I can reveal more of the Lord's signs, will you follow the word of the Lord? Will you put your faith in me that I am his messenger?"

The crowd, now reassembled and packed even more tightly than before the eruption, gave out a low roar of approval. Some shouted hallelujah. Some amen. And Barney, who had to acknowledge that even he had been temporarily stunned by the events of the last few moments, breathed again. Because no matter what forces were at work here, the play was back on track. After tomorrow's second helping of God would come the Wallop and after that Barney and the kid would be flush. He'd be hip deep in women, real scotch whiskey, and lighting dollar cigars with ten dollar bills. So lost was he in his fantasy, Barnabas Bixby nearly missed his cue.

"We'll just see 'bout that, Boy. 'Cause come tomorrow, I'll name the sign you have to produce for these good people. No more of your tricks and tomfoolery tomorrow. I imagine you won't get too much peaceful sleep tonight, thinking about all the possibilities and how you plan to pull one over like you done today."

"Maybe so, sir. Maybe so. Let us see what tomorrow brings."

With that, the Boy stepped off his crate, moved through the crowd and disappeared at the edge of town as he always did.

* * *

The gathering crowd was enormous. There was still near five minutes to go before the appointed hour and everything was set. Barney had managed to sneak out of town in the dead of night and get to the farm where the red heifer was being kept. He was feeling so confident in how things would turn out that not only did he pay the dairy farmer the twenty-five bucks he owned him, he threw in an extra ten spot on top of it. Now all there was left for Barnabas Bixby to do was to wade into the crowd, dare the Boy to produce a pure red heifer, and watch the yahoos be awed and amazed as the cow ambled down Main Street. Once that happened, the Boy would have them. He would beseech them to give up all their worldly goods as proof of their belief in their savior. Of course, the Boy would "suggest" they give their money and most valuable goods to that stubborn and foolish disbeliever, Barnabas Bixby.

Bixby was not without supporters among the townsfolk. That was perfect, because it was always the last minute converts who coughed up the most treasure to the disbeliever. His supporters clapped him on the back and applauded as Barnabas strode out of Bock's Boarding House in his best black suit, bible clutched in hand. They had even set up a fruit crate next to the Boy's for him to stand on. Just as he stepped up onto it, a small, blond figure strode barefoot down Main Street. The roar was deafening as the crowd parted for the Boy. He offered his right hand to Bixby, who, as planned, refused to shake it. God once again seemed to be taking a hand in it as the dark, roiling storm clouds moved in to blot out the sun. A vicious wind came up, blowing hats off heads. What great theater, Barney thought, no carnie had anything on this.

When he saw the crowd extended all the way to the end of Main Street and that it filled the wooden sidewalks so that they pressed up against the storefronts, Barnabas Bixby spoke the words everyone in Goshen had been waiting exactly twenty-four hours to hear.

"Speak to the sons of Israel that they bring you an unblemished red heifer in which is no defect and on which no yoke has ever been placed. Numbers 19:2-7," Barnabas bellowed as deeply and loudly as he could manage. There was a gasp from the crowd. Unlike yesterday's rumblings of the earth, which might very well have been a matter of lucky timing, they didn't see how the Boy could, out of thin air and with no preparation, produce a perfect red heifer. Although he kept his face stern, inside Barney was smiling. Then, he saw a man in the crowd, an unwelcome one, pushing his way toward him. It was the dairy farmer. He couldn't get to Barney, so he stopped in his tracks and mouthed, "The cow is dead. The cow is dead."

Barnabas Bixby kept his stern expression, only inside the smile had vanished. Without the red heifer, it would all fall apart. Everything depended on that damned red cow. Cruelty's words rang loudly as a thousand steeple bells in his head, "When it all goes right, it's all wrong." But there was no turning back now and the kid was so good, Barney hoped he'd be able to improvise something when the red heifer failed to make its grand entrance. Apparently, the kid had been paying attention and noticed the dairy farmer too.

When the Boy lifted up his arms, a hush fell over the crowd. "Is there an animal doctor among you?"

A heavyset man with wire-rim glasses raised his hand and called out, "I'm Franklin Dunbar, Doctor of Veterinary Medicine and I see to most of the livestock in these parts."

"Dr. Dunbar," the Boy said, "will you please go into the cow pen. There you will find a spotted brown cow fat with calf and about as ready to drop that calf as can be. Will you fetch her and bring it here presently?"

Dunbar did not make answer, but turned on his heel and headed toward the holding pens. What, Barney wondered, was the kid up to? He knew the kid was good, better than good, but was he *that* good? No, nobody, not even Willis Mansard was *that* good. Besides, the kid didn't have any money with which to work a side scam or to arrange a fallback. That was their deal: the kid only got his share if the play hit gold. Barney was still doing the mental permutations when Dr. Dunbar returned, a big bellied, spotted brown cow trailing behind him. Again, the crowd parted like the Red Sea for Moses and the Hebrews.

The Boy stepped down from his crate. He walked over to the cow and ran his hands along her flanks. He then stepped back up onto the crate. "Behold!" said the Boy and almost immediately, the cow laid on her side. Within seconds, hoofs and the nose of a calf showed out beneath the tail of the mother. It wasn't five minutes before she had dropped the calf to Main Street in the most effortless birth Dr. Franklin Dunbar had ever seen. And when the doctor was done cleaning off the newborn, the calf stood on wobbly legs as if to show the assembled masses her pure, unblemished red hide. The crowd was stunned silent.

Barnabas Bixby, his heart in his throat, carried on. "By what means of evil and sorcery have you done this, false prophet?"

"By the will of the Lord, sir. By his will a thousand such calves may be born, here or in the Holy Land. Even today, such a calf is born there as here," The Boy then turned to the crowd. "The end is at hand, brothers and sisters, but for those of you who truly believe, it is the beginning of heaven without end. Tomorrow, bring all your worldly goods, your cash money and jewelry, any such material thing you have ever loved before God and lay it down here in this street for soon the horn will sound and you will be risen." During the tumult that arose in the wake of his pronouncement, the Boy leaned over to his partner and whispered, "Meet me tonight on the other side of the animal pens just before sunrise." Then he stepped down off his crate and vanished as he always did.

Barney never met the Boy. He waited until Goshen was asleep and ran. He had been running ever since. He had left behind everything he owned, every stitch of clothing save those on his back. He'd left his bag of flim flam props and disguises, his fake money and false papers. Now the sun was leaking through the roof of the boxcar and there was a squealing of brakes.

"Come on, fella," one of the hobos said, pulling at Barney's arm. "Best get going while the getting's good or you'll catch a beating from one of the railroad bulls or the yardmen."

Barney jumped out when they yanked the door back and he tumbled down the side of a small hill. The 'bo who had urged him to jump told Barney he knew of a camp deep in the woods just a few miles from where they'd landed. Barney figured he was in no position to be choosy and he was so damned hungry he would have gone anywhere as long as there was the chance of a meal. Once into the woods, the hobo excused himself saying he needed to let a little water out. Barney took the opportunity to do the same. When he was done, he sat down, back against a tree and waited for his traveling companion to resurface. After a few minutes, when the hobo didn't reappear, Barney called out to him.

"Over here!" the 'bo answered back.

"Phewwww!" Barney said to himself.

Except when Barney followed the voice, he didn't find the man. Instead he stumbled over something. When he looked back to see what it was, he found he couldn't breathe. For there on the forest floor was the carcass of a perfect red calf, throat slit, eyes open and unseeing. Barney heard a twig snap behind him and spun his head around. The Boy!

"Behold," was what he said and laughed at Barney. Then he took his right index finger and rubbed it over his harelip. With that, the deformity vanished. "Come on, con man, we've got a world to save one town at a time."

Arbitraging the Blood Brain Barrier
Eric Stone

What was that? I hate it when I don't know. It's always right about now, right about hour 31 of my 36-on shift that peripheral vision starts to play tricks on me.

There it is again. It wouldn't be a problem if I didn't have to make sure it wasn't on the screen. I don't think it is. It's lower, maybe floor level. I shake my head and ignore it. If it's not on the screen, I don't care about it. I can't miss anything on the screen. Karl's happy with me when I'm making bank. But when I miss something, even if it's not costing him anything, he gets cranky real fast.

"A missed trade is a loss, my little pretties." When he yells that across the trading floor you know someone's going to get their skull rung.

What's he want from us, anyhow? It's a dying job. Soon as these kinds of outfits get faster connections, better software, we're all gone. It's 1993. Within a year, at most two, this currency trading craziness is going to be all computers all the time.

Thirty-six hours is far too long for any person to sit in front of a screen. They say it's so we can track movements, get a feel for fluctuations, spot trends. But we wear out. It's nothing that robots can't do better. And they don't need coke to keep on top of things, not that I know of.

I've already got a bloody nose but I need another line of blow, a big one to get my head straight, my eyes adjusted. I can't take my eyes off the screen so I tap the left foot pedal three times, blinking the white light above my cubicle three times, summoning the tea lady. You can ask her for tea if you want. No one does. She comes to your desk with a large mirror with neatly laid out lines of finely ground snow.

There it is again, lower right, more a sense of something moving than anything I really see. But I can't turn my head. I've got a feeling about the Singapore dollar. I'm pretty sure it's about to rise against the pound in London but stay steady against the U.S. dollar. If it does it won't be for long, maybe four or five seconds before it adjusts. If I catch it in time and play it right, I'm a hero. Eight point seven five million pounds in the black if my vision cooperates and my fingers are fast enough and it hits the 0.0175 offset I'm thinking it might.

The tea lady knows better than to make any of us traders turn our heads. That's what the last one got sacked for. She can get fired for all sorts of things. Look straight ahead, not down not up, don't look at the screens, don't talk to the traders, don't do anything but your job then move on to the next cubicle. If they could be deaf, dumb and blind and still do their job, that's what Karl would want.

She holds the mirror up to me with one hand, my straw with the other and I vacuum up the long, fat white rail. It blows right through my blood-brain-barrier and sizzles along my synapses. I can't help but close my eyes for just a moment as it surges through me. I hope I didn't miss anything. I better not have missed anything.

I straighten up, hands poised on the keyboard, eyes riveted to the screen. Everything is fine for a couple of minutes but then there it is again. Four hours, thirty-eight minutes to go on my shift and whatever is going on in my peripheral vision is getting persistent, distracting.

Next time it happens I can't help myself. I turn my head quick, just a little, just enough to see that it isn't on my screen, it really is something. I still don't know what though.

Then there's a bump against my chair and I can hear heavy breathing and shit, I've got to look. The line on the Sing dollar is holding steady, it's been that way since midnight, so I chance it.

Weathers' face looking up from the floor beneath my chair is cherry red. It's always red. I don't know how the fat Aussie does this job and drinks that much. But now it's a different red than usual, tinged with blue, a little purple. His eyes are wide, staring past me at something way out there, beyond the ceiling even, up and out through the 51 floors above us and deep into space, high above Hong Kong. It looks like he's trying to say something.

Karl's got eagle eyes. If he sees my head disappear below the lip of the cubicle for even a moment he'll be over here. I risk it, bending an ear down toward the man on the floor at my feet.

"Sil, sil, silver." The word puffs out on what sounds like his last breath. His eyes cloud over as quick as a storm darkens the sky when it rumbles over the mountains on the east side of the island.

I can hear Karl huffing across the floor toward me and I turn my eyes back to the screen. Singapore hasn't budged. Or if it did I missed it and it settled back to where it's been all week. Keeping my eyes on the screen I nudge Weathers with a foot. He feels like a filled burlap sack.

Karl shoves into the cubicle in front of mine, so that he can see my face without me having to pull it away from the monitor.

"Is there a problem, Ford?"

I drop a shoulder down and to the right and tilt my head in that direction, rather than taking my hands off the keyboard to point.

"It's Weathers. I think he's dead."

He leans over the partition and looks down at the bottom of my chair.

"Dead crocked, you mean. That's it, I'm cashing him out."

"No, really, check his eyes. I just caught a glimpse but those are dead guy's eyes, not drunk guy's."

He leans further over the partition and takes a longer look.

"Yup, shit, I think you're right. I'll come around and drag him out of there. He say anything to you before he..."

"He said 'silver.' Beats me. I'm just trying to get my work done."

"The body's not distracting you, is it?"

"Does it look like I'm distracted?" I am, no one's ever died in my cubicle before, but I'm not about to lose my job over it. I never liked Weathers anyhow. "I think the Sing dollar's gonna move. I'm waiting on it. Gotta concentrate."

"Good man."

Karl comes around to my cubicle and I can hear him drag the body away from my chair. As bosses go he's a pain in the ass, but you've got to give him credit for being hands on.

More people come and hoist Weathers up and carry him away. Then the cleaning guy comes with a spray can of disinfectant and a brush and finally the Hoover. I don't want to think about any of that.

Three hours forty-two minutes to go and Singapore still hasn't moved. In my head I'm willing it to budge, jump an inch, less than an inch, a millimeter is all it will take, tick just slightly before my shift's done. It's mine, I know it is, I can move the damn Sing dollar with my will. I tap my foot for the tea lady again. I've got to stay straight, ready.

I hear a voice. It's loud. It's in my head. No, in my ears, coming from Karl's office. It's his half of a phone conversation.

"Silver, fucking silver. How'd he know?"

Know what? No one's given a shit about silver since the Hunt Brothers turned the whole market upside down trying to corner it and went down in flames. I heard somewhere that fat fuck Nelson Bunker had to get a job in a 7-Eleven in a Dallas suburb. Before he got rich again, that was.

Silver, silver...sterling silver? Pounds sterling? That's got to be it. We're currency traders after all. Well, not really. What we really trade is bits, computer bits, endless long lines of ones and zeros that add up to millions of dollars if they order themselves in the right way at the right time. No one has to get their hands dirty touching any real money around here, at least not the paper and metal kind.

But what about sterling? It's been quiet lately. The U.S. dollar, the euro, the yen, the baht and the Spanish peseta have been where all the action's been the past couple of weeks. The Yankee dollar's been nuts enough that at the beginning of my shift I even made fifteen grand playing it against the Hong Kong dollar. And that's not supposed to happen because of the peg. It's always fixed at 7.8 Honkies to one U.S. But the briefest, tiniest gap peeked out and I threw together a quickie three-way with the Indonesian rupiah that was a marvel. That's the kind of thing a guy can do at the start of a shift, after 20 or so hours of sleep and then that first bright bump of good morning blow. I sure as shit couldn't do anything like that now.

Three hours fourteen minutes to go and the Sing's not doing jack. Just lying there in its hammock on the verandah, one of those awful drinks they make at the Long Bar in Raffles in its hand, fat and lazy. I know it's got to move. It's gonna move soon. I can feel it.

Now I've got to take a piss. I've been ignoring it for the past hour but I can't any longer. That's why I keep the big screw-top jug under my desk. I reach down without taking my eyes off the screen to unscrew the top. An acrid, ethery stench rises up. Shit, I forgot to have the tea lady empty it after the last leak I took.

I'm shaking off when the Sing dollar ticks up just the slightest bit of a notch but it's enough. My hands fly back to the keyboard. There's only seconds, maybe three to five of them, before London and New York adjust. I sell Sing for greenbacks, a lot of them. I buy the pounds sterling, tick tock, a flick of a key later. I hold my breath for the moment it takes the trade to register.

My nose registers something else first—the reek of highly concentrated, dark orange pee. I haven't been drinking enough water. I'd dropped the jug to make the trade and it's spilled all over my shoes and the thin carpet. No matter. There's millions of dollars at stake.

Got it. The spread is 0.0035 less than I'd hoped for but it still puts my working account up a flat, tidy seven million-seven thousand pounds, nearly eleven thousand U.S. at the current rate that goes into my own pocket.

Two hours fifty-one minutes to go and I can take it easy. I've made my nut for the day. My foot taps the button that lights the red light above my cubicle. Blink twice for maintenance but not an emergency, not like a computer problem or something.

The man with the cart pushes his way down the aisle to me, takes a look and a sniff, knows what happened and assembles his supplies. When he's ready he gives me the word. I roll far enough back in my chair to give him access and he's in and out from under my desk in about 30 seconds, leaving my cubicle scented with fake pine. At least that's better than piss. He even takes my shoes and socks. He'll bring them back clean.

One tap of the white light for the real tea lady who knows to bring me iced-tea, no sugar, and three more for another rail. The pressure's off, so I might as well do some bottom feeding. The Argentine peso is showing some promise. I wonder if there's anything I can pull off between it and Eastern Europe, maybe a *ménage a trois* with the South African rand. Times like this are when the job gets creative. Not a lot of money in it, the markets are too small. Still, it can be fun.

But Weathers is stuck in my head like a bad but catchy song you can't get out until you sing it. Pounds sterling, that had to be what he meant. It had to be. He might have been a drunk, but he was a smart one. Not much got past him. I open a second window on my screen and start poking around in my recent trade history.

I can see my own trades and the overall volume for the office. There's my Sing dollar, pound trade. Someone else must have got in on it, too, since the volume in both currencies is a little higher than mine alone. Not by much though, and that's strange. There's not much point in moving less than ten million of anything unless there is a whole lot of volatility. Which there wasn't.

Looking back over the past month I find three more trades where the money I moved accounts for all that day's volume in those currencies, except for a little bit more, two million in one case, a million each in the others, all ending up in British pounds sterling.

Two hours nine minutes to go and I miss a play between the shekel, the rand and the yen. There could have been a few million yen profit in it but I wasn't fast enough. I was distracted by the other half of my screen, the half I was trying to make sense of.

Karl will be back here any minute. He can see our live screens on the screens in his office and he keeps a tight eye on the money we're tracking. I shut down the history screen. I don't want him to see what I've been doing until I've worked it out.

"A missed trade is a loss, Ford." He's standing in front of me again, peering down over the wall of my cubicle.

"You did good on the Sing dollar, but that was then. No resting on your laurels. No sleeping on the job. Only excuse I'll take for missing your moment is the one Weathers gave. And that's because it won't do me any good to chew his ass anyhow. Got that, Ford?"

I nod yes. I know he wants me to shout it out, 'Yes, sir. I got it, sir.' But I'm trying to hold back a sneeze. I look toward him, my face screwing up, neck veins bulging with the effort to hold back.

"What the hell's the matter with you?"

It sprays out of me, snot and blood and whatever crap I've been breathing in all shift and maybe even some cartilage spew from my nose in a wide arc that covers my monitor and the wall behind it and much of my desk.

Karl steps back the moment he sees it coming but he isn't quite fast enough. The shoulder and monogrammed pocket of his shirt—one of those awful royal blue shiny ones with starched white French cuffs and collar—is lightly speckled.

He doesn't say a thing, just turns and walks back to his office. He's used to this. We all are. Put a bunch of people in an open floor-plan office on 36 hour shifts without sleep and snootfuls of all the cocaine they can snort and heavy air-conditioning and sneezing's the least of it. We all bring changes of clothes with us to work.

I tap the red light twice to bring back the maintenance man and the white three times to repack my nose. There's still two hours and two minutes to go by the time it's all cleaned up. I'm jolted back into a state of jerky chemical alertness and I'm tracking the forint against the euro on the main screen and those odd little transactions in the history window.

LuAnn sits three cubicles to my right. We used to go out, almost convinced ourselves we were in love. We weren't. We aren't. We got over it and are good pals. She's a smart trader, on top of things. Karl tracks our trades, but I don't think he can see when we message each other. I open my IM screen and send her a message.

"Hey, any small trades piggybacking on yours past few shifts?"

A couple of minutes tick by before I hear back.

"Maybe. Looking."

An hour and forty-nine minutes to go when I hear back again.

"Five in past month. One or two mil each at most. All Brit £. Strange. What do you think?"

"Someone's trading for himself. Who?"

"Dangerous biz."

"Yep."

This isn't one of the legit arbitrage operations. Legal, maybe, but serving some purpose that almost certainly isn't. That's for sure. We get paid in cash, commission only. That's enough to make it clear we're not working for one of the big banks, or even any of the regulated smaller ones. Probably not even one of the Chinese banks.

Once a day a couple of big guys with tattoos peeking out above the collars of expensive suits show up empty-handed, walk into Karl's glass office, talk with him for a minute or two then walk out again carrying a briefcase without a word to or glance at anyone else. Some days their visit leaves Karl in a good mood. Some days, not. In spite of the suits, they seem more like fancy messenger boys than like the boss. Whoever they are, it's obvious that they're with one of the triads.

None of us knows who the boss is. We all know better than to ask any questions. There's a phone number to call in case of an emergency, but it's really got to be an emergency—something we can't run through Karl. I'm pretty sure it's best that way.

Whoever's money it is we're trading, laundering probably, I know a whole lot better than to even think about skimming anything off the top. I'm banking more than enough cash just doing what I'm told and keeping my mouth shut.

I wouldn't put it past our unknown boss to have had Weathers killed if he was the one making the extra trades. But my Sing dollar deal happened after they'd hauled his body away. More likely Weathers had found something out. He was nobody's fool. And he wasn't the sort to keep quiet, either. Now he isn't going to say anything to anybody.

The forint isn't doing anything against the euro. I check the newswires to see if anything is going on that might agitate the currency markets. The army in Indonesia has uncovered a bomb factory and arrested some extremists. That could go either way. Maybe it means the country's becoming more stable and the rupiah will rise. Maybe it means there're more terrorists there than previously thought and it's going to fall. Thailand's in the middle of an election campaign and the almighty U.S. dollar is what it is. Maybe there's a triple play in the making. I pay attention and try not to think about anything else.

Got it. One hour, eleven minutes to go and the rupiah ticks up, the baht ticks down and I slip into the hole, coming out about five seconds later one hundred forty-two thousand yankee dollars to the good. That's only a hundred forty-two bucks to me, but this close to the end of shift, and having made the killing earlier, I don't have much money left in my account to move.

Close though, it was close. If my shift wasn't almost over I'd send for another line. But I've got to go home and get some sleep after this, a lot of sleep, and I don't want anything to interfere with it. I send for the real tea lady again and ask for ice water when she gets to me.

LuAnn pings me on IM.

"You just do a half million, Iceland vs. the Brits?"

"Nope."

"I did 120, someone jumped on it for 0.5."

"Nobody on commission. Why risk it?"

It's got to be someone trading on their own account. That's the only way the smaller trades make sense. There's not enough commission involved to make it worth the effort if that's the only pay off. But I doubt that anybody working here, not even Karl, has the kind of bankroll to be making all these trades for himself. Someone outside is staking them, or they've found a way to skim from the bosses. Either way it's a volcano of shit if the bosses find out.

And the toxic cloud is going to roll down the slopes of that volcano and smother any of us who know about it and don't report it. The scam's as clear to Lu as it is to me, and probably a few others also. Her IM asking the obvious question gets to my screen just as I hit send to ask her the same thing.

"Shit, Ford, what to do?"

"Don't know. Shift's almost over. Thinking."

Three, two, one and just an hour to go and Karl's looming over my screen again. He looks worried, or mad.

"My office, Ford, now." He turns and marches off. This cannot possibly be good. Never, not once, not for anything have any of us ever been called away from our screens during a shift. If a fire breaks out we'll be sacked if we leave our cubicles before being given the okay. That's what they tell us.

I close the IM and history screens and get up. Looking out across the trading floor I see Karl leaving the cubicle next to LuAnn's. She's getting up, too. We look at each other and I don't know which of us looks more nervous. We walk slowly together toward Karl's office, talking low out the sides of our mouths.

"Shit, Ford, you think he saw our IMs? Could it be...?"

"Him? Maybe. Weathers' dead."

"I saw them carry him out. Do you think...?"

"Maybe. He died in my cubicle. Last word he spoke was 'silver.'"

"What the hell?"

"I don't know. I've been thinking. Maybe 'sterling silver,' as in pounds sterling."

"Was he bleeding?"

"No, but he looked bad, choking or something. Poison? Maybe just a heart attack."

Karl doesn't have visitor chairs in his office. He's got two of those large, thick rubber balance balls and he tells us to sit on them. They're a little underinflated and it's hard to keep from bouncing. I'd laugh if it wasn't for the look on his face.

"Think you two are so fucking smart? Think I don't see everything, everything that goes on on this trading floor? Instant messaging, shit, idiots."

"I saw something odd, Karl. Didn't make much sense to me so I wanted to see what LuAnn thought, that's all."

He stands up and leans forward, bracing himself with his palms on his desk and puts a frighteningly neutral look on his face. I can see the effort it's taking. His voice is flat, too, though nearly cracking with the struggle he's putting into keeping it that way.

"You didn't see anything, neither of you. Nothing. Got that? Weathers thought he saw something and he had a big mouth. You don't need your mouth to do this job."

He stares at us for several beats after that, then sits down to face away, toward the bank of monitors on the wall behind his desk.

"Get the hell out of here, you two. Shift's not over."

LuAnn and I are afraid to look at each other on the way back to our cubicles. She speaks so low I almost can't hear her, and out the side of her mouth trying not to move her lips which doesn't make it any easier.

"It's him, isn't it?"

"At least he's in on it."

"What do we do? He knows we know. We're both fucked."

"Shift's almost over. Drink after work?"

"I won't be able to sleep anyhow. Okay."

"The Dogs. We should leave separately."

She nods her head as we split ways to get back to our desks.

Thirty-eight minutes, three, two, one and thirty seconds to go. Air conditioning keeps the temperature son the floor frosty all the time, but that's not the reason I'm shivering. The three white blinks tea lady has come and gone and I'm wiping powdery residue and bloody snot off my nose and upper lip. I don't care if it keeps me up.

The rupiah, baht and greenback are still up on my screen. There's probably not time for any more trades, certainly not to carefully track anything, but Karl's watching. He's got to be. So I'd better make it look like I'm back at work, business as usual.

To look like I'm doing something I call up the Swiss franc, the Brazilian real and the yen. The new software can do some very neat tricks. I align their movement graphs over each other, starting right now at point zero. I magnify the chart on the screen so the slightest variation will show up big, assign each of them a different ping tone that will alert me if they move, and sit back to wait out my shift.

The problem with coke is that if you don't want to crash you've got to keep doing more. At eleven minutes and, and, and twenty seconds to go I hit the foot switch three times again. Out the side of my eye I can see the look the tea lady's giving me. I don't blame her. Bloody tissues are dropped three, in places four deep around the base of my chair.

At six minutes exactly to go the real tone sounds and damned if the thing doesn't tick up against the Swiss and not a half-second later the yen rings, too. What to do, what to do? My head is swirling. I didn't expect this. It'll be gone any moment. Okay, let's see—buy francs for real in Zurich then instantly turn around and trade those francs for yen before the market can catch up in Tokyo.

Fingers crossed. It's almost like I can hear the seconds ticking on the clock at the top right corner of my screen.

Close, but no cigar. I got the francs for the real but was too late on the yen. No harm done in any case. Swiss francs are always good for something and I picked some up for the account at a good price. There won't be any commission in it for me, but it'll look like I was paying attention.

* * *

About eight and a half minutes after shift is over I walk into the Dogs—the pub across the street from the building's main entrance. It's not very crowded at nine in the morning, the breakfast crowd has gone to work, the mid-morning booze hounds haven't come in yet and they haven't even started setting up for lunch.

I manage to focus my eyes enough to make out LuAnn at a back corner table. I totter over the uneven wood floor and sit down across from her, not saying anything. A waitress comes over and sets a glass of water and a menu in front of me, a Bloody Mary with a salad's worth of vegetable matter and an egg in front of LuAnn.

LuAnn cracks the egg on the rim of the glass. It's raw and floats on top of the thick tomato juice, vodka and other ingredients. She picks up a fork, breaks the yolk, then stirs it into the mixture. The celery, green onions and long skewer of olives rest against her cheek as she takes a very long draught of the thing. She puts it down and gently dabs her lips with a napkin.

I watch her over the rim of my water glass.

She licks her lips and makes a smacking sound.

"That's better. Nothing like a hearty breakfast."

"Some breakfast."

She shrugs.

"When you think about it, it's kind of a deconstructed Denver omelet. You ought to try it sometime."

I shake my head, which turns into rotating it on my neck slowly, stretching the muscles, shooting out cracks as it unleashes the tension in the bones. When I finish I look at LuAnn. We've got to talk this over, then I've got to go home and try to sleep.

"So, what do you think?"

"I'm trying not to, Ford. Do we have any options?"

"Not many. I think we've got to rat Karl out."

"Why not just let it alone?"

"When it blows up in Karl's face the bosses are going to want to know if any of us were in on it. Or if we knew about it and didn't say anything. If they think either of those things, we're fucked, too."

"Shit, why didn't I just get a job trading for a bank, a real one?"

"Same reason as me. More money in this, more excitement, 36 hours on then five days off."

"Ford, you think it's worth it?"

"Not anymore. I'm not going back, too risky. Might be time to move out of Hong Kong. I've got enough saved up."

"Yeah. Same boat. I've had enough and I've got enough, too. And I sure as hell don't want the triads on my ass. So, how are we going to do it?"

I've been thinking about that and I've got a plan. I tell it to her. She gulps down the rest of her Bloody Mary, eats her vegetables and then drinks half my water before she says anything.

"That's nuts. Or brilliant."

I don't know which one it is, either.

"So, you in?"

"We probably shouldn't use our mobile phones."

"There are a couple of public phones in the hall by the bathrooms."

* * *

Twenty-six minutes and three, two, one, forty-five seconds after our shift ends we're sitting at a table with a view of the front of our office's building. We're each nursing a Guinness. LuAnn's has another raw egg cracked into it. I don't suppose it tastes like any kind of omelet. We're not talking. We're both too tired, too on edge.

Normally we'd be betting on something like this. Is Karl going to get dragged out of there for murder or skimming? And by who? Either way he's gone and we're out of here. We're just waiting and watching to see who pulls up in front first—the cops or the triads.

Occupy This!
SJ Rozan

Fucking drums were going to kill him.

Drum circle, what is that? Gavin had never even heard of a drum circle until a few weeks ago, when these jerk-off hippies started squatting in the park. Squatting, that was a laugh. Before the King Johns showed up—some Trustifarian was paying for them, Gavin had no idea who and could care less, but he loved the guy—the hippies really were squatting, taking turns taking dumps behind some rigged-up shower curtains. When you were done you were supposed to sprinkle some scary white powder into the buckets-full-of-crap. "Neutralizes the meat-eaters' toxins," he was told by a brown-haired girl who would've been hot if she hadn't had hardware sticking out of her ears, lips, eyebrows, nose, and Gavin didn't want to think about what other body parts. She was on Newbie Duty the night Gavin arrived and she showed him around: the cook tent, the People's Library, the shit pit. Gavin didn't ask where the buckets went once they were full, though the park being Occupied was only four blocks from the river.

Really short blocks, too.

Luckily for Gavin, the KJ's got there just a day after he did, so gross as they were—and they were gross—at least you could sit, not squat, and at least the door locked. Though as far as Gavin was concerned Richie Rich could've shelled out for a daily, instead of a weekly, service contract. He supposed it shouldn't have come as news to him, but shit really smelled.

Probably one reason for the grossosity was the sludge these people ate. Nothing came out of the cook tent that didn't have beans and fucking tofu in it. By the second day Gavin would have given his right arm for a roast beef sandwich from the deli around the corner. And a beer. They carried Tecate, shows you how many wetbacks there were around here, but the beer wasn't bad. Of course, he wouldn't have been allowed to drink it in the People's Liberated Zone—self-righteous pricks—so he'd have had to lurk in a doorway down the block, Tecate can in a paper bag. Which would've blended him right in with all the other losers who emerged from God knew where to zombie around the financial district at night, once the rich and powerful went home. That made a sick kind of sense. Once he was one of the rich and powerful. Now he was one of the losers.

Not for long, though. Not for long. Meanwhile, a different kind of blending in was working for him.

Coming to the park had been a stroke of genius. The whole fucking plan was genius, actually. Too bad no one would ever appreciate it. Not that they wouldn't feel the effects. They were feeling them already, $560,265 worth of effects. Gavin had counted the money when he'd stopped in the alley to change his shirt, his shoes, ditch the wig and the dark glasses, and switch backpacks. All of which he'd taken with him, no evidence left in the alley. That was how he knew how close the river really was.

In the beginning when he was making the plan he'd thought about using an accomplice, a getaway driver. He was used to looking at things from all angles, and while he loved his plan, it only made sense to think it through a couple of other ways. The problem: a driver meant, by definition, another person involved. That doubled the chances of a screw-up. Way more than doubled, because the chances of Gavin himself screwing up were between zero and nil. No, this was better alone. More risky right at first, between the bank and the presto change-o in the alley, but less risk later and a much bigger reward: Gavin got to keep all the money.

Risk-reward was Gavin's specialty. Those pricks at FirstCentralBank had loved him, fallen down and worshipped him, in the years when his bets paid off and he made them huge profits. *Huge* motherfucking profits. He was their young wizard, their Harry Fucking Potter of complicated financial instruments. Kobe steak dinners, sweet company car, raises and bonuses. Good times.

Later, after the crash, they told him to rein it in. First his boss, then his boss's boss, then a Big Meeting in the Big Conference Room. For one thing, he was supposed to stop thinking of what he was doing as "bets." How unbelievable was that, those hypocrites in their bespoke silk suits, lecturing him? When was the last time Gavin foreclosed on some asshole's house, threw his wife and kids into the street? Gavin just moved money around. So he kept doing it. And after a single fuck-up— not even his, some Chiquita Banana in Buenos Aires who was supposed to make one goddamn buy and couldn't get her manicured nails on the button in time—they canned him. They! Canned! Him!

So he moved some more money around. The day the ax fell two security guards were waiting to hustle him out of the building as he left his boss' office. Right through the bullpen, right in front of everyone. He knew what they were all thinking, too, behind those ashen silent faces: *if this can happen to Gavin it can happen to anyone.* Damn right, assholes. Because they did it that way, not even letting him go back to his desk for his personal stuff ("Your things will be packed and sent to you. We wish you luck in your future endeavors.") Gavin didn't get a chance to collect the severance package he'd earned, the private one that would've supplemented the pathetic package FCB gave him. If he'd just had the rest of the afternoon at his computer he'd have been able to do it with finesse. But no, they'd forced him into the approach he took, one that had all the subtlety of a Double Whopper with cheese.

He'd robbed the bank.

Specifically, the FCB branch where all the hardhats at the big construction site by the river cashed their paychecks. Of course he knew what day the cash was delivered, why the hell wouldn't he? He went down to the branch when he was ready and moved that money around as smoothly as he always had, only this time it was physically, not electronically, and he'd moved it not into a client's account but into his red backpack, which was now in the river, and the cash was now in his blue backpack, which was now over his shoulders, which were now pressing too damn close to the shoulders of some bearded, b.o.'d, bad-breathy revolutionaries down here in the People's Liberated Bite Me Zone. Around the corner from the FCB branch he'd knocked over.

The original plan had been to go home, chill, wait a few nice quiet weeks while he continued to collect his unemployment insurance, then leave this jerkwater town for good. The cash he'd netted was enough to get a hell of a start on a new life, if you knew how to invest it, and you bet your butt Gavin knew.

In the ramp-up phase he'd bought himself an identity, some dead guy's social security number, and slowly, carefully, he'd built up what he needed: driver's license, bank accounts, credit cards. The best part, neither the dead guy nor Gavin had ever been fingerprinted—God Bless America—so he'd gotten himself picked up on a traffic violation one night upstate when he was stone cold sober. After the Breathalyzer they'd had to let him go, of course, with apologies, which he'd squelched his pissedoffedness and accepted graciously. Now Gavin's fingerprints and the dead guy's ID were forever meshed. So he could get a passport, too, and dig in on some white sand, blue ocean beach with a beer in his hand, to watch all the tanned asses swing past him.

That plan was still good, except the part about chilling at home. He'd heard the sirens much too soon after he left the bank. Wardrobe change or not, a guy of his build, his age, with a backpack, so near the robbed bank—no, ballsy as Gavin was, he wasn't going to brazen it out. He went to Plan B.

Of *course* he'd had a Plan B.

He joined all the other backpacked guys and helped Occupy the park.

Brilliant, of course. He'd been here two days; he'd stay another two or three and then split. The cops were stretched thin anyway, keeping an eye on all these smelly hippies, and a bank stick-up where nobody got hurt wasn't going to lose the Police Commissioner any sleep. As long as Gavin didn't leave the park, as long as he scowled at the cops (not too hard, he wanted to blend in with the hippies but not get targeted as a ringleader) and didn't shave or bathe, he fit right in. He was just another anonymous jerkwad.

But the drums. Jesus Christ up a Christmas tree, the drums! Snares, toms, a bass, woodblocks, a freaking marimba, some hide-covered thing with a buffalo skull painted on it that two guys with braids took turns thumping. Worst was the giant red-painted wood tub, its skin held on with rivets, that two Asian guys whacked on with what looked like nightsticks. The goddamn drums never slept. You could hear them for a block around the park. At night no one outside the park gave a shit; nobody lived down here and these asshat revolutionaries were only keeping themselves sleep deprived. But during the day, everybody in the surrounding office buildings was being driven around the bend by the relentless, crazy-making pounding. Because one of those surrounding buildings was the headquarters of FirstCentralBank, it was almost worth it to Gavin to put up with this shit just to know his boss, and his boss's boss, and all the rest of the cocksuckers in the Big Conference Room were going out of their skulls.

Almost. It would be worth it in retrospect, once he was lying on the white-sand beach thinking about them getting migraines up there in that tower.

Right now, though, he felt like he could beat every one of the drummers to death with their own drumsticks.

Okay, all right. He stretched, trying to find himself some space on the pavement. At least lie down and try to rest. Would've been smart to bring earplugs. Damn, Gavin smiled to himself, a flaw in the plan!

He must have dozed off despite the rhythmic aggression, because he felt a moment of confusion when he sensed movement around him, heard murmuring, then shouts. He came fully awake when the bullhorn started.

"Let's keep it peaceful! Clear the park! Let's all stay calm!" Repeated and repeated, the instructions carried even over the noise of the drums, though the drummers stepped it up to try to drown the cops out.

"What's happening?" Gavin asked the guy next to him, who was clambering to his feet.

"Cops are moving in. It's a raid." The guy was jittery, excited. Moron. Gavin stood, too, and craned his neck to see the barricades. Didn't look like the cops were moving in. The opposite: they'd formed in ranks like a receiving line and pulled a section of the barricade away. With surprising restraint they seemed to be almost inviting the unwashed to step out.

"The park's going to be cleaned! Take your possessions. You can leave the kitchen, the library, the portasans. Just clear the pavement. You'll be allowed back tomorrow at noon."

Sounded reasonable to Gavin. In fact getting the joint hosed down for free was the offer of the decade, if you asked him.

The unwashed weren't taking it lying down, though. The revolutionaries didn't have a bullhorn—against police regs, they'd have needed a permit, and the only permit the city was granting this crowd was for the King Johns—but they used this "human megaphone" system. A scruffy guy standing on a barrel was yelling back at the cops, and every hippie in earshot repeated what he'd said as loud as they could. Actually, it was pretty cool.

"Ever hear of free speech?"

"EVER HEAR OF FREE SPEECH?"

"The mayor promised no raid!"

"THE MAYOR PROMISED NO RAID!"

"This is a public park!"

"THIS IS A PUBLIC PARK!"

"We're the public!"

"WE'RE THE PUBLIC!"

"We're not leaving!"

"WE'RE NOT LEAVING!"

"We're not leaving!"

"WE'RE NOT LEAVING!"

As the chants of "WE! ARE! THE NINETY-NINE PERCENT!" began, Gavin thought, *Maybe you're not leaving. But I'm gone. Occupy this, losers.* This had gotten way old anyhow and the cops were handing him a perfect exit. No one would take a second look at him now. He'd exit the park like a peaceable hippie, stroll home, and take a frigging shower. Then he'd start the process of leaving this shithole town.

Some of the other Occupiers seemed to have the same idea—come on, a shower and a nap in a fucking *bed* had to be tempting, even if you planned to come back and Occupy some more—so Gavin joined the line shuffling toward the barricades. The procession moved seriously slowly. Gavin didn't know why and he was almost at the front when he found out. Unbelieving, he jumped out of line and stared.

Fucking cops were searching people's backpacks.

On the way *out.* Searching them on the way *out.* What the fuck?

"What's going on?" Gavin asked some girl with a flower tattoo disappearing between her boobs.

"They think we have bombs. Someone said there were bombs in the park."

The whispers now swept past him, swirling and building. The cops had gotten a tip, probably from some planted undercover, some rat: explosives, bomb-making supplies in the park. That's what this was about, not cleaning up the place. That's why the mayor had gone back on his word. That's why the cops were so restrained, trying to low-key the whole thing. *They were scared*! the whisperers hissed. Some counter-revolutionary One Percenter shithead started a bullshit story about explosives and now the cops were scared.

Gavin thought hard and fast. Bullshit? Probably—these wusses, with their tofu and beans, making bombs? But he didn't really know about that and it wasn't his problem. His problem was cops searching his bag.

The drums were louder now, the hippies, too. Phrases passed back and forth through the crowd like waves in water, rolling one way, then another. *Search my bag? Where are we, Teheran? We have rights! Hands off! We're not leaving!*

But they were and Gavin knew it. Anyone who didn't go easily in the next few minutes would get his head smashed when the cops moved in to clear the place. Maybe they had some kind of blanket warrant to search people's bags, maybe not. Probably the People's Lawyers were racing to night court right now to file a challenge. If this search crap was illegal the Occupiers could sue the city's ass tomorrow. Great, but that wouldn't help Gavin.

Tight spot, but he'd been in tighter. That eyeball-to-eyeball with that jerkoff in Hong Kong last year—Gavin had had the bigger cojones, had made faster decisions, and every decision had been right. FCB had ended up three hundred million ahead on that one.

So, fast decisions now. Parameters: he had to leave. And the money had to stay.

It took him about three seconds to know what to do. The cops said the cook tent and the library would be allowed to remain, but they might be lying. If it came to a police action, or a hippie riot, who knew what could happen? Books, pamphlets, pots and pans and so-called food, all flung around, all ending up in the crapper. Not the literal crapper, but Dumpsters, by morning.

But the literal crappers. No one was going to screw with those.

No, even if they cleared the park and scrubbed away the last smudge of hippiness, the KJ's would stay right where they were. If Daddy Peacebucks cancelled the contract, it would still take the King John people a day or so to come get their property. Chances were he wouldn't cancel so fast anyway. He'd wait and see if the Occupation would be allowed to go on. If the Occupiers really were permitted back in by tomorrow, Gavin would drift on in with the rest. If they weren't, this was still a public park. They'd have to re-open it to innocent bystanders. Note to self: it was possible the KJ people—or the cops— would lock the potty doors. Remember to bring bolt cutters.

Excellent. Gavin sliced across the current, elbowing his way through world-changers getting more excited and angry by the minute. When he got to the KJ's he was momentarily stumped: each one had been slapped with a scribbled sign reading, "Tear Gas/Pepper Spray Refuge Area." What the hell did that mean? All the stalls were empty: no one wanted to get caught with his pants down when the cops charged in. Gavin picked the middle stall for no good reason, stepped in and locked the door. Ohmygod, the stinging stench made his eyes water. It was darker than it had been last night when he came here to piss, too. He squinted and looked up. The air vents, which were also the only light source, had been blocked up. Ah. Tear gas refuge. Gavin, almost choking, decided he'd prefer tear gas if it came down to it.

When he'd shut the door the rising chaos outside had gotten marginally quieter. Better get to work fast before he passed out from the stink. It took him under thirty seconds to figure out a way to pry up the seat platform. By then his eyes had gotten used to the dimness. He laid the seat aside, trying not to breathe while he decided how best to lift the actual crap container. "Best" would be with rubber gloves, but once he steeled himself and grabbed the thing it came up easily. Why wouldn't it? It wasn't like you'd ever need to bolt it down. And just as he'd expected—*God, Gavin, you're good*—there was at least eighteen inches difference between the depth of the container and the distance to the ground.

He knew there would be. You'd have to have that to account for sloping sites, rocky sites. He steadied the glistening, reeking plastic box with one hand and slung the knapsack into the hole. "See you soon," he told it, and resettled the box on the lip that held it. Then he put the seat back. By the time he burst out of the stall he thought he'd never been more grateful for sweet city air.

The drums rumbled louder, faster, and more ominously. So did the crowd. Time to blow this pop stand, and fast. Gavin shoved his way through to the front, making for the police barricades. He bumped into the hardware-sprouting girl, who grabbed his arm. "Where are you going?" she yelled, face up in his. "They're moving in! We have to stay strong!"

Gavin pulled away. "I seriously do not need this shit." He thought about adding, "I can't afford to get caught, I'm a fugitive already," to give her a thrill, but what would that get him? He pushed past guys with gray ponytails and girls with bandanas already covering their noses and mouths to make them tear gas-proof. Good luck with that, he thought. Try the Tear Gas Refuge Zone.

He had a heart-thumping moment when a dog-faced cop at the barricade peered at him, but the guy waved him through and then he was out. Thank you, Jesus. Gavin couldn't help grinning. He had an inspiration: First stop, the all-night deli, for a roast beef sandwich. And a fucking beer.

He got the counterman to put the beer in a separate bag so he could sip it on the way down the street. He was doing exactly that as he turned the corner again and heard the sound from the crowd change sharply. The drumbeats rose in volume and tempo, hippie voices roared, and a wedge of cops surged into the park. What had happened? Who the hell knew? Gavin stepped into the darkness of a doorway down the block to drink his beer and watch. Now he could see puffs of what looked like smoke but was more likely tear gas, and he could hear the percussion of the projectile guns over the beat of the drums. He was ready to boogie if the wind shifted but so far the gas was being blown the other way and really, he was enjoying this. Jackass hippies screaming and yelling, running every which way; jackass cops swinging nightsticks, cracking some heads, missing lots of others. A red flame sliced through the sky, then another. Some Occupier was throwing traffic flares at the cops. Seriously? Traffic flares? That totally proved what wusses these weekend revolutionaries were. Real anarchists would be throwing gasoline bombs, what did they call them? Molotov cocktails. Something that could actually blow stuff up. Not traffic flares, hell-o? Seemed to have cornered the market, though. Red flames were arcing everywhere now, and he realized some of the cops were picking the flares up where they landed and flinging them back. Another great idea, not. Talk about suing the city.

That was his last thought before the explosion. A huge BOOM!, some terrified-sounding shrieks, and Gavin was crouched in the doorway, hands over his head. After a minute, when nothing else loud happened except more shrieks and screams, he stood again. *Wow.* He stared wide-eyed into the park. A bunch of the tents were on fire. The panicked hippies were all racing around, some to get away, some to try to smother the flames, which only grew. But the drums—the goddamn drums had stopped! Hallefuckinlujah! What happened? What exploded? He searched and spotted it. There—a raging fire. A flare must have hit something—*something? The johns! The KJ's! The johns were on fire!*

Gavin took off at a run, but the cops had re-organized fast and he couldn't get near the park. He tried a couple of times but they pushed him with nightsticks. He kept trying; finally a cop grappled with him, tripped him, knocked him on his ass. Gavin stared up to see flames reaching like hands for the sky as the fire grew, encompassing all the KJ's, feeding on the methane trapped behind the stopped-up vents in the Tear Gas Refuge Area.

It was impossible. It couldn't be. It wasn't fucking happening. Lifting himself on one elbow, watching, Gavin had these thoughts over and over, until finally the flames started to run out of fuel. They fell back just as the first fire truck arrived—what was it, three minutes? His whole life, that's what it was—and because the firefighters focussed on the tents, Gavin was able to watch unimpeded as the King Johns folded in on themselves, collapsing to a bubbling heap of molten goo. The flames relaxed into a gentle dance, like this was some hearth in a mountain cabin. Stank, though. The sharp smoke, mixed with the remains of the tear gas, now drifted his way. Acrid and toxic for sure.

When the firefighters finally turned a hose on the smoking plastic mound, Gavin didn't stand up. He flopped onto his back, lay wondering vacantly whether the money, the $560,265, had been blown up, or burned up, or was still there, encased in boiled shit and melted plastic. If it was, whether anyone would find it, or it would end up shovelled into the landfill. He was still lying there, wondering these things, when the hardware girl stalked by, spotted him on the ground, hissed "Chickenshit!" and kicked him in the ribs. He didn't get up as she strode away, stayed right where he was, on his back, staring at the smoked-out sky. He was still there when the drums started up again.

94

Digital Dingus Four-Point-0
Bob Truluck

La Fée sat, as it always had, in a once-house it had bewitched then assumed years earlier. The experienced cracker house had grown as a result of the collision but had grown in a fashion disparate as the indigenous building was to the restaurant's name. Mad architectural ramblings eased off the main structure at unpredictable locals, related only by the unwritten low-roofline codes enforced by the fickle weather here. The original porch had been forced against its will to surround any and all annexing and see that it stayed in line. The porch had tables with happy table cloths fluttering in tepid air. The sun was showing off for the tourists south of town and no native in his right mind was buying into outdoor-dining opportunities.

The meet was set at La Fée not for the luxurious option of outside dining nor the dim interior ambience nor the ridiculous European food. Nope, was chosen because it had a nice, expensive reputation. The parking lot validated the rumor—loads of Teutonic nightmares and Bavarian heartaches tethered out there among a few SUVs the size of a two-story flat.

The Show used a set of faux-granite steps that couldn't have been OEM—lots of petrified leafwork on the vertical kicks that someone had maybe thought looked Old World. The Show crossed the porch that was certifiably OEM, caught his image bounce in the not-even-OEM etched-glass doors. Grin, pull on a door handle, watch a bored maître d' type unlean from a podium and react poorly to the Show's pedestrian ass. He corralled it, got out the two-dollar smile, played it straight but tight. "One, sir?"

The Show pointed off stage. "The bar. Waiting on a couple of guys." Smiled back nearly a buck fifty of the d'-man's rictus grin.

"Through the double opening, sir. Enjoy yourself." The d' served it up with a subtle back flavor of *fat-chance.*

The Show said, "You too," keeping it as sincere as the d' had.

* * *

The Show had shown on time, knowing he'd still have a twenty-minute, half-hour wait—nobody kept Suits waiting. No, they'd arrived fashionably late, look-atcha-wasting-my-time juice stinking their auras up, fidgeting like Big Money himself was sitting outside in the limo waiting.

The Show knew how it would play out, knew the lay. He'd been here before: Dinguses One-, Two- and Three-Point-0. Wondered had the Suits ever been in a sandbox like the one they were about to play in now. Doubtful, very doubtful.

The Show, affecting the Geek, slid in the bar, slid onto a barstool and ordered a Glenlivet, double on the rocks. Made the railtender grin pretty good. Then he informed the Show that'd be twenty-four bucks and change.

The Show, as the Show, would've put a lot of nothing on it and dropped something like: *is that all?*

Tonight he was the Geek. The Geek would never be so bold. Perpetually astounded—sure. Smooth—not in a million.

In his ear the Geek—the actual and factual Geek—said: "Easy, bro. I'd be acting impressed."

The Show muttered: "Fuck you," at the mic buried in his shirt, said, "Wow. I'll just have the one then," to the Tender.

The Geek, outside in a fairly hideous conversion van, laughed in the Show's ear, said, "Nice. Now, that's more like me."

"Get outta my fucking ear. I'm sitting in a bar talking to myself because of you." Pause. "Oh, wait: I am you, you talk to yourself in bars. Never mind. Get the fuck outta my ear."

The Show looked up, sipped, caught the barkeep watching. Big grin back at him, showing the old guy the detached eyes he used when he was playing the Geek.

The Geek didn't have a detached gaze or even dress totally like a geek, but a guy had to have a little fun, right? Didn't *all* work and *no* play make boys dull?

So the current case, sipping single-malt scotch, wearing the Geek's *iRIP* t-shirt, his baggy cargo pants. Un-huh: cargo pants. And the shirt. The Show had tried to explain to the Geek that it wasn't a tribute—was sarcasm. The Geek was left unswayed—nope, to him it was a tribute to the master of all Geekdom. Crown it with what the Geek considered his absolute sickest sartorial apparatus, a twenty-five dollar, department-store fedora, light straw, dented crown—for God's sake—brim turned down in front like Dick fucking Tracy or somebody.

The Geek would throw down with a geek-gangster lean, geek-gangster bad-ass looking for purchase in his rosaceous face, pull the rim down to right above his eyes. Give the Show some geek stinkeye thinking he was looking sinister or threatening or something, something he'd never be.

Thoughts vaped—the Suits were on scene.

Sure they were his Suits. May as well been wearing sign boards with their industry logo: a lily white sphincter winking out harmless, multi-colored pills. Below, the motto would say: *Hey, We're Big Pharma—Fuck You.*

The Show recognized the venom in the thought but appreciated it for its humble beginnings: Digital Dinguses 1.0, 2.0 and 3.0. And, actually, they'd sold 2.0 and 3.0 a couple of times each. Yep—been here, done this, know the people, know the game. Let's play dirty.

The Show tossed an engraving of Grant on the bar, asked for something fruity and colorful.

The Tender grinned, nodded a nod that said, *that's more like it.* "Like what?" Having fun with it.

The Show shrugged shoulders. "Who cares? I doubt I'll drink it anyway."

The bartender's Smokey-Robinson-caramel face wasn't sure if the Show was fucking with him or just slightly derange. He let the face go, called the Show's shrug with one of his own, got busy. Over a shoulder, he said, "Outta umbrellas. You want some Maraschinos with little plastic swords through them?"

"Sure, if they're not ten, twelve bucks apiece."

"The fifty on the bar covers the Glen, the girly drink and my needs, doc."

"Consider the fifty yours."

Deed done, happy libation in hand, the Show slid off the barstool, shook the baggy pant legs down, stamped his feet in the totally uncomfortable yet painfully lime-green Converse high-tops.

The railman leaned on his side of the boards. "Mind I ask you something, doc? You don't seem like the kinda gentleman would get the ass and cost a man his gig."

The Show stopped his turn, grinned, saw it coming. "Ask on, my brother."

Pause. Nod of a knowing sort. "Lot of different people come in here putting out lotsa game—it's that kind of establishment. The one's got it wanna make sure everybody knows they got it. Them that don't got it wanna be sure everybody thinks they do. See where I'm goin here?"

Yeah, the Show did, but he wrinkled his forehead, wagged the rest of his head.

"See, sir, after while, the Gots and the Don't Gots all homogenize cause you realize only thing separates them is the first lucky roll of the dice. I'm talkin, even if your first throw is comin out your dear mother's vagina into a world of wealth. But mostly, was just incredible luck at bein in the right place, right time."

"Marx or Lenin?"

"No, sir. Aristotle Onassis."

The Show laughed out loud some, wagged his head some. "Point being...?"

"You ain't neither, with all due respect, doc. You come in, sit down, I'm goin: *aw, shit, a goofy white boy gonna order a Miller Lite draft, leave a half dollar like he's doing me favors.* But, nope, you got a walk don't fit your...Outfit?"

The Show put an ass cheek back on the barstool, sat the silly drink back on the bar. It sat unaffected and blithely threatening like a child soldier. Fuck the Suits—he was getting good entertainment value here. "Sure, use *outfit.*"

A pause, a look. "You sit, order a true gentleman's libation: fine scotch whiskey. Drink it right: rocks only. Know exactly how long to let it chill and breathe. Sip like you respect the men made it and their history. You handle and carry yourself contradictory to your appearance."

"That it?"

Pause to look, saying he knew he was on it.

"Way you decked, you shoulda been rubber-neckin like my Aunt Estelle at a fifty-percent sale. Un-un, not you, doc. Didn't act like you thought you'd stumbled in a Waffle House, but you wasn't wowed— you been in better." Pause. "I'm sayin way better."

"Man, you oughta work airport security."

"Am I close?"

"Frighteningly." The Show dug down a few hundred feet into a front pocket, liberated a couple of c-notes. He folded them over twice, put them discreetly under the empty rocks glass. "Don't let your pride get all tender. I like your conversation, like your style..."

"But...?"

"You don't seem like the kinda gentleman would hink a man's gig either. Dig?"

"Most indubitably I dig, doc."

The Show and the Tender traded some eyeball for a beat or three.

"You ain't gonna tell me, are you?"

The Show watched the Tender, shrugged the Geek's tribute T. "Say I gotta friend's trying to sell something to a couple of fast fellas. Say my friend ain't so fast and these boys are about eighty, ninety percent likely to fuck him."

"Un-huh. And you dressed like your friend."

"Yeah. Wearing his pretties."

"Un-huh. Knew it was somebody else's clothes, knew it." A smile from the Tender. "And it's them two come in bout ten minutes back. Had on what had to be the monthly payment on a million-dollar mortgage between them."

"You're good."

"Naw. I just seen something finally piqued your interest."

"That obvious, huh?"

"On a fella your age, yeah. Y'all like house cats, people in your age bracket. Don't nothin move you till that bird or mouse or somethin interestin get your eye."

The Show stood. "We done?"

"So what happens they try and fuck your friend?"

The Show raised his eyebrows. "I fuck them first."

He said, "I see. I see," but he probably didn't.

The Tender grinned a little. "Last one. You seem awful comfortable, considerin where you're headed." Pause. "You done this some before, ain't you?"

"A time or two."

"Anybody beat you yet?"

"First guy. For a while, anyway. Let's say: we recouped our losses, broke even in the end."

"You makin money then."

A shrug. "Doin fine. Got more than I can spend."

"You ever got any loose stuff layin about, you bring it on down. I'll redistribute all the wealth you got needs a bit of redistributin." The Tender's hand came out. "They call me *Doc* cause I call everybody else *doc*."

The Show took the caramelized hand. "I'll do it, Doc. They call me the Show, cause that's what I am."

"I can see that, sir. The best of luck to you, and to your friend, in your endeavors. You givin hints on this item your friend's trying to sell?"

The Show grinned. Before he turned to go game the Suits, he said, "Insanity, Doc. Pure, simple, sinful insanity. Nice making your day."

***

Common courtesy on vacation, neither Suit found the Show stand-worthy when he braced their table.

Casual appraisal, practiced assembly of stereotypes, then the inevitable bleak assessment.

Suit One: a born leader born with lots of very domesticated hair, dark and suspiciously devoid of grey. Navy-under-grey pinstripes. Red and purple rep tie. Pastel-blue button-down. As boring a set of wing-tips as Macy's ever sold. Tall and broad as a Clydesdale. Late fifties, heavy faced, gobs of foie gras hanging over the taxed collar. The Show knew he had a fella wouldn't traffic in bullshit looking at him.

Suit Two: A dangerous little neurotic in an excellent Armani piece. Thin and quick as a ferret. Not someone you'd want having your back to unless you had an itch could only be scratched by a sharp stiletto. Toadie in training. *Watch him, baby.*

Suit One watched the Show drop his messenger bag next to a spare chair. Two opened his mouth to do the intro.

The Show put out a palm as he sat. "No names, okay?" And sat. He sipped the fruit cocktail silently, annoying Suit One a bit by wasting a few of One's precious seconds allocated for entertaining this foolishness.

One predictably popped first. "What you got, young man?"

Pause for drama and drum roll. "The future. Digital dope."

Dual subtle winces pained otherwise bland faces. "Let's stay away from words like that."

"What? Digital?"

A no BS stare from One. Two caught it and joined in. "Don't be a smart ass, okay?"

From the fancy van outside, the Geek says: "Easy, big man."

The Show took a deep one, let it go quietly. Zenned up a bit. Said: "Sure. Let's do the deal." He'd so rather have punched the smug fuck in the throat, watch him suck for air around a crushed larynx, enjoy the Suit's panic when he realized his breath wasn't coming back.

Just went in the messenger bag, came up with a laptop and a device that looked a lot like any knock-off old-school Walkman. He placed the laptop on the chair next to him, fired it up one handed. The other hand inadvertently placed the dingus on the table while four eyes above Windsor knots watched it like it was of Martian design.

The Show ignored the corner-of-the-eye action, got the company banking account on line. A smile, a: "There's your machine. Got my check?"

One: "Let's slow down."

Speed up. Slow down. Born leader for sure.

Two: "Exactly. We don't have a clue what we're getting for our—"

The Show and Suit One both hopped on Suit Two with cautionary eyes.

Two recovered his feet, said, "Our deposit."

"Who needs a test drive?" A blank nerd stare smeared on it.

Two: "Here?"

The Show nodded. "Why not? You've never been buzzed in public?"

Two ruddied from collar to eyebrows. "No, I haven't."

Show: "Please." He pulled the dingus onto his placemat. "Okay, gents, pay attention." Earbuds: "These are your transmitter and return bounce unit." The dingus: "This is the bomb. Your bass adjustment controls the narcotic modulation. The treble's the stimulant, coke being the current setting. Balance, dank krypie, complete with taste, bouquet and all." He slid the thing at them but no one touched it.

Two asked, "What's the volume wheel control?"

"The music. You like to do music when you're tweaking, don't you? I know I do." The Show hit the eject button and the Walkman popped open like a clam; a CD glistened on the drive spindle.

One found a bit of boldness, pushed at the dingus with an exquisitely manicured digit, pointed. "What's on that disk?"

"Different stuff. Got some Ryan Adams, some Wilco, some Steven Foxbury as far as stuff in that vein. Some early Modest Mouse, some Decemberists on that side. Hmm, let's see...Random shit, some Yeah Yeah Yeahs, some Cage the Elephant." Pause to recog. "Oh, and Black Keys' *Goodbye Babylon*. Love that song, don't you?"

Two: "What does that have to do with the apparatus?"

"Nothing. Other than intrinsically, as mentioned. Who's game?" The Show held out the earbuds.

No one seemed game and the Show fought a valiant battle with the nasty grin colonizing his face. Shake the cape at the big bull: "Can we move along here?" Glance at a watchless wrist, pull the Geek's absurd lid down to his eyes, peek under the brim to deadpan Suit One.

One: "You wanna give us a minute?"

Circle the bait, bitch.

"Sure. I gotta pee anyway." The Show grabbed the dingus as he rose, leaving his cell unit on the table. "Be back, gentleman."

* * *

The Show grunted out, "Hold on," to his chest while a guy with a holy collar flung water from his hands. The priest continued flinging as he walked past the blower and used the door.

"Clear. They scheming heavy?"

The Geek in his ear: "Oh, yeah. Arguing about which cloning outfit in Hong Kong to use. The older guy thinks it's straight scam. Thinks you're a poor imitation of a con-artist."

"I am. They planning on fucking us?"

"Oh yeah. Gonna get it cloned, hand it back to you, tell you it didn't work out back at the office. *So sorry—gimme back my money.*"

"Un-huh, well I am shocked to my socks. Didn't the note say the chip had seventy-two-hour use-by encoding?"

"Yeah. They think they can make it in forty-eight. Chumps."

"Superchumps."

Beyond the audio bug, the Geek had the dingus rigged with both a GPS device and a remote chip destruction mode. *Go ahead, Suits, fuck us.*

Someone used the door behind the Show. He shook his unit even though he'd not pissed. Said, to his chest, "Let's do 'em."

* * *

Alright—predatory smiles all around. *We're dealing.*

The Show sat, smiled like he was a nitwit.

Suit One was goddamed near fatherly when he pitched his woo. "Son, look, we can't give you six zeros on something like this." An indicative four-finger point at the Geek's creation. "I mean, even it if does what you say it does, that's a considerable amount of earnest money."

The Show sat pat on his pockets.

One: "What say, we take it back to the shop, give it a test spin or two, kick the tires, then talk in sensible half-millions? What say, son?"

"Three point four billion."

Two: "What?"

Suit One's mouth nearly smiled, invisible threads tugging at its corners.

"Three point four billion."

One: "Our profit last year."

It got a face puzzle from Two.

One clarified: "Onan Pharmaceuticals' profit last year." His gaze on the Show. "I suppose you know what percentage of that amount a million is, off your head.

"Point-oh-two-nine percent. Less than one-thousandth of your *declared* gross. Pay up and let's all get on with what we were doing before we were doing this. What say?" Earbuds up. "What say, slim? You game? Because if somebody doesn't do something productive here, I'm gone."

One looked at the Show, Two looked at One. The Show watched them wrestle with the dilemma.

A waiter the Show hadn't seen before slid in with a tray of drinks. One of them was amber as an October sunrise, two cubes of ice bobbing.

The waiter said, "The gentleman in the bar you were conversing with earlier sent this for you, sir."

The Show grinned but didn't turn and salute Doc.

The waiter dealt out cola and who-knows-whatskeys to the Suits and drifted to where good waiters wait. He dragged the sound with him leaving their table an audible black hole in the fizzling waspish hum of the broad low room.

One held the Show's eyes, spoke to Two. "Put the ear things in."

"Excuse me?"

"You heard me, put them in. Why the hell do you think I brought you? I don't know about narcotics, but I do know you snort cocaine and smoke marijuana. I've seen you. Put the goddam ear things in."

Jesus, more dead air around than a college radio station.

Suit Two breathed deep, filled his spare chest and looked like he was going to mutiny.

Ever the Byzantine little capitalist above all, he yanked at the ear buds, said, "You owe me big."

Suit One gives him some: yeah, yeah.

The Show slid the dingus to him, asked, "What's your pleasure?"

Two thought he'd start with a little of Humboldt County's finest sativa-dominant, but only a puff or two.

The Show plugged him up, sparked him up, tuned him up, turned him on. Had him giggling like a sixth-grade girl in about forty seconds. Had him insincerely begging *no mas* in like a minute and a half.

The Show balanced him out, took him down a little with a smooth Indica skunk. Got him blissful, balanced him on zero, shot an inch-and-a-half-line equivalent up his virtual nose. Said, "I hope you've eaten since I just ruined your appetite."

Suit Two smiled, said, "That's fine. Yeah, I'm fine."

One had seen enough. "Shut it off. Let's talk dollars."

While Two asked what happened, the Show said: "Talk whatever you want, but you won't walk outta here with that handy little gadget without I'm holding a cashier's check of some sort for a million bucks. Do I need to go to the restroom some more so you can consult with your esteemed colleague there?" A point at Suit Two.

Two was still out there a bit but coming back to ground slowly. "Me?" He pointed at his chest. "Am I a colleague?"

"Shut up, you idiot," to Two. To the Show: "Gimme your routing numbers." Fingers wiggling for them.

"Fuck you. Cashier's check, like we agreed." The Show scooped the dingus toward himself.

Suit Two whined a pretty miserable, *no*. Suit One clamped a large hand on the Show's wrist.

The juice gushed in like a tsunami, dragged the Show's facade out to sea. "Get your fucking hand off me, asshole." Cold, serious, certified: the real Show in the Suit's face now.

The Suit moved his hand, put the palm at the Show. "Hey, easy." But reading the last scene, sniffing with a gene that was about a million years old—the Show called it the *cockroach gene.*

He had the gene himself. An unvetted survival warning so strong it's distracting above all else. All systems start firing, trying desperately to locate the inevitable can of Raid, the flyswatter, the hard leather sole.

So what if the Suit got a peek inside his game—didn't make a difference to anyone. The hook was set.

Suit One dropped an abstruse: "I see." Then, "Give me the check." He snapped his fingers at Two, held out an expectant hand.

Suit Two wasn't real sure on which check was being discussed. Turns out, it was the one in his inside suit-coat pocket for a cool million dollars, a cashiers' check.

Suit One gritted his teeth and mumbled while the Show held the chit up to the laptop's camera eye, snapped its pretty picture and routed the big load to an account in a bank in a place far, far away.

The Show tore the check several times, dropped the confetti in the frou-frou cocktail, stirred it with a plastic sword.

Straight faced, he said: "Listen, guys, don't do this thing alone. It can get outta hand and bad things happen."

One was loosening up, blame it on the alcohol. "You've had incidents?"

Smile. "That's why we're at a four-point-oh version." Straight faced again. "We've tweaked it considerably, but it's still a dangerous gadget."

Suit Two amened that. "What went down with the first three?"

Stock shrug. "One-Point-0 and Two-Point-0 had a sex option. Didn't work out."

"Wait, wait. Sex option?" Two was back from Alpha Centauri seeing possibilities. "Talk to us."

One's ears had perked up but he was playing it cool.

The Geek, in the Show's ear: "The check cleared, daddy. Tell them it makes the head of your dick explode and you come like a Roman candle."

It made the Show smile and he was tempted. But the truth was more fun. "The initial research that led to all this comes from Yerkes in Atlanta, so we knew going in how dangerous manipulating or—more accurately—modulating the pleasure centers can be. Simian test subjects will starve themselves when modulated for stimulants and allowed to self-dose. They'll tweak on narcotics until they pass out if left to their own dosing. But sex-center modulation? Death to the males in days."

Suit Two brought the discussion back to profit-margin sensibility with: "Don't humans have enough self-reserve to use it effectively? I mean, the potential to treat sexual dysfunction is tremendous."

The Show grinned. "No. No it isn't tremendous. It's ugly. Women seem to be able to handle it, appreciate it for what it is. Men?" Headshake. "It's awful to watch someone drain themselves of life."

One was curious. "You've seen it?"

"Twice. One-Point-0 was sorta accidental." Apologetic face. "We just didn't know. Turned a test participant loose with it."

Two: "He died?"

Show: "Yes. Still dead too, unfortunately."

Two: "Who else?" like he wasn't too sure he wanted to know.

"A guy from one of the control groups on the Two-Point-0 project broke in while we were outta town. He lay in our lab for ten days coming. He looked like he'd been at Auschwitz. Terrible thing to see someone just wither the fuck away."

The Show closed his laptop, slid the Four-Point-0 across the table. "I'm sure I'll be hearing from you within seventy-two hours. Enjoy, and please heed my warnings. This thing is nothing to play around with. It'll still kill you with an overdose just like the real deal. And when you come back with your offer for the engineering, please don't insult me." Bag up laptop and cell unit, dump the rest of the Glenlivet in the smart mouth, leave them with: "Enjoy your evening, gents. I'm sure it'll be interesting."

The Show's hand pantomimed a phone. He put it to his head, mouthed: *call me*, and drifted.

As he passed the opening to the bar, he turned a bit, grinned like a fox, discreetly showed the smiling Doc the print side of a thumb.

* * *

The Show really had no idea if any of the shit he'd shot the Suits was for real. It's what the Geek said, but the Geek believed everything he read on the internet. But, to the Geek's credit, he had done an internship at Yerkes while he was cheating his and the Show's way through college. The triple-doctorate degree the Geek was apprenticing under died suddenly and inexplicably. Seems he had cocaine-opiate poisoning trauma but showed up with no speed-ball in his blood. Go figure, huh?

The Geek, as had been previously instructed by this his chief alchemist if such became the case, had spirited away all data, computers, equipment and the first-aid kit. Again to the Geek's credit, he may not have initiated the phenomenon, but he got it. He poured over the shit for nearly six months, killed the neighbor's German Shepherd first run. Got it right in the next six months, produced a sleek model all nested inside a broke-down Walkman case.

The rest is, as they say, historical. Along the way they honed their game, found the dingus better as bait than a lotto-win-never-work-again thing once they learned how the Suits played the game. Learned that Suits would rather fuck you—and fuck the hand that fed them—than find a legit use for Geek's genius.

Nope, no saving mankind. Had to try and fuck the Geek. Every time. The Show was astounded at how people viewed the Geek, and even viewed the Show playing the Geek, as totally one dimensional. Like, because he had an odd genius, he was some sort of idiot savant or functional autistic, like he could modulate your brain but couldn't swing matching socks most days. It wasn't that people like the Geek couldn't—they just don't give a shit about matching socks and the things that bother the rest of us.

The Show knew another Geek. He knew a guy too inventive to work in a corporate lab. Too weird to be much of an academian. Too corrupt to be a priest. But if you were his friend and a big guy came along and kicked your ass, he'd get to kick the Geek's ass too—the Geek would insist on it.

Met in high school, both in bad situations. The Show had nearly served his time in the wonderful foster-care system in this country, finishing out with a lovely couple so big that jokes off the fat-joke rack didn't even fit them. Grotesque creatures left breathless going from bed to couch. Long as the checks from Tallahassee kept showing in the mailbox in front of the trailer and the Show hostled beer and fast food in, they didn't care much of a damn what he did.

The Geek was in the same sand-spur patch of a mobile-home park, actual and biological parents. Well, the mom anyway—the Geek and the father had always been skeptical. The Geek was tall and skinny like the Show; the dad was a squatty, mean-natured bastard. Made his living mixing over-the-counter meds together in his bathtub. Not a long-term issue—pops stroked out most of his gray cells as a grand finale to a six, eight day meth binge. Walked over, got in the seventy-eight Firebird sitting on cinderblocks, closed the door, adjusted the headrest, leaned back and went into an open-eyed slumber he never really woke up from. The Geek's mom got busy partying, leaving the Geek to be an orderly for the old man.

The housing market had burst like a water balloon, splashing vacant houses everywhere. The Geek used his computer to find one that the mortgage holders walked on and he and the Show simply moved in. The Geek then slipped into the mortgage company files, manipulated them a bit and they spent their senior year as the two very popular guys who lived unchaperoned in the niceville party house.

Then off to Atlanta to do some more school. Then the Geek strikes digital gold and the Show mines it. Ah, life is good, then it's better, then better still, and here they were now.

And here Suits One and Two were, coming from the restaurant's porch, animated in conversation. Uh-oh, having words? Come on, fellas, plenty of cheese to go around.

They were watching from the Geek's Trojan Horse, down a half block from the restaurant's doors.

The Geek said, "Hang on," disappeared into the back of the van. A light came on. The Show looked back at the Geek in headphones.

"This is good," pointing at an earpiece. "Now they're arguing over which Chinese clone factory they can trust."

"How about: *none of the above?*"

"Get this: the older guy wants to call his brother-in-law, the attorney. The skinny guy wants to fly to Hong Kong tonight."

"They GPS at the airport, rape the chip, but I think no problem. I'm betting we don't make the airport."

"How much?"

"Five grand." Being easy on the Geek. They could afford that a hundred times over, no strain, but betting wasn't even fun anymore. Hmm, neither was anything else, thinking on it. Maybe this decadent wealth wasn't all it was cracked up to be. More data needed, as Geek would say.

"Ten."

"Five. Where we headed?" The Show moved to the captain's chair as the marks loaded into a black limo. The limo's taillights came up and the car pulled onto the street.

The Show fired the beast up and fell in a few cars behind the limo full of Suits, the Geek still back there on headphones and hardware.

The Geek said, "I'm thinking that company condo I found when I read their drives," meaning a corporate condo down in Fantasyland the company honchos used for vacationing with the family, impressing clients and doing the bed-dance with their kept pussy.

"Shit. I'm losing audio. Fuck, fuck, fuck." Headphones got flung.

The Geek climbed forward again, asked, "You want me to drive? I know how you hate the Love Wagon."

"I don't hate it. I just find it absurd. You could drive a brand-fucking-new Bentley. A Lamborghini. Here." The Show slid out of the helmsman's chair, slid in the passenger seat as the unattended van slowed. "I gotta get outta your ugly-ass clothes."

The Geek stumbled by, slid in the vacated chair, took the wheel, got back to speed. Rolling good, he said: "I like old-school."

The Show stood in a half-hunch thing, wobbled aft. "Dude, you could get someone to hand-build you a Tucker. Where're my fucking clothes?"

"The wagon's cool. I couldn't get all this shit in a Lamborghini."

Wasn't the point but don't bother vibrating your larynx arguing points to the Geek. An early nineties big box van, one-way bubble windows with the appropriate reddish tint. Head-sized pop-top hatch in the roof. Fridge and equipment both sides mid-ship. Three-quarter futon full aft.

The Show lay on his back on the futon and shucked geek duds. He felt around until he found his skinnies, slid in and hitched up. Sat, found an ugly-ass, green Fleet Foxes shirt even they should have been ashamed of, slid into the shirt. He stuck his feet in a pair of black-and-white striped Tom's laying on the floor and stumbled his way back to the passenger seat. He plopped a Tom's on a carpeted dash, said, "We're off flight plan for the condo."

"Yep, seems that way. There's a Motel 6 up ahead. Maybe they're trying to hold on to some per diem."

"Right. More likely just being conscientious employees, trying to save the stock holders some money." The Show put his eyebrow up, looked at the Geek, said: "I'll kiss your pimply ass if they do a Motel 6."

No time to argue now—the limo used an almost semi-circular drive around some spoiled ivy, tethered up. Mount Vernon Inn—a local three star with a pick-up bar nestled inside. Ah—the Suits weren't on company time, had gone entrepreneurial and didn't want Papa Pharma clued to their scheming.

Suits deploy, no love or yack lost.

Limo loses a couple of pieces of luggage, rolls on.

The Geek tethers his tugboat curbside on a side street.

Suit Two goes in, does hotel business. Exits with a couple of plastic keys. He pokes one at One, hefts a carry-on over a shoulder, grabs the two bigger pieces of luggage. The pair hikes to a room.

The Show said, "Down and out. Bet they've got a rental car out front."

Number Two sat one of the bags down at a door, went wordlessly to the next door. Both used plastic keys, swung doors open.

One picked up the big bag, disappeared behind his door. Two remained for a heavy beat or two, staring at the void his superior had left, then the Geek said, "Oh my, looks like we've caused a lover's spat."

"I hear you. You take a gazillion-dollar idea and toss it among the greed-is-good crowd, things happen."

Nothing happened for fifteen, twenty minutes, so time decided to drag on like a Star Wars sequel.

The Geek went to his equipment again, looking for audio. He said *shit* and *fuck* a good bit but it didn't improve his reception.

"Ah. Here we go. I locked on one of their cell phones in the restaurant. Not sure which, but I gotta hit. Hold on." The Geek put an earphone to an ear. He smiled, shuffled his fingers on a mouse pad.

Sound came up: the Suit-in-Chief, being abrupt, telling someone to get his ass down here now. Hmmm, wonder who was on the other end. Then Two saying give him a minute. Dead air.

The Show asked: "The boss's phone?"

The Geek wagged his head. "Nah. His little toadie's. The hair-do was incoming—I got them both now. Here we go—Junior's dialing out. Long distance. Bingo. Super-long-distance. And the lucky city is—Hong Kong."

The Geek pushed up the sound.

A purr. A feminine voice in a strange tongue. Two says: "Michael Chang, please." The voice transitioned into: "Thank you, sir. Please hold for Mr. Chang." Muzak shit as boring in Mandarin as in English. A new voice, a man's, said, "Chang."

"It's me. I've got it."

"Yes, I talked to your counterpart minutes ago." Pause. "I think his plans do not include you, my friend."

"I'm sure. I'll be coming in tomorrow."

"Alone?"

Pause in conversation, then, "Yes."

Counter-pause, then, "Yes. More convenient for all. I will have a car pick you up."

"Are your lab people ready?"

"Of course, my friend. We are always ready. That is how we prosper. From your description we believe we should have completed functional cloning within the seventy-two hour parameters you mentioned."

"Nice. Very nice."

Civilities and straight-up buddy fucking covered, the conversation went to the required re-negotiating. Seventy/thirty went to forty/sixty, deteriorated its way back to an even fifty/fifty. The barter was left there even if only temporarily.

A few minutes, Two's door opens, he dances on scene, waltzes to One's door like he's sprinkled pixie dust on his happy feet. Ah, the way the smell of deceit hangs on a pleasant evening is enough to make anybody buoyant.

Knuckle up One's door, gain entry, disappear from scene.

The Show popped a van door. "I'm taking a walk. Stay loose."

Per usual, the Show wasn't sure the Geek heard. The poor chump was intermittently oblivious to the fact that a world full of people was spinning around him. You could go to his place, use his never locked front door and the Geek might notice you're there—after an hour or so. Say something like: "Hey, where you been?" after you'd spoken to the goof two or three times.

The Show used the sidewalk to the hotel's far entrance off the side street. There, he cut across to the sheltered walk. Maybe halfway to Suit One's door, the Show's cell unit vibes him: the Geek.

"Talk to me."

"Our boys are test running the Four-Point-0."

"Oh shit. Get ready to roll."

"*Aa sou*, grasshopper. Is how we prosper," channeling the guy involved in Suit Two's phone call to Hong Kong. The Geek could be a relatively funny guy if you knew him.

The Show hot-footed across the parking area to the van. Climbed in asking: "Where're we at?"

"Dank. Started way low. Now we're at about stoned-stupid."

The Show said, lowly, levelly, "You see this shit coming, right?"

The Geek disengaged from his electronic extensions, said, "Yeah. It bother you?"

The Show smiled. "No. Live by the dollar sign, die by the dollar sign." Shrug.

The Show figured he and the Geek didn't invent this game—it had invented itself as it was unfurled. If the end-game was as it was, then that too was forged by these greedy bastards, and it left no visible marks on the Show's karma.

The Geek: "Here we go—little ride on the dragon. Blast off: black tar. Good Housekeeping Seal of Approval: Mexican mud. Junk of the Month Club: Eighty-nine percent pure China White. This won't last long. Who's dosing who, Mr. Analytical?"

"You were gonna off a guy, would you do it in your room or his room?"

"Good point. What happens now? The usual?"

"Yeah. The Suit-Left-Standing'll be checking out real soon. We'll drive very carefully to an interstate motel out toward the airport." Signature smile. "Then we get to see what our boy's made of."

The Geek: "You don't sound optimistic."

Signature shrug. "We'll see. I'm just saying he'll play hell making that flight to Hong Kong."

"He does seem to have an itch for the powder."

"Yeah, but the boss made him do it."

***

Per script, the Armani zipped through One's door after dousing the lights. He spent maybe thirty seconds in his own rent-a-crib, hauled luggage and accoutrements to a black Chrysler-something. Zip—he's gone, rolling toward the predicted airport.

The Geek pulled off the curb, followed along.

The juice was burning off now, now that the game was winding down. The Show leaned his head back, closed his eyes. "Wake me when it's over, doc."

* * *

"Hampton Inn. Good choice—free USA Today, nice gratis breakfast offering," woke the Show from a half-sleep, half-daydream detachment.

"Free porn?"

"Pssht—who pays for porn anymore? The cow's free, why go buy milk, huh?"

"Or something like that. Put us on the far end down there." The Show pointed his intention.

"To bad you're not driving. Oh, you are, you're just doing it virtually."

"Shut up. Park this fucking shipping container."

The Geek backed the van in at the parking lot's end. Two's Chrysler sat under the travel lodge's will-lit porte cochère.

Suit Two exits double glass doors, looks both ways like a TV crook, mounts the big black sled.

Down and out again—run the Chrysler aground in front of a numbered door, unload a few cases, toss a crafty glance each way, slide in the room. Lights came up as the door closed.

The Geek abandoned the wheel house, stooped his way to the equipment deck. He tinkered, cursed quietly, hummed off-key, made clicking noises from back there.

The Show slumped, watched a door.

A few minutes, the Suit exited with a plastic ice bucket, took a short walk to an alcove. He reappeared with ice, went as he'd come.

Quiet between big birds screaming in and out of the airport.

A leasable lawman carried a styro cup of coffee around a corner.

The Geek shouted: "Goddam, I'm a fucking dumb-ass."

The abrupt segue from a white-noise lull to self-effacing scream made the Show jump. "Old news. What's new?"

"I was the problem with the audio—had the wrong coding in the..." Pause. "Fuck, you don't care."

"Whatcha getting?"

The Geek pulled the headphones against his head. "TV—news. Ice clinking now—making a drink maybe? Ah, here we go—we're cranking baby up."

The Show asked what was the Suit's pleasure.

The Geek took a super-deep breath like he was hitting a joint, let it roll painfully unencumbered across his vocal chords with, "Couple of good tokes—between mids and decent dispensary grade stuff." He turned the breath loose loudly, said, "Uh-oh—little baby bump of the real thing."

Here we go. The Show moved to sit on the engine cowl, said, "Put the audio on speaker."

The Geek complied but the news was blaring. He moused around until he calmed its particular noise to a filtered whisper. The man could be heard moving around in the room.

"And, we're off. Steady tweaking now—got her set on about third full rate. Un-huh, feeling good now, feeling great. Yep—kick her up a notch."

Seemed to the Show like the Geek enjoyed this part most, calling it like a sports event, a little Cosell in his voice.

Vomiting noises in the speakers.

The Geek went on with blow by blow commentary. "Oops—little too stiff at half rate. Back her down." Off commentary, back to the Geek's voice: "Bro, check it—dude's hitting the opiates."

The Show figured the Suit was looking to knock the edge off the electronic buzz, told the Geek as much.

The Geek, back to commentator: "Okay—enough of that, ease the treble up again. Nice—a third. Better—half and no puking. Oh, check out this risky move—bumping in a tad of morphine grade opiate into the modulation. And, ladies and gentleman, we all know where that goes."

"Yeah, you end up dead on the floor of a room at Chateau Marmont."

"Shit can happen. Man, this dude's riding. Coke up to about three-quarters full, he's into low grade street junk on the down side."

He could be heard clinking again.

The Show said, "Nothing like pouring copious booze on a tight-rope. This won't go long. You got my rake?"

The Geek looked in a couple of places, came up with a small nylon bag, tossed it at the Show.

The situation elevated quickly over the next half hour or so. A couple more drinks gulped down, running the opiate mod at a notch above excellent street shit, running the coke mod nearly wide open.

Then the final commentary—the two minute warning. "Dude went past pink Peruvian flake, jacked it straight to clinical blow." A turn to watch the Show.

The Show tossed him some deadpan, said, "Let's give him a half hour."

"Five minutes would work."

A shrug. "We'll give him a half hour."

* * *

They gave the Suit his thirty minutes, and the Show slid down to his door while the Geek put the van closer.

The Show used the electronic rake and popped the door, eased inside.

The Suit was in boxers on the bed, legs splayed out and ending in fine argyle-socked feet. A motel glass was in his right hand but had spilled most of its contents on the boxers and the bed. The earbuds sprouted from the sides of his head, the deadly little machine in his left hand.

The Show took in the scene, shrugged it off, grabbed the Four-Point-0, popped out the earbuds and left the Suit otherwise as found.

* * *

The Show climbed in the passenger door and poked the dingus at the Geek.

The Geek gave the little machine cursory inspection for signs of abuse and misuse and stashed it. He fired up the wagon and rolled them onto the access highway, put on some rap music the Show immediately turned off.

No talk for a mile or two, then the Geek asked if the Show was cool.

"Yeah, just getting tired of it, or bored. Something."

"Well, you know, at this rate, we're never gonna get an FDA label on the thing."

"Yeah, but we've made over four mil off it. I think it's time to call it quits."

Couple more silent miles.

Geek: "It's still a nice money-maker."

"Yeah, till we get nailed."

"For what? Contributing to greed?"

"They'll think of something. *They* always do."

Quiet miles.

Geek: "So what're we gonna do? Get out all together?"

A shrug, a: "Maybe. Or maybe we move laterally, find an industry that would be more open to the potential of this dingus."

"Yeah. And that would be what industry?"

The Show dropped the beat old-school style: "The music industry, doc."

The Geek started in a slow nod that grew to a bobbing laugh. "Ah, bro. See, you're the fucking genius here."

"No, you're still the genius. I'm just the bright-idea guy. Like it?"

"What's not to love—sex and drugs and rock 'n roll."

The Show put his eyebrows up. "I don't know about the sex thing."

The Geek said, "Yeah, I gotta work on the sex thing, don't I?"

"Yes you do, doc, yes you do."

Easy Money
Pamela Samuels Young

In the beginning, the overriding goal had been justice for their clients. Now, six years later and a few million in the bank, it was all about the money.

Kendall stood just inside his law partner's office, hands at his waist—cop style—trying to think of some persuasive argument to put a stop to this snowball of greed headed straight for the nearest jail.

"Look, Cedric, it's time to call it quits," Kendall said, venturing further into the office. "We're lucky that we've gotten away with it this long."

"Man, you gotta cool it with all the gloom and doom. It's bad for business." Cedric rested his massive forearms on the desk. With his shiny bald head and hulking frame, he could easily pass for a bouncer.

"And luck has nothing to do with it. We're rich because I know how to pick my clients." He winked and flashed a gapped-tooth grin.

The two partners' approach to the practice of law had always been at opposite ends of the reasonableness spectrum. Cedric had a hustler's mentality. If making a buck was even a remote possibility, he was quick to roll the dice. Kendall, by contrast, shamelessly described himself as risk averse. He typically jumped to the worst-case scenario long before he'd heard all the facts.

As thin as Cedric was thick, Kendall at 33 was of average height with decidedly Nordic facial features. He hailed from a real-life legal dynasty: a brother and father at L.A. mega-firms, an aunt on the federal appellate court bench, and a grandfather and great-grandfather who were legends in the legal community decades before he was born. Kendall ended up in law school because it was expected of him. And he'd hated every minute of it.

While Kendall grew up constantly hearing that the sky had no limits, Cedric—raised by his grandmother—had been bred to aim low. A decade older than his law partner, Cedric defied the odds and graduated from Long Beach State in six years and spent the next eight with the Long Beach Police Department. Law was not his dream career either. He'd tried twice, but had been unable to pass the psychological portion of the detective's exam. Too aggressive, separate teams of psychologists had noted. After his sixth excessive force complaint, he quit before he was fired. He'd ended up in law school on a dare.

Both men had a tough time learning the law—Kendall at UCLA, Cedric at an unaccredited online university—but somehow earned the necessary grades to graduate.

They'd met at a bar review course after Cedric had taken a seat next to Kendall, cosmically drawn together by their mutual insecurities. Cedric had failed the bar exam once, Kendall twice.

When Cedric Paine formally introduced himself to Kendall Fear at the first break, the same sly smile instantaneously graced their lips. *The Law Firm of Paine & Fear.* The decision to jointly hang out a shingle had begun to percolate in both of their heads that very day.

"We only have two pending cases left," Cedric said with a frown. "I'm not leaving that money on the table."

"You don't have the money yet," Kendall pointed out. "If one of these guys calls our bluff and goes to the police, we'll lose our license and end up in jail."

Kendall took a reluctant step closer to Cedric's desk. He had always been repulsed by the office, which like Cedric, gravitated toward the outrageous. The south wall was covered with loud gold wallpaper. Two red-velvet Queen Anne chairs sat in front of a mirrored desk rimmed in gold. A circular table large enough to seat a family of eight had been jammed into one corner of the room. Giant sculptures shaped like phallic symbols were positioned on opposite sides of the door. The ego wall behind Cedric's desk boasted poster-size photographs of Cedric with Mike Tyson, Eminem and Michael Jordan. Vegas meets South Central.

"We've been doing this for three years without a single glitch," Cedric reminded him. "It isn't illegal."

Perhaps not technically, Kendall thought. *But ethically, no way.*

Kendall was not proud that he had allowed himself to be enticed into his partner's easy-money scheme. A mortgage, three kids under ten and two alimony payments left him no real choice. Being able to rake in more bucks than the pompous, Ivy League lawyers in his family was another significant motivating factor.

But now, with his half of their six million in legal fees properly invested and hidden from both his current and former wives, Kendall had announced his desire to dissolve their partnership. He wasn't a genius, but he was smart enough to get out while the getting was great.

"Okay, let's compromise," Kendall offered. "Go ahead with today's meeting at Simpson Pharmaceuticals, but let's forget about going after Barry Mantel."

"Here we go again," Cedric sighed, hanging his head. "That guy's really got you spooked."

Barry Mantel, CEO of American Financial Investments, the nation's largest investment banking firm, was not like the other men they had threatened to sue. He wasn't only wealthy, Barry Mantel was powerful. And powerful men weren't easily played. Kendall understood that because he'd grown up with an entire family of them.

"I just don't think it's wise to go after a guy like Mantel," Kendall pressed.

Cedric ignored his partner's angst and glanced at his watch.

"I gotta go. It'll take me more than an hour to make it to Irvine in traffic. We can finish this conversation when I get back. You'll feel a lot better about Mantel once you see how well it goes today."

* * *

Cedric pulled his recently acquired Ferrari into a parking stall outside the headquarters of Simpson Pharmaceuticals and turned off the engine. After a quick call to the twenty-six-year-old stripper he'd been seeing—another benefit of his booming business—he dialed Kendall's cell phone. Cedric always called his law partner right before commencing his settlement discussions. Never once had Kendall picked up.

"I'm about to head up to Robertson's office," Cedric spoke into Kendall's voicemail. "I'll let you know how the negotiations go when I'm done."

"Punk," Cedric muttered as he pressed a button on the steering wheel, ending the call. If he was ever charged with a crime—a possibility Cedric considered highly unlikely—the phone records would show that Cedric had called Kendall minutes before. If he went down, Cedric wanted to make sure there was sufficient circumstantial evidence to take Kendall right along with him.

After straightening his tie in the rearview mirror, Cedric grabbed his briefcase from the front seat and climbed out of the car. He could feel his pulse quicken. Cedric had experienced the same rush of adrenalin during his cop days when he was on the verge of getting a suspect to confess.

He smiled at the comforting memory and took off for the entrance of the building. "Show time."

Wearing his only pair of wingtips and a too-tight, pinstriped blue suit, Cedric stepped into the glass and granite-filled lobby of Simpson Pharmaceuticals. After giving his name to a nice-looking blonde, he received a stick-on badge and was escorted ten floors up to a private waiting area outside the office of CEO Paul Robertson.

Cedric did not expect the meeting to begin on time. Making him wait was a pathetic power play he'd experienced before. Robertson did not want to appear overly concerned about his visit. Pulling out his fact sheet, Cedric used the time to review his research.

Paul Robertson, 57. Ten years at the helm of Simpson Pharmaceuticals. Four daughters, two in college. Married to his high school sweetheart for 37 years. Longstanding member of Mason Presbyterian Church. Both parents still alive. Combined annual salary, bonus and stock options: thirteen million. Next month, Robertson would be honored by the local chapter of the United Way as Humanitarian of the Year.

The final sentence made Paul Robertson an ideal Paine & Fear defendant. *Kailey Jones, recently discarded mistress of two years.*

At Cedric's urging, Ms. Jones, a Simpson Pharmaceuticals administrative assistant, had filed a workers' comp stress leave and had been on bed rest for the past three weeks.

The previous day, Cedric sent Robertson an email—labeled *Highly sensitive! To be opened by intended recipient only!*—enclosing a demand letter and a copy of the sexual harassment complaint Paine & Fear planned to file on behalf of Ms. Jones. The demand letter informed Robertson that Cedric had been authorized by his client to broach a pre-litigation settlement. Unless Cedric was advised otherwise, he would report to Mr. Robertson's office at 3 p.m. the next day to commence negotiations.

A much older and less attractive blonde showed up to lead Cedric into the CEO's office. Cedric inhaled. The opening minutes were always the most uncomfortable.

"This is—" Robertson was poised for an attack, his fists clenched, his face taut. But he paused as soon as he got a good look at Cedric. The CEO obviously had not expected to see such a big black man.

"This is bullshit!" Robertson continued after a gap of several seconds. He was on his feet, but remained behind the safety of his desk.

Cedric had only witnessed two types of emotions during these meetings. Restrained indignation and outright fury. He had correctly guessed that the pudgy, red-faced man who'd grown bored with Kailey Jones would be the temper tantrum type.

"I see you've read our complaint. May I have a seat?"

"What is this? Some kind of shake down?" Robertson's thin lips quivered with rage.

"Not at all." Cedric bypassed the two chairs in front of Robertson's desk and took a seat on a couch a good ten feet away. "I'm simply offering you the opportunity to resolve a legitimate legal dispute prior to litigation. My client wants this mattered settled as quickly and as quietly as you do."

"Fuck your client!"

Cedric struggled to suppress a smile since that would likely enrage the man even more. "As I understand it, you already have."

He was relieved to see that they were alone in the monstrously dreary office. Way too much mahogany for Cedric's taste. Only once had he walked into an executive's office to find a lawyer present. In that case, it had turned out to be the CEO's brother, who was a bit of a philanderer himself. Cedric never worried about his targets sharing his correspondence with their company lawyers. In matters of the groin, even the smartest womanizers preferred to proceed without the advice of counsel.

"Did you put Kailey up to this?" Robertson demanded.

"That would be unethical," Cedric replied, avoiding a direct answer to the question.

He had found out about their affair when a woman he was seeing canceled their date to spend the evening consoling her best friend, who'd just been dumped by some rich CEO. After learning the sugar daddy's identity, Cedric promptly arranged for Ms. Jones to drop by his office to discuss her legal options.

Paine & Fear's first sexual harassment case years earlier had been a legitimate unwanted sexual advance, complete with the grabbing of breasts, offensive comments, and threats to put out or face termination. Kendall had suggested the idea of a pre-litigation settlement discussion. Not because he thought the motion picture executive would buckle, but because they knew nothing about sexual harassment law and he feared a malpractice lawsuit after they botched the case.

Their opening demand in that initial case had been $500,000. Neither Kendall nor Cedric expected the guy to pay that much and were prepared to go as low as $50,000. But the executive, fearful of what the lawsuit would mean for his career, his marriage and his stellar reputation in the community, folded and folded fast. Their take—$165,000—was more than the firm's annual profit the year before.

That's when Cedric figured out that they were on to something. If they kept their settlement demands affordable—affordable in proportion to the W-2s of their targeted execs—they'd never have to see the inside of a courtroom again. After their third case, Cedric upped Paine & Fear's contingency fee to fifty percent.

"I never harassed anybody," Robertson spat. "My relationship with Kailey was completely consensual."

"That's not my understanding."

"Then you need to go back and check your goddamn facts!"

Cedric extended both arms along the back of the couch and waited a few beats before responding. He didn't mind letting the guy rant a bit. Then they'd at least be able to communicate at a normal decibel level.

"I'm not here to discuss the facts, Mr. Robertson. That's for a jury. I'm here to help you avoid the embarrassment of an ugly, salacious sexual harassment lawsuit."

Robertson fell into his chair. His teeth were so tightly clinched Cedric thought they might crack. "How much?" he seethed.

"As you know the cost of litigation can be—"

Robertson gripped the edge of his desk. "I said how much?"

"One million dollars."

"This is extortion!" He pounded the desktop with one of his meaty little fists. "I should call the cops right now!"

"There's nothing criminal about this discussion, Mr. Robertson. California courts are so backlogged, they actually encourage pre-litigation settlements."

Cedric popped open his briefcase and pulled out a folder. He walked over to Robertson and handed him two photographs. One showed Robertson and Kailey—who was a good six inches taller—on a private beach in Maui. Kailey, like Robertson, was topless. In the other, they were smooching in the lobby of Trump Tower. Cedric had been impressed with Kailey's foresight. She'd had a friend secretly snap a few pictures as proof of her tryst, just in case she might need them.

Robertson stared at the pictures, his eyes widening with dread.

"You can deny the harassment, Mr. Robertson, but you won't be able to deny the affair. These photographs, of course, will accompany our press release."

Robertson was on his feet again and had to look up at Cedric. "How do I know you can really guarantee confidentiality?" His voice was now low and monotone. Beads of sweat dotted his receding hairline.

Now we're getting somewhere.

Cedric retrieved the photographs and pulled a document from his folder.

"Here's a copy of our settlement agreement."

He extended it to Robertson, who didn't reach for it. So Cedric tossed it onto the desk.

"The confidentiality clause on page seven provides that if our law firm or Ms. Jones discloses this matter to anyone, the settlement amount must be paid back in full. It also provides that neither my law firm nor Ms. Jones may approach you for any additional sums. Of course, Ms. Jones will immediately tender her resignation. You don't see these types of provisions in other settlement agreements because most lawyers aren't willing to guarantee the actions of their clients. We are. We've never had a breach of one of our agreements."

"Oh, so this is a regular scam of yours?" Robertson snorted. "Who else have you extorted?"

"This isn't extortion," Cedric replied calmly. "And as I said, we take confidentiality very seriously. So I'm barred from disclosing any information regarding my other cases."

Robertson's left eye began to twitch. "And what if I told you and your client to go fuck yourselves and just file your damn lawsuit?"

Cedric hunched his heavy shoulders and smiled for the first time. "Then we will."

The CEO turned away and gazed out of the window. His physical gesture of retreat told Cedric everything he needed to know. He had a deal.

"If you are amenable to our offer," Cedric said, placing his business card on the desk, "A cashier's check payable to The Law Firm of Paine & Fear should be messengered to my office within forty-eight hours. As you'll see on the last page of the settlement agreement, my client and I have already signed the document. You should sign on page twelve, make a copy for yourself, and return the original to me along with the check.

"And before you ask, the settlement amount is non-negotiable. If we fail to receive payment within forty-eight hours, I'll assume you prefer to litigate and I'll file the complaint in L.A. Superior court on Friday morning."

Cedric lumbered over to the couch, retrieved his briefcase and showed himself out.

***

Robertson's cashier's check arrived by messenger at 4:45 p.m. the following day, along with the signed settlement agreement. Cedric dashed across the hall to Kendall's office.

"One down and one mo' to go, bro!" He happily waved the check in the air.

Cedric pretended not to notice the stacks of boxes lining the north wall. It still irked him that Kendall was jumping ship *after* he'd made him rich. "You'll have another two hundred and fifty grand in your account by tomorrow."

A smile tugged at Kendall's lips, but disappeared before it could fully take shape. "I still don't feel good about going after Mantel," he said, eyes on the check. "We've made a lot of money. It's time to quit."

Cedric shook his head. He was glad they were dissolving their partnership. He needed a law partner with balls.

"We don't know enough about Rita Washington," Kendall continued. "I just have a bad feeling."

"I told you I've thoroughly checked her out," he snapped. "The same way I check out all of our plaintiffs."

While he was admittedly sloppy in all other aspects of his legal practice, Cedric researched his sexual harassment clients with the intensity of a scientist closing in on a cure. He dug into their personal and financial backgrounds, requested graphic details of their trysts (the part he enjoyed most), and hammered them about the importance of non-disclosure. And so far, so good. The threat of having to pay back hundreds of thousands of dollars was a great silencer.

He found Rita Washington nothing like the other women they'd represented. Physically speaking, she was a looker like the others, but was slightly older, just shy of 39. She was also savvier than their typical airhead plaintiffs, who actually believed they would eventually go from mistress to wife. Cedric's online research confirmed that Rita had a master's degree from San Francisco State, a Westside condo and no children. She had not worked since quitting her job as an analyst for American Financial Investments three months earlier. That explained why she needed the money.

Rita Washington was also their first black client. After reading up on Barry Mantel, Cedric never would have guessed that the straight-laced, former Texan had a thing for brown sugar. Cedric would have hit on Rita himself, but the haughty way she carried herself told him he wasn't even in the vicinity of her league.

"She's coming in this afternoon for a final chat," Cedric said. "You can join us if you want."

"No thanks," Kendall grumbled. "I'm trying to get packed up by the end of the week."

A tweak of rejection hit Cedric again.

Kendall had begun trying to distance himself from their money-making machine about a year ago when a plaintiff admitted her relationship with the owner of a construction company was consensual and she hadn't really been sexually harassed. Revenge, not money, was the woman's main motivator.

That revelation sent Kendall's griping into overdrive. Knowingly filing a meritless lawsuit was grounds for sanctions from the state bar, he had harped. Thereafter, Kendall refused to sit in on client interviews, but grudgingly agreed to use Cedric's notes to prepare the lawsuits. Despite his ethical misgivings, Kendall didn't want to return to handling nasty divorces or petty slip 'n falls any more than Cedric did.

In truth, Cedric did have some trepidation about going after Barry Mantel. The man was several stratums above the guys they normally targeted. At only 46, he was number five on Forbes' list of the richest CEOs. He regularly rubbed shoulders with Bill Gates, had been mentored by Warren Buffett and was close friends with Deepak Chopra. And like many of the rich men they targeted, not only was he respected in the business arena, he presented himself to the world as a committed family man.

"Sophisticated women like Rita Washington don't have affairs with CEOs then turn around and sue them," Kendall insisted. "What if she gets cold feet?"

What the hell do you know about sophisticated women? Cedric thought, *his wife doesn't even shave her legs.*

"I already told you," Cedric repeated as he headed back to his office, "Rita Washington won't be a problem."

An hour later, Cedric showed Rita to a seat at the table opposite his desk. She was a towering 5'10", with skin the color and texture of melted caramel. Her jet-black hair was gathered into a neat bun at the base of her neck, which drew greater attention to her large brown eyes and pert lips.

Cedric didn't know much about women's clothes, but he could tell that the matching knit jacket and skirt Rita was wearing came with a hefty designer's price tag. Unlike his other clients, he had never seen Rita in a low-cut blouse or sweater with her boobs bunched-up, screaming to be noticed. It made complete sense that a powerful man like Barry Mantel had a mistress who was a class act.

"Thanks for coming in," Cedric began. He couldn't help licking his lips. "I wanted to have this brief meeting to emphasize the importance of confidentiality one last time. We're able to resolve our cases as quickly as we do because we guarantee absolute confidentiality. Once we reach a settlement, your lawsuit, the money you receive and your prior relationship with Mr. Mantel must never be disclosed to anyone. If you breach that obligation and Mr. Mantel comes after you, you'll have to repay the entire settlement amount. Do you understand?"

"I do," Rita said, the picture of professionalism. "Confidentiality on my end won't be a problem."

She crossed her fabulously long legs and Cedric started imagining what was between them. He felt himself go rigid and enjoyed the slowly heightening sensation. He completely understood why Mantel risked it all to be with her. If Cedric thought he had a shot, he would too.

"Needless to say, you should have no further contact with Mr. Mantel. The sexual harassment complaint was emailed to him about an hour ago. He'll probably call you. It's imperative that you ignore his calls. If things go as my other cases have—and I fully expect that they will—this matter should be wrapped up within forty-eight hours of my meeting with him."

Rita's perfectly arched eyebrows rose slightly. "You really expect Barry to pay up that quickly?"

Cedric grinned. "Absolutely. He won't need long to ponder his options. By the time we meet tomorrow afternoon, he'll be more than ready to pay up. Trust me."

"And you're still asking for four million dollars?" He didn't sense the usual greed-filled intent behind Rita's question.

Cedric nodded and remembered another point he'd forgotten to make. "You understand that your agreement with the law firm of Paine & Fear only entitles you to fifty percent of the total recovery, correct?"

She smiled and nodded. "Two million dollars will be more than sufficient. But what if Barry wants to negotiate a lower amount?"

"We don't negotiate. It's four million or we're filing suit."

"I'd really prefer not to go through that," she said, wringing her hands.

"Don't worry. I'm confident we'll reach an agreement."

There was nothing else to discuss but Cedric did not want her to leave. He imagined handing Rita her two-million-dollar check and having her show her immense gratitude by dropping to her knees to give him a top-notch blowjob. As he was pondering this never-to-be-realized fantasy, he noticed a look of worry on his client's face.

"You aren't getting cold feet are you?"

She pursed her lips and hesitated as if that might indeed be the case.

"No...It's just that I...I know Barry pretty well." She paused again. "I can't see him parting with four million dollars without a fight. When he's put on the defensive, he goes for the jugular."

"According to *Forbes* magazine, your ex-lover made one hundred and ten million dollars last year. Parting with a measly four of 'em shouldn't be a big deal."

"It won't be about the money with Barry. It's the principle. I wasn't sexually harassed. We were lovers."

Thank God Kendall had turned down his invitation to join the meeting. He'd be shittin' bricks after hearing that admission.

"Just because you were a willing participant, doesn't mean you weren't harassed. Barry Mantel is a powerful man who took advantage of his position as your employer." Cedric spoke with an air of lawyerly authority. He was certain he could find some legal decision to support that proposition. "Mr. Mantel won't want the embarrassing publicity. He'll pay up."

Kendall's statement suddenly nagged at him. *Sophisticated women like Rita Washington don't have affairs with CEOs then turn around and sue them.*

Cedric shook off his partner's apprehension. Kendall was a perpetual worry wart.

"Well, Ms. Washington," he said with a playful wink, "I'm about to make you a millionaire."

* * *

When Cedric arrived at the west coast headquarters of American Financial Investments, a security guard escorted him to the corporate dining room on the thirtieth floor. His previous targets had all held their discussions in the privacy of their office. Cedric didn't like this departure from the norm.

It was well after the lunch hour and the dining room was empty except for a handful of waiters milling around. Sweat dripped from both of Cedric's armpits. He was only nervous, he told himself, because Barry Mantel was such a titan. Anyway, the fact that he was on edge was a good thing. That would keep him on his toes.

The table where he was seated was sufficiently secluded behind a wall divider that offered semi-privacy. As he waited, a swirl of nausea inched up his throat. Just when he thought he might need to run to the men's room to throw up, he spotted a tall, sharply dressed man approaching the table in long, determined strides.

"Mr. Paine, good afternoon." Barry Mantel extended his hand and greeted Cedric with a good-natured smile.

Mantel was a handsome man with a rugged face and a full head of dark hair. His wolfish gray-blue eyes radiated the power and ruthlessness Cedric had read about. Only a man this imposing could get a woman like Rita Washington to spread her lovely legs.

Mantel pulled out a chair and took a seat directly across from him. "I missed lunch. Figured we could talk over an early dinner."

Cedric had never had a defendant greet him so warmly. He began to relax.

A tuxedoed waiter appeared and directed his attention to the CEO.

"I'll have a gin and tonic, Alberto. And the rib eye, medium rare." Mantel turned to Cedric. "What about you, Mr. Paine?"

Cedric was too nervous to eat, but he could sure use a shot of whiskey.

"Coke," he said, the word barely squeaking out.

The waiter took off in the direction of a bar that stretched the length of the dining room.

"I read that piece of fiction you sent me," Mantel said with a chuckle. "And you really got me with the name of your law firm—Paine & Fear. I had to look you up to make sure somebody wasn't pulling my leg. Looks like you're just a low-level ambulance chaser. Thanks for giving me such a damn good laugh."

Cedric stiffened. "Well, sexual harassment is certainly nothing to laugh about, Mr. Mantel."

He needed to show this rich prick who was in control. "Since you're such a busy man, perhaps we should get down to business. My client's demand is four million dollars. Four million paid by cashier's check within forty-eight hours and our lawsuit is never filed. You'll receive my personal guarantee of complete confidentiality."

"Four million dollars?" Mantel's laugh started as a low chuckle, then grew into a loud rumble that filled every crevice of the empty dining room. "I've never paid more than a grand for a piece of tail. And I've had some damn good pussy in my day. You've sure got a huge pair of balls."

Mantel was laughing so hard the table shook.

Cedric struggled to keep it together. Mantel was obviously playing some kind of head game, but he wasn't falling for it. The CEO had shown up. That meant he wanted to play ball.

"You're here," Cedric said, "so I'm assuming you want to deal."

Mantel was smiling now, but his eyes fired arrows of intimidation across the table.

"The only reason I let you in my building was because I wanted to meet the asshole with the chutzpah to try to pull a shakedown on me." He angrily tapped his finger hard against his chest. "*Me.*"

Okay, now we're getting somewhere, Cedric thought. In this game, anger masked fear. And fear was a good thing.

"I tried to reach Rita last night, but she wouldn't answer my calls," Mantel said, as the waiter set their drinks on the table and disappeared. "You must've put her up to this. She would never do this on her own."

"I didn't make up the facts in that complaint, Mr. Mantel. Your mistress came to my office with her allegations."

"Bullshit." Mantel's voice was still level, but his clenched fists portrayed his true emotional state. "I ain't paying you or her a dime."

"Then we'll sue you." Cedric's chest expanded with a bravado that his face was unable to duplicate.

Mantel took a sip of his gin and tonic. "Okay, then," he said with a shrug. "So sue me."

A long, wordless stare-off followed. Cedric had trouble coming up with an appropriate response on the fly since he had never faced this kind of reaction before.

"Uh...okay then...I um...we will."

He shot up from his chair and snatched his briefcase from the floor, but stood there as if he was waiting for Mantel to change his mind.

"Get out of my face," Mantel finally said.

Slithering out of the dining room had taken Cedric much longer than his entrance. He had just stepped through the door and into the elevator bay when the waiter called out to him.

"Excuse me, sir. Mr. Mantel would like you to return to his table."

Cedric closed his eyes, exhaled, then slowly turned around. *Thank God!* Their conversation had probably been some kind of test to see if he would blink. The mighty Barry Mantel was going to bite after all. Just like all the others.

Cedric did a military turn and practically jogged back to the table. He was about to take a seat, when Mantel stopped him.

"No need to sit." Mantel cut into his steak and folded a healthy piece into his mouth. "I forgot to give you something," he said, talking and chewing. He pointed his knife at a document sitting on the table. "That's for you."

Cedric picked it up and scanned the first page. "What the hell?" All of a sudden he was having a hard time catching his breath. "You're suing us?"

"Damn straight," Mantel said with an ominous grin. "Extortion is a crime. Didn't you know that?"

* * *

It was another six minutes before the elevator arrived and carried Cedric thirty floors down to the lobby. Fifteen minutes later, he was still sitting in his Ferrari, gripping the steering wheel, as pissed as he was embarrassed.

Rita's words echoed in his head. *When Barry's put on the defensive, he goes for the jugular.* That was certainly one hell of an understatement.

He pressed his forehead against the steering wheel. How was he going to tell Kendall the law firm of Paine & Fear was being sued by one of the most powerful CEOs in the country?

He drove to his favorite bar and spent the next two hours searching for the courage to face his law partner in a pint of Jack Daniel's.

When he finally limped back to the firm, a frantic Kendall met him in the hallway.

"It's been over three hours since your meeting with Mantel! Why didn't you return my calls?"

Cedric plodded past him and into the comfort of his office. "It didn't go as planned," he mumbled, flopping into the chair behind his desk. "Mantel didn't bite."

"Didn't I tell you!? Powerful men like Barry Mantel—"

Cedric tried to signal for time out, but couldn't seem to coordinate his hands. "You might want to wait a minute before you start with the *I told you so*," he slurred. "Because that's not the worst of it."

Kendall froze, then lowered his body into one of Cedric's gaudy velvet chairs. "What did you do?"

It took him three tries before the latch of his briefcase finally popped open. He pulled out Mantel's lawsuit and hurled it across the desk.

Kendall read in silence for several excruciating minutes, then looked up, his eyes ablaze with panic.

"Yeah, I know," Cedric conceded before his law partner managed to find his voice. "You told me not to go after the guy, but I did."

"You're not taking me down with you!" Kendall cried. "I'm not—"

"Excuse me, Mr. Paine, do you have a minute?"

They both looked up to find Rita Washington standing in the doorway dressed in jeans, a white silk shirt and a snazzy leather jacket.

"Oh...uh...hello, Ms. Washington." Cedric tried to sit erect, but his head refused to stay in place. "What are you doing here?"

She timidly entered the office. "You said you would call me after your meeting with Barry. I guess I was a little anxious. I left a couple of messages, but you didn't call me back."

Kendall locked his arms across his chest as his face stretched into a sneer. "Go ahead," he ordered. "Tell her."

"Why don't you have a seat." Cedric massaged his left temple. "Things didn't exactly go as planned."

Rita sucked in a breath and perched herself on the edge of the chair next to Kendall. "What happened?"

"I guess you were right when you said Barry goes for the jugular. He's refusing to pay and he's..." His voice trailed off as he gave his brain a second to unscramble itself. "... he's suing us for extortion."

"*Us?*" Rita looked from Cedric to Kendall. "Exactly who is *us?*"

"Our law firm," Kendall announced. "And you too."

Rita covered her mouth with both hands. "Oh my God! I told you Barry never harassed me. You put me up to this!"

Kendall sprang up from his chair. "I had absolutely no knowledge of that and I want no part of any of this!"

He swung around, ready to flee, when two uniformed officers entered the room.

"Everybody on their feet!" one of the officers shouted. "Put your hands in the air!"

Cedric wobbled to an upright position, but he was mentally unable to comply with the rest of the officer's request. "What...what's going on here?"

Rita ignored the command and inched her way around the desk toward Cedric. He spotted the gun holstered at her left hip at the same moment she pulled a shiny gold badge from the inside of her jacket.

"L.A.P.D.," she said in casual, but firm voice. "You're both under arrest for extortion."

Kendall shrieked, clutched his chest and started hyperventilating.

"You...you...you're a friggin' cop?" Cedric sputtered.

"Detective," she corrected. "Detective Deidra Baker. I guess I was a pretty convincing plaintiff, huh? My team set up a nice profile for Rita Washington on the internet."

She snatched Cedric's arms behind his back and slapped handcuffs across his wrists. The two officers had to drag a hysterical Kendall from the room.

"We got an anonymous tip," Rita explained as she shuffled Cedric into the hallway. "I suspect it was from one of your other shakedown victims, but we'll never know for sure. It was my idea to reel you in with a big fish like Barry Mantel. My sister's his administrative assistant. He was glad to play along in our sting operation. That extortion complaint he gave you was a little added joke on his part. I don't think he likes lawyers."

Cedric's drunken haze had miraculously cleared, but his vocal chords were now immobile.

"We've been watching you and Mr. Fear for the past five months," Rita continued. "We have more than enough evidence for a criminal prosecution. You're going to need a very good attorney, Mr. Paine."

"You can't do this!" Cedric whimpered. "I'll...I'll—"

"You'll do what?" Rita asked with a smug smile. "Sue me?"

The Biggest Fish in Texas
Darrell James

He was almost there—almost there, sweet Jesus!—when his cell phone rang.

Fremont's first instinct was to let the damned thing ring, finish what he was doing, but—SHIT! That Jay Z ring tone, that repetitive gangsta thump, like driving nails in his skull when he was trying to concentrate.

Fremont rolled his eyes to the heavens, fished the phone from his pocket, and answered. "Who's this?"

A soft, female voice on the phone said, "Is this Mister Lilly?"

"Just a minute," Fremont said.

The skinny little redhead he'd met in the bar, just an hour ago, was still working to get him off. *Bless her heart.* But, he pushed her back on her heels and zipped his pants. There was *b'ness*, and then there was *business*, the way he saw it. "Go on, take it elsewhere!"

"You owe me a twenty!"

"I didn't finish."

"That's your problem, dude. I still get paid!"

Fremont took a twenty from his pocket and crushed it into her hand. "Go on, get out of here."

"Fuck you, man!" she said, showing him she still had pride. Still, she tucked the twenty into her shirt pocket, turned on her heels and headed off.

"Now where were we?" he said into the phone.

"I saw your flyer, Mister Lilly. I'd like to talk to you about your offer."

He was behind the Quickie Mart on Goedown Street—neither of the ironies completely lost on him. A place to do business if he had too. He said, "You see my flyer, yeah? You need to make arrangements?"

"How soon can you be here?"

"How's, say, thirty minutes.?

Thirty minutes was fine. Fremont took down the address on Prairie Dog Road and ended the call.

Most of his clients were in their seventies, eighties, nineties, looking for peace of mind in their final years.

Peace of mind was what Fremont was selling.

This caller sounded young, though, in some kind of all-fired hurry. Could be dying of something terminal, he guessed. Or calling for someone else who was. Either way, the sweet-sexy sound of her voice had given him a rise again. He wanted to picture her as blonde, attractive—God, please!—something decent to look at for a change.

Fremont adjusted himself inside his slacks, and made his way to his car, still parked in the lot behind the bar.

* * *

Fremont wasn't all that fond of the Bible Belt. He'd come to Notrees, Texas, outside Odessa, all the way from Tucson, Arizona, bringing with him another of his fantastic ideas.

This particular idea had come to him that night smoking a bowl with his friend Lougie. They were flying high at the time, two in the morning, watching Oral Roberts on cable TV. Making fun of the man and his God-fearing beliefs. "How 'bout this!" Fremont said, framing the idea for Lougie with his hands. "Sell 'Christian Only' burial plots to the Bible-thumpers. I mean, check it out, what righteously saved motherfucker wants to be laid to rest next to fornicators and thieves? See what I'm sayin'?"

Fremont took another hit, as he rolled the idea around in his head a little more. "Get this...'Stairway To Heaven Cemetery. No Sinners Allowed.'"

"You'd have to go where the Christians are, where The Man himself is, Oral," Lougie said, zeroing in on important particulars. He could spot flaws in the plan even through the haze of Mexican Brown.

"You way ahead of me, little buddy," Fremont said, through clinched teeth, holding the smoke in, feeling it go to work. "Let the man do the job of working them up." He wheezed, letting it out in a rush. "Get them Biblically right, ahead of our calls. Be like shooting fish in a barrel."

Fremont remembered the two of them falling all over themselves with laughter at that. *"Fish in a barrel!"* Thinking about the little emblems the Jesus freaks put on their cars. Or maybe it had been the weed.

There was another small problem they'd have to contend with, Lougie pointed out. They didn't actually own any burial plots. Nor own any land, in fact, on which to lay the dearly beloved to rest.

"See, the way I see it…" Fremont explained. "They don't have to actually know that."

It was the perfect score—at least with the weed talking.

The next morning, however, Lougie couldn't see it. There was, after all, his job bussing tables at the truck stop, and what if no one bought any plots? There was that. You'd be out the travel money. And, man, humping up and down the street knocking on doors, well…

There was that too.

But Fremont liked the idea. Said he'd be back in a month. Money in his pocket.

Well, it hadn't worked out as well as he'd imagined, really. And he'd already been in Notrees more than a month. The fish here, it seemed, were a little more savvy than he'd expected. *"Where exactly is this Stairway to Heaven?"*

Fremont had seen a giant white cross erected in the middle of a farmer's field just outside of town. He took pictures of the cross and the open field surrounding it, and started referring to what he was selling as *futures*. "See, the actual cemetery is still in development. We in the early subscription phase. Drive out Route 158, toward Goldsmith. See that big cross? Now picture being laid to rest beneath that cross. Your neighbors are lining up. Don't wait. Act now. But only *God's Chosen* need apply."

He'd actually sold a couple of subscriptions so far, giving him hope that, maybe, all he needed was to get his pitch down. An avalanche of orders to follow. *"Climb on board the Salvation Train. Don't be left in the dark."* The dark referring to hell in this case.

Fremont made it up as he went.

Still, what he'd earned, so far, amounted to chump change. And— fuck!—you had to hustle.

Every damn minute…hustle!

* * *

Fremont found the address on Prairie Dog Road, turned in past the mailbox, and took the long dirt driveway down to the front of the house. There was a single tree in the front yard, in defiance of the town's name, Notrees, a spreading Elm. A rusted-out pickup sat abandoned beneath the tree. All four tires were flat. Weeds were growing out from beneath the running boards.

Fremont pulled his eight-year-old Camaro up next to it and killed the engine.

The farm house was a simple, white frame structure in need of paint. A long covered porch ran the width of it. There were a pair of wooden rocking chairs at the top of the steps, facing out toward the road. Wide open prairie behind and all around. Pump jacks could be seen off in the distance, going through their slow, monotonous, up-down revolutions. Central Texas into its lazy workday.

There was also a For Sale sign in the front yard that read Notrees Realty with the name of the listing agent on it, Henrietta Cox.

Fremont gathered his briefcase and stepped out of the car and into the sulfurous smell of Texas crude. Nauseating, unless you were the one reaping the big-oil profits, he supposed. He stiffened his back against the smell and crossed the yard onto the porch.

The front door to the house was standing open. Only a screen door lay between him and the narrow foyer. Fremont took note of the cross, hanging on the wall just inside, fish people. He gave the door a knock and waited. In a second, a woman appeared, drying her hands on an apron. "Mister Lilly?" she said from behind the screen. "Thank you for coming." She stripped the apron off as she approached and tossed it on a small settee, then opened the door to welcome him inside.

Her smile was the nature of sunshine, wilting Fremont where he stood. Whatever her interest in burial plots, it was obvious it wasn't intended for her. She was maybe late twenties. She wore a man's denim work shirt over cut-off Levis. Barefoot. Smooth, shapely legs showing. Her hair was cut medium length, blonde. Pretty in a wholesome country girl way. A flush of pink to her cheeks, smelling of shampoo and wildflowers. The Norma Jean version of Marilyn Monroe.

"Won't you come in," she said, holding the screen door wide for him.

Fremont stepped inside, the nearness of her as he passed making him dizzy with lust. "You called about the cemetery plots," he managed.

"Yes. I'm Peyton Harris's daughter. Call me Charlene. Please, follow me inside?"

The request seemed almost flirtatious, something Fremont believed the girl hadn't really intended. It was simply who she was. She would be sexy in a strait jacket. "Thank you, ma'am," Fremont said, falling into his practiced Texas drawl.

She moved off down the hallway, letting the screen door close on its own.

Fremont enjoyed the view from behind as she led him down the hallway and through a small kitchen, that was simple and neat. Then out a door and onto a screened-in porch at the rear of the house. There, an elderly man sat in a recliner that faced the vast prairie beyond the screens. His gaze was fixed on the slow-churning pump jacks in the distance.

"Dad, this is Mister Lilly. The man I was telling you about. He's come to help us make arrangements."

The man said nothing but continued to stare out across the prairie.

"You'll have to pardon my father," Charlene said. "He's only fifty-eight years old, still physically strong, as you can see. But suffering the early onset of Alzheimer's."

"Sorry, to hear that," Fremont said. "Does he know I'm here?"

"Perhaps. On some level."

"Jimmy Hoffa is under the haystack!" the old man suddenly blurted, his eyes still on the beyond.

"He doesn't know what he's saying sometimes," the daughter said.

Fremont was staring at the father, a little unnerved by him. He braced himself, however, and turned his attention to the young woman. "You said you saw one of my flyers?"

Charlene gestured him to a seat on the sofa.

She took a seat as well, across the small table from him, sitting forward, clasping her hands together in front of her. "I saw one on the bulletin board at the grocery store. The message of your offering hit home in a big way, what with Daddy and all."

"Then you understand what we offer is a final resting place away from the taint of sinners, those not cleansed by the blood of the Lamb?" Still making it up as he went.

"Oh, yes. My father and I are devout followers of Jesus Christ, our Lord. Your service is just what God would have."

"I shudder to think of this dear man of God," Fremont said, "being laid to rest in your typical cemetery. Lying side-by-side with fornicators, thieves and child molesters."

"Please, don't even say that!"

"Well, I'm just happy to be of service," Fremont said.

Fremont launched into his routine, telling the woman about the need in the marketplace for believers to have a "sin free" place of rest, unsnapping his briefcase as he spoke and drawing out a colorful sales brochure.

He then introduced her to Stairway to Heaven, a Christian Only cemetery. "Sinners need not apply." He spread the brochure before her on the small table. "A resting place specially reserved for God's chosen."

The cover of the brochure showed a verdant meadow with a huge, brightly shining cross standing in the middle—a creative design element Fremont had drawn from the real cross standing in the farmers field outside of town. Happy little birds could be seen playing among the flowering foliage. You could almost hear them singing.

From the billowy clouds in the sky above the meadow, a giant set of hands—God's own hands—reached down from the heavens, welcoming the saved into waiting arms. Fremont considered the brochure did most of the selling. Look upon those images and what else could you do but sign on the dotted line?

"When the day of atonement comes, where will your father be? " Fremont quizzed. "Shall we pray?" He extended his hands across the table for her to receive. The woman closed her eyes and placed her hands in his.

Fremont could feel a soft warmth radiating from her. Leaned forward, the way she was, he could see the swell of soft white cleavage through the opening in the denim shirt. She wasn't wearing a bra, he realized.

Her father continued staring into oblivion.

Fremont got down to business. He closed his eyes and led the two of them in prayer. "Dear Lord..."

In his best evangelical preacher voice, Fremont implored God to guide this woman's decisions today. Consider her father's greater salvation. Make the right choice. Do the Godly thing. Go with Stairway to Heaven burial plots. *Pay Fremont the money.* He didn't use those words exactly, but Fremont believed he had a buyer, a fish, in this woman.

When he finished, he opened his eyes to see tears rolling down the woman's cheeks. She rose and came quickly around the table to him, wrapping her arms around him in a tight embrace. "Thank you, Mister Lilly! Thank you! You don't know how comforting it is that you have come."

Fremont could feel her soft breasts pressed against him through their clothing, the clean scent of her swirling inside his brain.

The woman's closeness gave him cause to ponder, if he took her right here, right now... would she object? Further, would the old man be aware of them going at it? Or, if aware and unable to respond, would it torment him somewhere deep inside. Then, would it jeopardize the sale?

The woman lingered in his embrace, making Fremont wonder further if this wholesome, country girl image was a façade. Perhaps, underneath was a wanton tigress, a sexual hellcat. Fremont considered taking a nibble from her ear, see what kind of flash-fires he might ignite. But, he reminded himself again that there was *b'ness* and there was *business.* He'd been without a sale for more than a week. Funds were dwindling low. And he really couldn't afford to blow what he viewed as a sure thing.

Against all his urges, all his screaming instincts, Fremont drew apart from her. He held her at arm's length, then used the back of one crooked finger to wipe a tear from her cheek.

Charlene straightened and composed herself. "I'm sorry. It's just...it gets so..."

"Lonely," Fremont said.

Charlene nodded.

"Damn the Redcoats!" the old man suddenly cried.

"It's only Dad and me. And I don't know how much longer he has. That's why I need to get this business completed."

Fremont cleared his throat that had suddenly gone dry. "Well, let's see what we can do."

He pulled an official looking contract from his briefcase and laid it on the table in front of her. "It's all pretty straight forward. This is a subscription transaction. The land will be cleared any day now, and construction will begin just as soon as we reach a minimum subscription base, you understand."

"Oh! You mean it's not complete yet?"

"As I said, we're in the subscription phase, see. It will be ready to receive your father in a few days and other God-fearing souls like him."

"Days?"

"Maybe a week," Fremont amended. "I'm sure you understand. God is with us on this. He takes no soul before its time." Fremont thought he was reaching a bit this time, making God a partner in his scam. But he saw the acceptance settle into her eyes and leaned in for the close. "If I can just get your signature at the bottom of the page." He produced a pen, as if by magic and handed it to her.

"We haven't discussed cost yet."

"I'm sure you'll find our fee is reasonable." Fremont slid the contract an inch closer. "Only two thousand dollars."

A worried look suddenly crossed the woman's face. "Two thousand?"

"Down..." Fremont said, going for broke. "Two thousand down. And another two thousand within thirty days of contract approval."

"Approval?"

"Did I mention we're very exclusive. We screen our applicants closely."

"Oh, dear. I'm afraid we don't have that kind of money. All we have is this house, and that old pick-up in desperate need of new tires."

"Well, you're in luck, see...my company has authorized me to offer a one time, special-needs discount. Let's say, twelve hundred dollars and be done with it."

The look in the woman's eyes was near panic.

"How 'bout eight hundred?" Fremont amended again, seeing the fish suddenly flopping on the line. "Seven hundred, and now I'm givin' up my sales commission. Just because I can tell you're such a fine Christian family and deserving of this opportunity." Fremont grasped her pen hand and urged it closer to the contract.

For one brief moment, the woman looked as if she might sign. Then she released the pen, letting it clatter to the floor, and rose off toward her father in tears. "I'm sorry, Daddy. I so wanted this for you." She drew herself close behind his chair and hugged her arms around his neck. The tears streamed down her cheeks.

The old man blurted a reply. "The prairie dogs stole it! Fuck the prairie dogs!"

Fremont had never dealt with this particular situation before. He slumped back in his seat unsure of how to proceed.

"Will the sun bake the pumpkins?" the old man asked sincerely, of no one in particular.

"It's okay, Dad," the daughter urged the father. "Take it easy."

"Call brother Bill! The crows are into the corn!"

"He's not going to stroke-out on us, is he?" Fremont asked.

"He just gets a little distraught at times." Charlene calmed her father then crossed back to where Fremont was sitting, eyes wide. "He'll be alright. Why don't we take our discussion outside so as not to upset him."

She led Fremont out through a door and down off a small porch into a backyard that was overgrown with weeds. Lying about were discarded car and truck parts, tires, axels, a rusted engine block, an old fender, a busted transmission.

"The place is in such a wreck," Charlene said.

He could see that. "You tryin' to sell it?"

Charlene nodded. "I returned to take care of my father. I had no idea how bad things had gotten."

"So, you don't live here?"

"No, I grew up in Moline, Illinois, with my mother. She's gone now too. I live in the Chicago suburbs these days, work in a law office in Lyle. Daddy has lived here alone all his life."

"So you, the good daughter, come back to settle his affairs."

"Doctor says Daddy won't have long, after full-on dementia sets in. He's led such a hard life—"

Her voice caught, and Fremont thought the tears might come again. He crossed and put one hand on her shoulder.

"I wanted to get Dad into a care facility over in Odessa. There's only one remaining spot left and I fear we'll lose it if we don't act now. The house hasn't sold as quickly as I'd hoped. And I don't even have a car to drive him there. His ongoing care will cost money. I need to get back to my job in Chicago, so I can afford to pay for it. I feel so stuck, Mr. Lilly, and I so wanted to get his burial arrangements completed." Charlene collected herself, bucked-up the way Fremont saw it. "But, I guess that's life."

It surprised him some, his tenderness toward this girl, but there was just something about her that touched off feelings deep inside. Fremont let his gaze move from her to the distant pump jacks. He wished there was something he could do.

When he brought his gaze back, Fremont noticed something out in the yard, a large black spot amid the weeds. He left the woman's side and took several steps closer to get a better look.

"What is it? What are you looking at?" Charlene called. She came to join him, followed his gaze toward the spot.

"Nothing Fremont said. "Just studying the ground."

"Oh? You mean the black spot...some kind of yucky...I don't know...ooze."

Yucky ooze was right. The spot was oil—no doubt about it—shiny and black, partially obscured by casual debris. It was something he might not have paid a second thought to, but for the dozens of pump jacks in the near distance. *Could it be?*

Fremont had heard of places where oil was so abundant that it pushed its way right up out of the ground. And this was central Texas, where yucky ooze had made zillionaires out of everyday dirt farmers. "It's nothing," he said, turning the woman quickly away from the find and leading her back toward the house.

Back inside the screened-in porch, Fremont continued to consider the curious oil spot in the yard. Was it possible the woman and her father were sitting on a fortune and didn't know it?

"You'll excuse me," Charlene said. "I have to give Daddy his medication. It's in the bedroom, it will just take me a minute."

Fremont nodded. And the woman went off through the kitchen and disappeared down the hall.

Across the porch from him, the old man still hadn't moved. Fremont decided to use the time to poke around.

He stepped into the kitchen, seeing morning dishes still in the sink. Across from the sink was a chrome dinette piece, table and chairs. And in the corner a three-drawer hutch, filled with decorative plates and ceramic figurines, shakers and the like. Lying in the open atop the hutch was a sales contract, the words Quit Claim Deed, were printed across the top of it in bold official looking type. The top half of the form was already filled out with the seller's information, in optimism of a buyer soon to walk through the door.

"Poor pilgrims," Fremont thought. "Who'd want to buy this busted-ass place? 'Less of course..." He was thinking about the mysterious oil spot in the yard again.

He then opened one of the drawers, finding nothing significant—a flashlight, some spare batteries, candles and the like. The next drawer was filled with more of the same—couple of ball-point pens, various books of matches. In the third drawer were papers of all kinds. Electric bill receipts, mortgage payment, late notices. Fremont was just about to finish snooping when one of the papers near the bottom of the stack caught his eye. It was a contract reading: Oil Lease Agreement, Odessa Drilling Company. The contract, three pages of it, was filled with official sounding legal clauses. It had not been executed.

Fremont quickly returned the paperwork and shut the drawer. Was it possible the oil company had actually made the old man an offer he'd forgotten about in his advancing dementia? An unsigned gold mine just lying around in a kitchen drawer? He shot a quick glance down the hallway, hearing the young woman heading back his way. He quickly stepped back out onto the porch.

When Charlene found him, Fremont was bent over the old man, talking baby talk to him. "And out there, see the oil rigs, pump...pump...pump..."

"I'm not sure he knows what you're saying," Charlene said, coming with a handful of pills and a glass of water.

Fremont watched as she hand-fed the pills to the old man one at a time, and forced them down with water.

"Well," she said. "The money thing is my own hard pill to swallow. But I've had time to think about it, Mister Lilly. And I guess Daddy and

I just can't afford Stairway To Heaven. And I'm sure the final slot at the care facility in Odessa is out of the question too. I was so hoping the house would sell so I could see to Daddy's needs."

Fremont thought he could see tears welling in the young woman's eyes again.

"This house," he said, his mind spinning dollar signs before his eyes. "Your father holds the deed?"

"Why...yes... of course," Charlene said, appearing inquisitive now.

"Perhaps...and shit...I don't know...it's just a thought...but, maybe I could take the place off your hands for you." He didn't look right at her as he made his pitch, but stole a glance from the corner of his eye to see if she was receiving.

"You wish to buy Dad's house?"

"Well, it's just something that came to me. What with your father's condition, the one space left at the care facility and all. The house is in poor condition, no offense, and not likely you'll ever get it sold. And, I can't imagine it's worth much." Fremont ventured another look at Charlene. Her eyes were shining with hope. "I'd have to pay to get the backyard cleaned up. There would be repairs. All money out of my pocket, you understand. But, seeing as how time is of the essence for you, my Christian ways would have me do this thing to help you good folks out."

"Well, that...that would be great, Mister Lilly. How much might you offer?"

"I don't have much cash," Fremont said, mentally sizing-up what he had in his pocket. "First think of it more as a chance to cut your losses, get a fresh start. Have enough to get your father to Odessa, and for you to get back to your job and your life in Chicago. Once working again, you could afford his care. I would offer say...eight hundred dollars."

The air seemed to go out of the room.

"Eight hundred dollars?" Charlene queried. "That's not very much."

"I understand," Fremont said. "It doesn't sound like much for a house to me either. So, how about I throw in my car, the Camaro parked under the tree out front, it's worth five to six grand. And, of course, I would cover the cost of the Stairway To Heaven burial plot, myself. Now, that's a four thousand dollar value. We're talking close to eleven thousand dollars altogether. Nothing to sneeze at. And keep in mind I'm doing this out if the goodness of my heart."

Charlene seemed to consider his offer.

"It accomplishes all your goals," Fremont reminded.

She hadn't said yes yet.

"You'll have a vehicle to get your father into that care facility. Travel money to get you back to your job. And! You'll have the peace of mind of knowing his eternity will be spent in the hands of our Maker."

Back selling peace of mind again, Fremont thought.

He waited.

"I...I don't know what to say..."

Fremont quickly retrieved the Stairway to Heaven contract and a pen and placed them in her hands. "It's the righteous thing to do," he affirmed.

Charlene looked at the contract for a long moment, then let her gaze move to the deteriorating man in the recliner. "Well...maybe it would be for the best. It does free me to get on with my life."

"It's God's will," Fremont added, sealing the deal.

The daughter signed the contract and handed it to him. Then she went into the kitchen and returned with the Quit Claim Deed. "The real estate lady had this drawn up, knowing we had just a short amount of time to act. It's a Quit Claim, or Quick Claim as it's sometimes called. It transfers ownership of the property from *Grantor*, Daddy, to *Grantee*, that would be you. It will require Dad's signature, but...well...maybe between the two of us, I could sign his name for him. No one would have to know. I'm also a notary in my law firm, I could notarize the document, make it totally legal."

Fremont had never actually purchased property before and all the legal terminology was foreign to him. But the woman did work in a law office; she seemed to know what she was doing. He watched as she forged the old man's signature on the title. "Your full name?" she asked.

"Fremont...Fremont, Alphonse, Lilly," he replied, spelling it all out for her. His head was spinning with anticipation.

She finished filling in the blanks. Then brought out an official looking stamp and applied her Notary seal. She signed the document again, this time with her own name and Notary title.

"I'll need the title to your car now," she said. "And of course, the eight hundred dollars."

Fremont took out his wallet and produced a title for his car that he unfolded for the woman and signed. He wasn't sure how he was going to get around, while he closed the deal with the Odessa Drilling Company, but he would work that out. Make it up as he went along, the way he figured. After all, shit, he was going to be a very rich man soon.

The woman notarized his title transfer and stuffed it into her shirt pocket. Fremont dug eight-hundred dollars from his pocket, all he had left in the world, and handed it to her, along with the keys to the car.

Deal complete, they stood looking at each other, the woman's eyes wet and shining.

"I can't tell you how grateful I am, Mr. Lilly."

The flirtatious light had returned to her eyes. This time, Fremont wanted to believe it was intended for him. Business done, it was time for b'ness. He crossed to her intending to get his hands full of whatever was beneath her shirt. But the woman sidestepped him and crossed quickly to her father.

"I must get Daddy to the care facility."

"What's the rush?" Fremont said, "I'm thinking we maybe do a little celebrating."

"I really need to get Daddy to the facility before they fill the last opening."

Charlene helped her father from his chair and began leading him out.

"At least, let me help you to the car."

"No need," she said, with a wave. "Enjoy your new home, Mr. Lilly."

Fremont wasn't sure about the sudden change of temperament, and there was a worrisome nagging at the back of his mind. He watched them go, off through the kitchen, down the hallway, and out through the front screen door. Seconds later he heard his Camaro's big V8 engine crank and roar to life.

They didn't even pack a bag, he realized.

Fremont took a quick glance toward the back yard, to the glistening black circle of muck. It eased his sinking concerns somewhat. He loosened himself from where his shoes seemed glued to the floor and made his way out toward the front.

When he reached the screen door, he spotted a car pulling into the yard, a late model sedan. His Camaro, with its new owners inside, made a wide turn through the yard and passed the new arrival on its way out.

A heavy-set woman quickly clambered from the sedan, a briefcase in her hand. She seemed surprised, agitated by the departing Camaro. She spotted Fremont behind the screen door and came charging onto the porch.

"What are you doing here?" she asked. "Who are those people? Who are you?" The woman's face was flushed red, lips drawn into a thin, angry line.

"Who's asking?" Fremont said.

"I'm Henrietta Cox, Notrees Realty. This is my listing."

"Well, you can remove your For Sale sign, lady. I just bought the house."

"Bought? From who?"

"From the owners," Fremont said, gesturing confidently to the Camaro that was making its way up the long driveway toward the road.

"Those aren't the owners! The owner is dead! I represent the bank in this transaction. There has been no sale."

Fremont stepped onto the porch. The Camaro had reached the pavement. Now its tires were spinning, issuing a loud screech, and speeding off up the road. The young woman, Charlene, was oddly in the passenger seat, her hair flying in the breeze through the open window, a smile on her face. Which meant—Jesus!—the senile old man was driving.

Fremont watched in disbelief as his Camaro wound through the gears and disappeared up the road.

"You have to leave before I call the police," the real estate lady was saying.

Fremont had fallen into a trance, trying to comprehend what had just happened. "But...the house...the old man...the oil...," he said.

"Oil! What oil?"

"The spot, in the back yard, oozing up from the ground."

"Spot?...You mean that big ugly black area? That's where the previous owner used to change the oil in his car. You know, some people can be so thoughtless, draining their crankcase right out there on the ground. Not giving first thought to..."

Fremont didn't hear much of what the real estate lady had to say after that. He was thinking of his friend Lougie and Tucson, and where he might find the money for a bus ticket home.

He'd come to the Bible Belt looking to score some cash. Now he was broke, homeless, and without his car—his beloved Camaro. Somewhere, out there on the road to nowhere, was a fine looking not-so-country-girl and her not-so-senile-father.

They were hustlers. Grifters. Scoundrels, Fremont realized. And obviously much better at it than he.

He'd just become the biggest fish in Texas.

Sentence of a Lifetime
Brendan DuBois

The Cessna CJ3 executive jet finally took off from the small runway on Crabstone Cay, Henry Wallace took a deep breath as he watched it climb up into the warm blue sky. He had made it. Practically the entire American law enforcement apparatus—FBI, Secret Service, and U.S. Marshal's Service—had been after him ever since he had skipped out of a Manhattan court hearing yesterday. But now he could finally relax. Henry loved learning new things, and now he was learning how to be a fugitive from justice.

The island was small, with a luxury hotel at one end and a collection of cabanas nearby for the hotel's workers, and this private landing strip. Everything here belonged to Henry, and as an extra bonus, it was also part of an obscure Caribbean island chain that had no extradition treaty with the United States.

Beside him, his long-time bodyguard, driver and trusted keeper of secrets, spoke up. "Looks like a beautiful day, Mister Wallace," Courtney Knox said. He was powerful, squat, with thick hands that had once carried weapons for the U.S. Navy's elite SEALs before Courtney decided to make a career change that meant lots more money and less opportunities to get blown up.

"First day of the rest of our lives, Courtney," he said. "Let's get going. I'm starving."

At the side of the runway a black Lincoln Town Car with tinted windows was parked, engine idling, with Henry's luggage piled at the side. Henry got into the rear and waited as Courtney loaded the trunk. At the bar before him was a freshly opened bottle of Champagne, a Krug Clos du Mesnil. He poured himself a flute of the Champagne, took a sip. Delightful.

Courtney ducked in. "Here, sir. Something to read while we get to the hotel."

His bodyguard passed over a copy of *Time* magazine, with Henry's face on the cover. The headline said, "The next Bernie Madoff?"

Henry snorted and tossed the magazine aside. "Bernie Madoff was a piker."

During the short drive to the hotel past the bright flowers and plants, Henry sighed with contentment. Not bad for a kid who had grown up in a scrappy small town on Cape Cod. Hell, transporting this Town Car to this spit of land cost almost as much as the car itself, but Henry wanted it here, and got it here. Simple as that. And that had been his entire life philosophy. See what he wanted and take it. From the very start, no physical labor for Henry, not like his dad, running a landscaping business, or his high school pals, service station jobs or working in hardware stores. From learning deal making on Wall Street, to working in the bowels of some financial service companies, and then running his own successful hedge fund...it had been a very profitable run, without once getting his hands dirty or sore.

The Town Car purred up to the entrance of the ten-story luxury hotel, made of light pink concrete, as Henry put the Champagne flute down. A good run, he thought, except for the nitwits from all over the country who had decided to invest in him and who were now broke.

* * *

Dinner was at a restaurant at the top of the hotel, adjacent to his penthouse suite. He sat by a curved window with a view of the Caribbean, the round green shapes of the nearby islands and sailboats at play. For dinner he had rock lobster tails sautéed in garlic and butter, with a side of blue cheese risotto and a green salad, with a bottle of a rare Château Pétrus to wash it all down. Courtney sat across from him and ate a cheeseburger with hand-cut fries.

When the dishes had been cleared away, Henry looked over the empty restaurant with pleasure. Only his friends ever came here, and with the latest news, they were staying away. So what. Once things quieted down and the FBI decided to chase the next big time white-collar criminal, his friends would come back.

"This morning, the Manhattan D.A. said I deserved a life sentence at the Federal Supermax prison," Henry said reflectively. "But instead, my sentence is going to be here. Good Lord, look at that view. Isn't it the best?"

"Very true, sir," Courtney said.

"I'll never get tired of it...but after a while, once the heat is off, we'll be able to travel abroad. Switzerland for skiing. Argentina for barbecue. Thailand for Thai food." And he laughed at the last sentence, though Courtney didn't join in. Instead, Courtney held up the magazine

Henry had earlier tossed away with contempt. "Have you read this yet, sir?"

"No, of course not."

Courtney said, "I've read it a couple of times. It says you bilked billions of dollars from investors, from charities to colleges to families."

Henry shrugged. "You know what really happened, what's not in that story? People got greedy. And I provided what people thought was an opportunity to make lots of money, with annual returns that consistently beat Wall Street averages. If any one of them had done a bit of research, they wouldn't have come to me. They would have gone someplace else safer."

"So you don't feel guilty?"

"For what? For giving greedy people what they deserve? Not on your life." He reached over, plucked the magazine out of Courtney's hand. He read aloud the headline: "'The new Bernie Madoff?' Not hardly. Bernie thought he could get away with it. Me, I always knew I'd get caught. But thanks to you, I had a plan. The minute investigations started, I flew to this little slice of paradise. My funds are in untraceable accounts in the Cayman Islands, Switzerland, and even Vatican City. I'm set for life."

"But didn't you say earlier you couldn't touch those funds for years?"

"That's right," Henry said. "If I start dipping into them now, the FBI and their forensic accountants will be able to connect the dots and seize them all. So it's just a waiting game at this point...but lucky for me, this is a wonderful place to wait it out."

Courtney didn't say a word. Henry pushed his chair back, tossed his napkin on the tablecloth. "I think it's time to retire."

As Henry walked down a paneled hallway from the restaurant, an elevator door was open and his bodyguard said, "I need to show you something in the service area, sir."

Henry nodded and followed Courtney into the elevator and about thirty seconds later, he stepped out into the heat and the noise. This was his least favorite place to visit in the hotel, where the food was cooked and the laundry was washed. It was noisy and dirty, and tonight, it was crowded. The basement was filled with islanders in white and black uniforms who worked for him.

And to a man and a woman, each was carrying that issue of *Time* magazine.

He felt chilled. "Hey, what's going on?" Henry asked.

Courtney put a hand on his shoulder. It felt as heavy as stone.

Courtney motioned with his free hand, and a young male worker in a waiter's uniform stepped forward.

"This is Andre," Courtney said. "His uncle lost his bodega in Dorchester because he invested in one of your companies."

Another gesture, and a woman in a maid's uniform also came out. "This is Maria. Her two sons are being kicked out of college because the charity sponsoring them is now broke."

The hand on his shoulder squeezed harder. "Everybody else here...their friends and families have lost everything due to your dealings, because they trusted you. And my own mom...she's being evicted from her home in Daytona Beach."

Henry started speaking quickly. "Look...give me some time...I'll figure out how to make everybody whole, make it right, I can do it and—"

Courtney shoved him forward, as the workers stepped away. Behind them was a concrete cubbyhole, with a cot, mattress and blanket. Next to the cubbyhole were three large sinks, overflowing with used pots and pans. "Say goodbye to the suite and the restaurant, sir. This is where you're going to live and eat, for the rest of your life. And to earn your living, you can begin by cleaning those dirty dishes."

"You can't be serious!" Henry said, feeling desperate. "And you can't get away with it!"

"I'm all serious, Mister Wallace," Courtney said. "And I *can* get away with it. I have control of this island, this hotel, its employees, phones, the Telex, and the Internet connection. And since you've trusted me all these years, I know the keys and codes to your funds."

Henry thought frantically. "I can pay you. I can pay you all! I can pay you—"

Courtney shoved him hard, toward the sinks. "But I already have all your money, even if it can't be touched for a while. Time to get to work, Mister Wallace."

* * *

And later that night, in a daze of exhaustion and fear, Henry learned one more thing: washing pots and pans was *hard.*

Leverage
Lono Waiwaiole

"Delilah," she said, the soft hint of music rolling off the word as she said it. Robbie heard both the word and the hint of music perfectly, which was one of the things he liked most about *Sirens*—you could hear well enough there to have an actual conversation if you wanted one.

Another of the things Robbie liked about the club was the relative quality of the dancers, a very high standard that this Delilah had nevertheless surpassed with ease. He had just finished watching her two-song set on the stage and now believed she could not have been put together more perfectly, but somehow she was even more entrancing fully dressed. He looked at her for a while without a word, and she looked back at him exactly the same way until the while was over.

"Is that your real name?" he said finally.

"What makes one name more real than another?"

"Is that your original name, then."

"No," she said, the bluest eyes Robbie had ever seen still sparring with his insistently.

"Sounds kind of dangerous," he said.

"What does?"

"Delilah."

"Is your name Samson?"

"No."

"You should be fine, then," she said, and she wrapped a smile around the words this time that suddenly raised the temperature in their vicinity by several degrees.

"I'm Robbie," he said.

"I know. The girls have told me all about you."

"The girls don't know all about me."

"You might be surprised at how perceptive the girls tend to be."

"Did they tell you I drop more cash here than anybody else?"

"Of course."

"Do you want me to drop some on you?"

"Absolutely."

"I think I'd enjoy that very much."

"So would I. Unfortunately, that can't happen tonight."

"Why not?"

"I promised tonight to someone else."

"I can make it worth your while."

"So can he," she said. "But I'm *very* pleased to meet you, Robbie." She extended her right hand in his direction and he took it. Her grip was simultaneously both soft and firm, and he was still puzzling that out when she withdrew her hand and walked away.

"Wow!" Jackson said, which was when Robbie remembered that Jackson was sitting there to his right and had been since their arrival.

"No shit," Robbie said as he watched Delilah walk the way these girls always walked, only more so—with a tantalizing roll of the hips that somehow said more on the subject of a woman's sweet magic than any words Robbie had ever heard.

"She's not the only girl here, though," Jackson said.

"Yes, she is," Robbie said as he rose from his seat. "Tomorrow at seven, right?"

"Yes," Jackson said.

"What about Lobosan?"

"A definite maybe."

"There's no point to the meeting without Lobosan."

"I'm working on it."

"Just get him there," Robbie said, and then he walked out of the club with delicious thoughts of Delilah pushing all thoughts of a meeting with anyone else straight out the back of his head.

* * *

"We met."

"You'll be seeing him again?"

"Of course."

"I appreciate the call."

* * *

"He won't be there," Jackson said on the phone the following afternoon.

"What's the problem?" Robbie said.

"I don't really know. He hasn't shut the door, either."

"Push the meeting back with the other two. They won't do anything without Lobosan."

"Will do," Jackson said. "See you at *Sirens* later?"

"That depends on whether or not we're both there, doesn't it?" Robbie said before he cut the connection and walked into his favorite jewelry store.

Danielle materialized at his side almost as soon as he walked in the door. "Mr. Robertson," she said. "So nice to see you."

"Are you ready for me?"

"I think so, yes. Right this way." She led him to a counter near the back of the store where a young man Robbie didn't know produced two pieces displayed elaborately—a string of white pearls and a diamond-encrusted pendant on a delicate silver chain.

"There is a story with each of these selections," Danielle said. "Would you like to hear them?"

"This is like apples and oranges. I don't think the stories will help me."

"I can see why you might think that, but it's not really true. Some people don't like both apples and oranges, but I doubt very seriously that you know a woman who wouldn't like both of these."

"Wrap them both for me, then."

"Very good. Will that be on a card?"

"Danielle, how many alarms would go off around here if I put almost ten thousand dollars in cash on this counter?"

"I don't think more than one or two," Danielle said with a smile. "Some government agency or another would probably want to know."

"A card it is," Robbie said. He produced one, and a couple of minutes later he was back on the street with the card in his pocket and a pair of small packages in a classy gift bag dangling from one hand.

* * *

Robbie watched the way the long blue gown flowed over Delilah's perfect curves as she moved toward him and was richly rewarded every step of the way. "Hey, there," she said when she reached him. "You came back."

"Had to deliver your present," he said, pointing to the gift bag on the small table in front of him.

"Already? Aren't you the impetuous one."

"I want to make it clear from the beginning."

"Make what clear?"

"How serious I am."

"I see," she said. She bent over to peer inside the bag, a move that convincingly cut the number of undergarments she might have been wearing under the gown by half. "Which one is mine?"

"Whichever one you pick."

She removed one of the packages and hefted it for a moment. "How about this one?"

"Open it."

She did as he suggested, and after a close look at the pearls she took an even closer look at him. "May I sit?"

"I'm sorry," he said. "Please do."

She stepped between him and the table and slipped into a small fraction of the space beside him on the couch. The right side of her slim frame brushed the left side of his as she crossed one long leg over the other, but her eyes demanded his full attention and they received it.

"This is a *very* expensive gift," she said. "Do you imagine you are buying something with it?"

"Not at all."

"Expensive gifts don't signal that you're serious," she said. "Extravagance is *way* too easy for you."

"What would be more effective?"

"Share something about yourself that you don't throw around as easily as money."

"Like what?"

"I don't know, Robbie. You could start with what you do to get all this money, maybe."

"I was born with it."

"I'm betting you have more now than you started with."

"True."

"How'd you make the difference?"

"Kind of like you, actually," Robbie said, but he thought it over for a while before he said it. "People just give it to me."

"What do you give them in return?"

"Not a thing, generally. That part's not like you, obviously."

"Obviously? What do you imagine I give in return?"

"I guess I'm a little ahead of myself. I don't know yet, do I?"

"No, you don't," she said. She handed him the necklace and turned slightly, her body still snug against his side while she did it. "Would you fasten these for me, please?"

Robbie slipped the pearls around her neck and fastened the clasp, his fingers slightly brushing the soft hairs on her skin as he did it.

"Who is the other gift for?" she said.

"That's for you, too."

"You know this is crazy, don't you?"

"No," Robbie said. "I don't know that at all."

* * *

"He says he's serious."

"Excellent."

"He might also be certifiably crazy."

"Not an unknown phenomenon in your experience, is it?"

"No. But for some reason it still surprises me a little every time."

* * *

Robbie looked around the gleaming oval table in Jackson's high-rise conference room when the meeting finally happened and almost laughed out loud. Four local fat cats who should have known better looked back at him as though they took him seriously, a mistake of catastrophic proportions.

Dinosaurs may have been dangerous in their day, Robbie thought, *but that was many, many days ago. All they are now is old—way too old to keep up.*

"This company is garbage," Cho said.

"That's the beauty of it," Robbie said. "The company *is* garbage, and we can buy a controlling interest at garbage prices. Meanwhile, the subsidiary buried in all that shit is solid gold."

"So you're saying we get in the driver's seat, flush the garbage and then sell the subsidiary for more than we paid for the company?"

"Much, much more."

"Who's gonna sell us that many shares?" Lobosan said.

Robbie shifted his focus from the ancient Asian to Lobosan, an obese car dealer pushing 70 if he was a day who already had more money than he knew what to do with. *That's why you deserve what's gonna happen here*, Robbie thought. *I know what the fuck to do with that cash.*

"United Capital," Robbie said with a confident nod. "They have the majority position now, but they want out."

"Why don't they do what you propose to do?"

"They're either too stubborn or too stupid to do it." He looked from one set of eyes to the next while he waited for that point to hit home, and when he thought the mission had been accomplished he said the rest: "But I think we can all agree that someone is gonna do it. Is there a reason it shouldn't be us?"

"Sounds pretty good to me," Jackson said, but Jackson didn't count because he had been Robbie's bitch from the beginning. Jackson's job was to bring this particular flock to market and say "sounds pretty good to me" whenever appropriate, and he was right on task.

Lobosan, however, counted big-time, because Robbie knew the other two would go whichever way Lobosan went. Robbie floated the question out there for everybody, but he kept his attention focused on Lobosan. The old man looked back like he couldn't quite see all the way across the table, but after a quiet minute or two he shook his head a little. "No reason that I can see," he said. "Count me in."

Mikkelson and Cho fell all over themselves to join him, as Robbie had predicted, and he was ready to whoop it up when Jackson delivered his next line: "This calls for a celebration, gentlemen."

"And I know just the place," Robbie said, thinking it was the truest thing he had said all night.

Lobosan shook his head a little more. "I'm out past my bedtime already," he said. "You guys'll have to do the rest on your own."

"It won't be the same without you," Robbie said, although he didn't believe it for a minute.

"The little woman'll kill me," Lobosan said through the hint of a smile.

"Your wife is half your age," Jackson said, temporarily scaring Robbie a little by heading in that direction. "She's gonna kill you anyway."

The five of them rode the laughter that boiled up around that comment all the way down to the ground, but by the time they got to the garage everyone had demurred on the celebration in favor of heading home. *Yeah,* Robbie thought, way *too old to keep up,* but he knew exactly who he wanted to help him celebrate and was anxious to take off in her direction.

"We need their oars in the water by Monday," he said as soon as he was alone with Jackson. "We run the risk of a bidding war if we don't get this nailed down."

"They're good to go," Jackson said. "We should be able to close on the Cap United shares by the end of Monday."

"I'll be back by then," Robbie said as he climbed in behind his driver. "Anything changes, I need to hear about it *before* it happens."

"Back from where?"

"Heaven," Robbie said, "or Las Vegas. Whichever I get to first."

* * *

Sirens was humming quietly when Robbie arrived, as usual, but he had to cool his heels for almost an hour while Delilah entertained someone else. "This has been a real buzz kill so far," he said when she was finally seated next to him. She quietly considered his comment for a moment, then brushed her lips across his left cheek so lightly that he wasn't sure if they had actually touched him or not.

"Quite the opposite is true, actually," she said after she settled back into her own space.

"What do you mean?"

"Does waiting for Christmas kill the buzz?"

"You're comparing yourself to Christmas?"

"Waiting for something you really want *creates* buzz, Robbie," she said, her insistent eyes not giving an inch. "That's the fundamental verity of what I do."

"What was that fool worth to you, two or three hundred? You could have doubled or tripled that with me."

"It's not really an either-or situation, though, is it? He gave me what he wanted to give me when he had the chance, and now you have an opportunity to do the same."

Robbie looked down at her without speaking until his head began to shake back and forth on its own accord. "You're not like anyone else here, are you?" he said when he finally said something.

"There are some obvious similarities, but no. Not really."

"What would it take to get you out of here?"

"For how long?"

"All weekend."

"I work for a living, Robbie."

"How much would you make on a good weekend?"

"How good?"

"Let's say the best ever."

"Ten grand or so."

"Get outta here. A guy could get two or three of the top hookers in the world for that."

"You probably know more about that than I do," she said, pulling back a little so she could see into his eyes even more clearly. "But why would guys looking for hookers be spending their time with one of us?"

"I see," Robbie said, although he was not certain that he did. "I can't say there has always been much of a distinction between the two."

"That's one of the ways I differ from the others, then."

Robbie looked into her unblinking blue eyes for a moment before he spoke again, but the pause didn't change what he wanted to say. "I can cover ten grand. How soon can you leave?"

"There aren't many places other than here that I'm dressed for."

"They've got clothes where we're going."

"Where might that be?"

"Vegas."

"We can just take off for Vegas at this time of the night?"

"I have a plane waiting."

"Wow," she said. "Aren't you a surprising one."

"I thought the girls told you all about me."

"The girls don't know all about you."

"I feel like celebrating, Delilah. Join me."

"I'm not going to fuck you, Robbie."

"Vegas is already full of people I can fuck."

"Then yes," she said, and she said it twice at least—once where Robbie could hear it, and again where he could see it in her blue, blue eyes.

* * *

"You won't believe it."

"What?"

"He's taking me to Vegas."

"When?"

"Tonight."

"That was fast, even for you."

"Thank you, but I didn't have that much to do with it."

"What do you mean?"

"He's a little different."

"Different from who?"

"Different from everyone."

* * *

"The price on the shares just went up," Jackson said.

"How much?" Robbie asked.

"Almost half a million dollars if we get 'em all."

"Who the fuck are we up against?"

"This doesn't necessarily mean there's someone else. Cap United could just be pulling our chain."

"Tell those pricks we'll have the original offer in their hands within the hour and we are out the door if they don't take it."

"The only thing about that is we don't have the paper from everyone yet."

"Who the fuck is missing?"

"Lobosan says he needs to move a few things around first."

"What the fuck does that mean?"

"He says tomorrow, no problem."

"I'll call you back," Robbie said. He cut the connection and pushed hard against the impulse to throw the phone across the plane.

"Problems?" Delilah said from the seat next to him.

"The deal we've been celebrating all weekend is about to blow up in my face."

"What are we gonna do to put it back together?"

"We?"

"I'm part of the celebration. I have to protect the reason we're celebrating."

"Good point."

"What happened?"

"The sellers just jacked the price up."

"Is there another buyer in the picture?"

"I doubt it, really."

"Then you're just playing poker with the seller."

"Probably," Robbie said, but he looked at Delilah with a new set of eyes before he said it. "Pretty perceptive, aren't you?"

"Don't you mean pretty *and* perceptive?"

"Yes. That's exactly what I mean."

"So what's our move?"

"We should call the bluff if we really think it is one."

"How exciting!"

"Only problem is we're a little short right now. I'd have to use my own money to cover until one of my marks gets his money in the pot."

"Marks?"

"Investors."

"You've lost me."

"Let's just say this thing has more levels to it than most of the players realize."

"That's even more exciting!"

"Yes," Robbie said as he punched Jackson's number and put Jackson back in his ear. "Fuck Lobosan's end," he said. "I'll cover it myself until he gets his cash in."

"I'll let you know what they say," Jackson said, and Robbie cut the connection again.

"Now what?" Delilah said.

"Now we wait."

"Oh, goody. I love waiting." She rose from her seat and settled down on his lap like having his hips straddled between her knees was the most natural thing in the world. She moved ever so slightly where their bodies met and drew his mouth to hers, continuing the long series of similar maneuvers initiated on the flight heading in the opposite direction at the beginning of the weekend.

"You're a *really* good kisser," she said when their lips finally parted.

"I'd forgotten how much fun making out can be."

"That's another fundamental verity."

"What is?"

"You can think about getting off for a *lot* longer than you can actually do it."

"So in some ways it's a lot more fun."

"Exactly."

"And potentially lucrative."

"Very."

"How the fuck did you turn out to be you?"

"The same way everyone does, I suppose." She put her hand on the back of his head and drew him close again, and they were deep into another kiss when her phone brought her up for air.

"I know who that is," she said. "I have to answer it."

"Why?"

"I owe him at least that much," she said, her eyes focused on his relentlessly.

"Who?"

"I have other admirers, Robbie." She put her phone to her ear, but her eyes didn't waver for even a moment and neither did Robbie's.

"Hey," she said, and then she waited.

"There is something I have to tell you," she said finally, still locked into Robbie's insistent gaze. "I've met someone."

"I can't tell you exactly what it means," she said after another pause, an edge beginning to emerge in her voice. "But right now we're all in, understand? I promise you're the first person I'll call if that changes."

"Where were we, Robbie?" she said as she put the phone away, and Robbie showed her where they had been for several more sweet moments until *his* phone interrupted them.

"Within the hour will get it for us," Jackson said, "but they won't go back on the price."

"What the fuck?"

"They're saying they have a real offer at the new price, Robbie."

"I know what they're saying. Is it true?"

"I think we'd have to wait to find out the answer to that question, and then we might not like the answer we get."

"The only question that really matters is does the deal still make sense at half a mil more to start with?"

"It still makes sense at twice that, but your personal exposure goes up significantly until we get Lobosan's end."

"What kind of a problem is that?"

"I don't think it's a problem at all."

"Do it then," Robbie said, and he put the phone and the deal away for a while.

"Problem solved?" Delilah asked.

"Probably."

"Do we get to celebrate some more?"

"We get to celebrate a *lot* more."

* * *

"Can I call you?" Robbie asked as she slipped into the limo.

"What's the number of the phone on your belt?" Delilah said.

Robbie told her and she punched it into her phone. When his began to ring, he put it to his ear.

"Of course," she said, and this time she said it three times—once over the phone, once straight from the back of the car and again from the blue eyes that somehow turned Robbie inside out every time he stared into them.

* * *

"I'm back."

"Everything worked out perfectly on this end."

"What happens next?"

"I end up with a lot of his money."
"I mean what happens after that."
"Does it matter?"
"If you are seriously asking that question, you aren't as smart as you need to be."

* * *

"What?" Robbie said the next morning.
"You won't fucking believe it," Jackson said.
"Spit it out."
"Lobosan's walking."
"What the fuck are you talking about?"
"He pulled out fifteen minutes ago."
Robbie felt the heat rise in his face while he stood in front of Jackson's immaculate desk, but his internal thermostat clicked in comfortably short of the boiling point. He started running the tape in his head of the past few days, and the more he looked at the tape the fewer questions stared back at him.
"Why did he do this?" he said.
"There has to be money in it for him somewhere," Jackson said.
"Do you see any money going anywhere except to Cap United?"
"Not yet."
"Then somehow, some way, that fat motherfucker *is* Cap United."
"I don't see what you're saying."
"What actually happened here? Somebody got half a million dollars more than the original deal, and *my* money ended up in the pot instead of Lobosan's."
"You might be right."
"I'm fucking right for sure," Robbie said. "And that only leaves one more question."
"What's that?"
"How did he know my money was in?"

* * *

"May I pour?" Delilah asked.
"Please," Robbie said.
Standing, Delilah messed around with the bottle in the bucket of ice for a moment or two, and when the bubbly started bubbling out the top she poured some into each of the glasses on the table. She handed

him one and picked up the other. "What are we celebrating this time?" she said.

"A truly world-class performance," Robbie said, raising his glass in her direction before sipping from it. "I especially liked 'But right now, we're all in, understand?' Considering what happened next, he understood it very well."

Delilah sipped a little from her glass in response, but wriggled her nose and returned the glass to the table. "May I join you?" she said.

"Please do."

"I wasn't sure I would be seeing you again," she said as she settled in beside him.

"But you thought you might?"

"Yes."

"Please don't tell me you thought I wouldn't figure it out."

"Not at all. I thought I *might* see you anyway."

"Very astute of you, as usual."

"Thank you."

"It's not quite over yet, is it?"

"No."

"The subsidiary?"

"Not nearly as golden as it looks, apparently."

Robbie nodded appreciatively. "You guys played me like a fucking drum. How long ago did he target me?"

"When you first showed up here, I guess. This is his club."

"Better and better. He was working me before I started working him."

"Are you going to tell me why you're having this conversation with me rather than him?"

"I want to be sure I know the why for you."

"Why is the easiest part."

"Was it only money?"

"Only people with too much money ask that question. I *work* for a living, remember?"

"It's time you stopped. You're selling yourself short."

"What do you mean?"

"He got at least half a million dollars more because of the work you did. What did you get?"

"I can count, Robbie. I'm asking what you mean by bringing it up."

"You need to be a partner instead of a hired hand."

"In a world where an investor is a mark, what is a partner?"

"I love that you asked that question," Robbie said, but he laughed out loud before he said it. "In fact, I love a lot of things about you."

"Does that mean you will or will not answer the question?"

"I'm gonna roll that fat motherfucker if it's the last thing I ever do, Delilah. A partner gets half of whatever I get."

"That could be *extremely* lucrative."

"Yes."

"But hardly worth it, Robbie, if it's the last thing you ever do."

"Oh, it won't be," Robbie confessed. "I imagine another celebration would ensue immediately thereafter."

"If not sooner," Delilah said. She reached one hand behind her new partner's head and drew him close enough to speak without words, and she kept that wordless conversation going until not another thing needed to be said.

Eight Ballers
Gary Phillips

Steve Durkin guided the new SLK350 Mercedes roadster onto the Carmatage lot. He had to brake suddenly as a dented family van zoomed across his front end. He looked to his left and watched as the van joined two other vehicles, blocking a parked decade-old Nissan Sentra from forward or backward motion. He sighed inwardly as he turned off the ignition and got out of the luxury car.

"Oh, come on, Brad, don't do this to me. I need this damn car."

"Sorry, Mona, but I've let you slide too long. It's four months you're going on now."

The woman put up her hands in an exasperated gesture. "I made some payments. You made me come down here and pay in cash. Shit." There were two children with her and the younger one made a funny face at the older one, hearing their mom using a bad word. The older one shot her sister a stern glare.

"That was just on the interest, I told you that. Francine told you that too."

"This isn't right," Mona Novienez protested. "You've got to let me have my car. I can't get the girls to school and to work without it. I can't."

"Look, I don't like being the Scrooge here, Mona, but you forced my hand. You know what's expected. Everything is spelled out in the contract, and you've violated our agreement—repeatedly." Brad Casin led his hands apart to demonstrate he was at his wit's end.

The woman—dark-haired and pretty, a few extra pounds on shapely hips highlighted in worn jeans Durkin assessed admiringly—looked vehemently at Casin. She toted a large purse and she possibly contemplated laying that bag alongside his head. Durkin certainly wouldn't blame her. But two of the lot's mechanics, good-sized men in work clothes and heavy shoes, were also standing nearby. They'd driven the other vehicles to cage her car. Durkin knew the drill because he'd used it before. Sound like you understand and ask the customer in arrears to come on down and let's discuss a change in your payment plan. But really what you wanted to do was save yourself the repo fee and have the chump drive the car to you so it could be seized on site.

"How do you live with yourself, you goddamned bloodsuckin' vampire?" she spewed at Casin. Her two daughters exchanged sheepish grins at their mother's anger. The woman looked away, touching a fingertip to a corner of her wet eye.

Casin pointed toward Manchester Avenue and said, "Get the hell off my property, deadbeat."

"Come on, girls," she said to her children, putting her hand on the shoulder of her younger daughter, who wore a pink and white backpack proportional to her size. Durkin estimated she was seven, the older one no more than ten. Their mother wasn't yet thirty though. They left the steps leading to the office and walked slowly off the lot. Durkin entered after Casin stepped past the open sliding glass door and stationed his rangy frame into his old-fashioned wooden swivel chair. It was behind a metal and pressboard desk.

"The fuck, huh?" An Angels' baseball game played on a compact flat screen on a wall of the office. Two of the home team were on base. A leatherette couch faced this. There were a few softball trophies atop a file cabinet in one corner. "These ungrateful people."

"Yeah. I hear you." Durkin put the Mercedes' keys attached to an alarm fob before the man.

Casin added, pointing at his crotch as he rolled backwards from the desk some. "Now if she wasn't such a ball buster, and kept that big mouth of hers open for the ramrod special, we could have worked a deal." He guffawed at this. Durkin remained stone-faced.

Casin grinned as he rolled back to his desk and grasped the keys, squeezing them tight like a baby did a rattle. "Aw hell yes. My sweet ass sled."

"As long as you make the lease payments."

For a beat Casin took umbrage at this salesman who would dare infer he was akin to one of the bad credit customers of Carmatage. He then shook it off. "You're funny, Steve. Really you are."

A wide-bodied but solid woman in a black business skirt and stiffly starched white shirt, sleeves at half mast, entered the office through an inner door. She wore stylish black framed glasses and her hair was pinned into a surly pile. She held a sheaf of papers in a strong hand.

"When you get a moment, Bradley." She and Durkin exchanged curt nods. "Steve," she said.

"Okay, Francine," the owner said to her.

"Enjoy your car, Mr. Casin. Any problems, please don't hesitate to call me. We appreciate your business at Grantha Motors."

"I plan to enjoy the hell out of that car, Steve. Most assuredly." He shook his fist, the keys and fob in them.

Durkin left and, hands in his pockets, walked to where Julio Menzana, the detailer from their dealership, waited for him on the street in a late model Cadillac CTS.

"Say, homie," Durkin began, "you mind catching a cab back?" He was talking into the open driver's side where Menzana in his light blue shirt and dark blue pants sat behind the wheel. Durkin held out two folded over twenties. "Something for the bother as well."

Menzana, rummaging in his fifties, took the money, shaking his head briefly. "Damn, Steve, can't you let that heina grieve at least?"

Durkin's practiced smile was about as innocent as a cobra curling on a doorstep. "I'm just a caring kind of guy."

Menzana handed him the keys and walked off, chuckling. Durkin made a U-turn in the Cadillac to roll up to the bus stop about a block down from the Carmatage lot. This was where the woman and her kids had walked to after the dust-up.

"Let me give you a ride," he said as the power window went down.

The older daughter crossed her arms, screwing up her face. "My mom knows karate."

"Stranger danger," the younger one declared.

The woman said to them, "He was over there. Bringing a fancy car to the nasty man."

"Then he must be his friend," the older one huffed, concluding Durkin surely was as repulsive as that octopus faced guy in the *Pirates of the Caribbean* movies.

"I'm not his friend," Durkin said. "I wanted to show you not all car salesmen are like the nasty man."

Now it was the mother's turn to look dubious. A bus was pulling in behind the Cadillac and the driver bleated the horn.

"Our bus, Mommy." The younger one was on her feet, heading toward the public transport. Her small tennis shoes matched her backpack.

Durkin, leaning across the Cadillac's passenger bucket seat, extended his business card for the woman to see. "I bet you're tired of dealing with these clunkers. How about handling some beauties on the high end of the scale? Both my numbers are on the card, cell and to the office."

Novienez herded her children toward the bus. But as the younger one got on, she turned back and took the still offered card. She joined her children, Durkin watching them in the rearview as the bus went around him and roared away.

* * *

"How about you bite me, huh, Brad? How would that be?" Novienez stood in the cubicle in grey slacks and a Donna Karen blazer, off-white blouse and medium-heeled Jimmy Choos. Her hair hung loose and two gold bracelets clacked on one arm. She had a hand on her hip and was talking into the handset of the landline. On the back of the upraised hand was a tattoo of an eight ball.

"Yeah, how long you gonna hold that over me?" She listened, boiling. "You know what," she broke in, lowering her voice, "screw you, you parasite. I'm tired of begging."

She was about to slam the receiver home but stopped mid-way and then gently cradled the instrument. Hands pressed together prayer fashion, she put them on either side of her nose and took a few moments to get herself together. There were cars to sell and commissions to be made after all. For at Grantha Motors of Beverly Hills, it wasn't just the sparkle of that silver BMW in the window that beckoned the Industry insiders and the wannabes. What Grantha provided was image of being with it, cool and trendy.

Back in the day the men, and it was mostly men then, dressed in suits and ties—designer suits and ties but uniformed nonetheless. But a visionary sales manager at Grantha named Kel Ritchie got the smart idea the sales force should be character types as that's what their clientele would respond to best. Not something so over-the-top as some dude decked out Goth black with black nails and a top hat, such would be too Halloweenish. But you had the ones who dressed country club casual chic and they had a breezy approach. You had one woman who dressed severe and her ice queen thing rocking the libidos of the older, established studio exec. There was even a salesman who dressed in labeled jeans and pressed shirt, not tucked in and damned if he didn't click with whoever was the hot young director of the moment. And a gym-toned, raven-haired Latina with the barest of her Boyle Heights accent perceptible was just exotic enough—but not too much as too ethnic was off-putting don't you know? Ritchie had moved on and was now a talent manager.

Durkin had suggested the silly eight-ball tattoo. Novienez had initially rolled her eyes at the idea. If one of her homegirls saw that, they'd pee themselves laughing so hard. But he convinced her it was a way to give her just enough bad girl image with people who only knew about gang culture from the doc they saw that time on MSNBC—after all, they were limousine liberals who more watched that cable outlet than the odious Fox News. She agreed. It worked.

Composed, Novienez went back onto the lot to scout prospects. Steve Durkin was waving good-bye to a hipster-looking couple and their terrier as they walked away.

"Goddamn vegans asking if we sold Priuses," he cracked at Novienez. He held his hands wide. "This look like Culver City around here?"

With a sideways look she remarked, "They can't all be high rollers, Steve-O."

"I saw you in there on the phone. Now while I pride myself on reading body language, it was pretty obvious you were having another go-round with your boy, Brad."

"Bastard won't lift a finger to help me remove the bad credit report he put on me."

"Despite your sterling performance here."

For the last five months, Novienez, after initially calling and meeting with Durkin, had been working on commission selling high-end autos at Grantha. At first she'd stay up half the night absorbing the stats and differences in horsepower and wheelbase say of a Jaguar XKR-S convertible versus a Porsche 928. This came in handy, but after stammering her way through several no closings, worried she was headed back to her part-time job at the Walmart on Crenshaw, which she probably couldn't get back anyway, she listened as only the desperate can to a piece of advice from Durkin.

"Watch a couple of Bette Davis' films. One when she was young, like *Now Voyager* and when she was an old gal. *Dead Ringer* is not known too much, but that's one of hers I'd suggest."

"I don't need to be entertained, Steve," she said, "I need to make a sale."

"It's all about the attitude, Mona. Check out how she carries herself. How even when she's jammed up, she struggles through."

She watched those Bette Davis films along with a couple starring Katherine Hepburn and mixed in some of the episodes of *Desperate Housewives.* She got into being a student learning what made the characters these actors portrayed distinct one from another, when were they assertive and when did they play into men's stereotypes for their own benefit. She even watched a few classic male dominated gangster films like *New Jack City* and *The Roaring Twenties* to get a feel for the swagger these actors put across.

It wasn't automatic nor instantly something she could pull off without seeming artificial. But once she got it in her head she was playing the part of a luxury car saleswoman, who in real life had two children she'd do what it took to provide for, she perfected her role.

"It's not just me," Novienez was saying later as the two had their afternoon cup of coffee standing in the showroom, each scanning the exterior. "These damn buy-here and pay-here used car places are vultures preying on poor and low-income communities. Brad has four Carmatage lots in the 'hood and varrio, and is president of the goddamn association."

Durkin smiled lopsidedly. "Don't be getting all redistribute-the-wealth on me, comrade. You're now making a comfortable living selling and leasing these over-hyped bourgeois rides to your one-percenter customers."

She sipped. "I'm aware of the contradiction. But life is nothing if it's not that, right? It's the in-between where the fun is found, isn't that what you say?"

Durkin's mouth creased. "Look, Mona. The only thing you have to worry about now is how you're going to spend the money you make on you and those two cute kids of yours in the house you'll plunk a cash down payment for."

"What a corn dog you are," she said, grinning.

"Am I right or am I right?"

"Yeah," she admitted, "money is way better than no money."

"Fuckin' A. Up top." They patted palms, high-fiving.

Hands coming down the two simultaneously spied a Range Rover pulling onto the lot. But just then the service manager called to Novienez from a doorway requiring her attention.

"Mrs. Horsley is on the phone and won't believe me about the repair unless she hears it from her number one gal." The service manager mimicked the older woman's voice snidely.

"Shit," Novienez swore softly, having gotten to the glass door of the showroom first. The sixty-plus widow replaced her Rolls Cornice every other year. It just so happened when she came in recently she took to Novienez who, Durkin told her later, smirking, reminded her of a housekeeper she used to employ.

Novienez bug-eyed Durkin as she stalked off to placate her well-off customer.

"Time to cash up," he said under his breath, walking back into the sun to work his spell.

That evening, after getting homework squared away, with the requisite procrastinating by the youngest, Mira, Novienez sat at the kitchenette table with a beer in their apartment in Inglewood near Darby Park. She was making enough now to move but her less than stellar credit report, which Casin wasn't helping improve any, forestalled that being accomplished.

"Mom?" the oldest, Suzy said.

"Yes, *mija?*"

"Are you rich now?"

"No, honey, but we're doing okay. Why do you ask?"

"Taylor said we'd be getting new friends soon." Taylor was a friend of hers at school. "She said she heard her mom and dad talking about your new job, and said you would forget where you came from. Are you going to forget?"

She pulled her daughter close. "No, baby, I'm not going to forget. I'll always knew where we came from, okay?"

"Okay."

* * *

Most Thursdays Francine Albrecht played Pai Gow poker at the Jockey Casino in Gardena. This Thursday was no exception and that's where Steve Durkin found her as she and five other players plus the dealer sat at a table in a section reserved for this particular card game. Essentially each player had to derive the best two card hand, two and five card combinations, to beat the banker, who was another player. In California, different than Vegas, individuals strictly played against each other, not the house, but the house got its cut for hosting.

Sipping a meager marked up scotch, he knew better than to interrupt her as he orbited nearby. He got his chance to take a seat when a retiree in a ratty baseball cap cashed out. Grumbling about his loses, he walked away tugging his oxygen tank on its rollers, the mask tethered around his neck bumping on his thin chest.

"Steven," Albrecht said, nodding. Carmatage's Chief Financial Officer was dressed in a charcoal grey skirt with a slit at the side, and a blue starched man's shirt.

"Ma'am," he answered, new cards fanned out from the dealer.

An hour later he was $600 down to Albrecht's $400 up. Another forty-five minutes he was done getting whipped and went off to the bar where a local female tatted comedian was riffing about ethnic hairstyles on the small stage. Albrecht joined him not too long afterward.

"What brings you around here, slick?"

"Can't a man unwind over cards and seeing an old friend?"

"Unwind is not in your vocabulary." She accepted the drink he offered her.

"How loyal are you to Brad?"

She held two fingers apart. "Oh yeah, we're as close as a Taliban soldier and a rabbi."

"Heh," Durkin uttered.

Albrecht downed some of her beverage. "Anyway, I expected better foreplay from you, Steve."

They were sitting on stools and Durkin swung toward her, bumping his knee against hers. "I can sell it to you anyway you like, Francine. Hard, soft or in between."

She chuckled and it was harsh and throaty. "We're going backward here, aren't we? Seems when I was chasing you a few years ago with that idea, it didn't take. A lonely middle-aged broad hoping the smell of money would be my aphrodisiac to hook you." A hint of bitterness came and went in her voice.

"I didn't lead you on, Francine."

"No you did not."

"So what about my question?"

"You're pulling down, what? A hundred and twenty, hundred and thirty a year hustling to the luxury lames? Why take this risk now? Surely you haven't been getting all hot and bothered about me in the wee-wee hours, now have you?" She put a hand on his thigh and slid it back and forth languidly.

"What if I have?"

"Tell me anything, you forked-tongue devil you." She removed her hand.

"Given my astute ability at judging character, seems to me you just told me you're still willing to take a chance."

She made a clucking sound. "Don't kid yourself, our ship has sailed." She didn't look off as she continued. "Could be I'm as hungry as you are, only no west-of-Robertson car mover is going to hire my plus eight size. Not like that packed in the right places *chica* you brought in."

He held up his glass. "Here's to hunger."

"And keeping the pantry stocked," she said, clinking hers against his.

* * *

Fay Horsley laughed as she moved swiftly across the length of her media room in her Los Feliz mansion. As mansions went, the two-story structure wasn't as expansive or ornate as say one of the Frank Ghery-inspired wonders of opposing angles and cantilevered bisecting roof lines found on the Malibu bluffs or socked away behind gates in the Palisades. Her home was designed along the lines of a Bavarian chalet and had originally been built by a women's undergarments magnate in the 1920s.

"Goodness, you mustn't catch me, you villainess you," she said. She was wearing lacy lingerie under a silk kimono and matching slippers. Her dyed reddish-brown hair was piled high but tendrils of it splayed about her handsome face as she pretended to be running from danger. She skirted into a wood paneled hallway.

Coming after her was Mona Novienez in a clingy white dress of diaphanous material and revealing neckline, wide belt, stilettos, and wearing a sequined domino mask. She had a peacock feather in one hand and said, "You can't escape me, secret agent Double-Oh-Trouble. I've seen through your disguise as a humble homemaker. You are doomed." After a month of this, Novienez was used to saying such lines without cracking up or twisting an ankle given the steep heels. Out in the hallway she stopped as the widow had stopped giggling and could be behind any of several doorways.

"You know it's useless to hide from me, don't you?" She went forward and after entering and prowling about the upstairs study for a few moments, emerged again and saw the door was ajar leading to the sun room. Sure enough the older woman was laying on her old-fashioned Greek-style divan, one foot on the floor. She had an arm over her eyes as if she were the heroine in a two-reeler from the era when her house was constructed.

She said, "My, my, that devilish powder you slipped into my wine at dinner has done something to me." One tanned and toned leg was propped on the divan, the kimono open. Horsley did yoga three times a week and laps in her pool.

Novienez stood there, hands on hips, head cocked to one side, a suitable haughty look on her masked face. "I have corralled you, my conniving spy. You will not have the chance to reveal my secret plans for world conquest to your masters in Washington." She stalked forward. "Indeed, I will use my exquisite torture techniques, learned from the Fifth Potentate of the Order of the Lotus Dragon, from whom there is no recourse but to yield unerringly to the will of she who must not be denied."

The other woman turned her head to look up at the younger one who now stood close to where she reposed. "What fiendish horrors will you enact on me?"

"That is for me to know and you to experience."

"I...I see," she theatrically stuttered. She placed her hand on the side of Novienez's leg, rubbing it a little. "You must know I'll never give in."

Their sexually charged playacting hadn't, so far, resulted in making physical love per se. There was touching and caressing but no down and dirty. "We will see my little spy," Novienez replied as the widow moved her hand up and down the inner thigh of her supposed captor. Novienez put the feather between the reclining woman's open legs on the satiny material of her undergarment.

Fay Horsley moaned softly, her leg moving to-and-fro slightly as she was pleasured with the feather. Her hand had moved back to the outer part of Novienez's leg and she alternately gripped and released the muscle.

"That's wonderful, darling," she said excitedly, "simply delicious." She took her hand from Novienez's leg and put it around the other woman's wrist as she continued with the feather. Six weeks ago when Horsley called, for once it hadn't been to complain. She wanted to get an extended warranty on her Rolls and requested her favorite saleswoman to deliver the paperwork. Of course this could have been accomplished over the phone and really, what was the need of that kind of coverage on a car she was going to replace in two year's time? But she wanted what she wanted and when Novienez got to her place, the housekeeper, a small but wiry Filipina, took her out back to the pool. She had an odd look on her face and Novienez soon learned why.

"I have found," the widow began after her guest had taken a seat and was offered iced tea, "that as the years pile up, and three marriages to men of varying quality, you shouldn't limit your vistas." She was laying down then as well, on a padded Adirondack lounger. She'd been doing laps and was in a one piece bathing suit, large towel around her, a floppy hat on and wearing sunglasses. "For instance I know you come from humble origins but now have a chance to make something for yourself and for your children."

"I hope to," Novienez said, edgy as to what was coming next.

"My folks had humble origins too. Grandpa was in the schmatta trade in New York in the Depression. His wife, Grandma Edna, was a firebrand, an organizer in a Communist front group. Workers of the world and all that." She stopped, the dark glasses enhancing the bemused expression on her face. "You know what I mean by a front organization?"

"No," Novienez admitted.

"The public face is different than who's calling the shots."

"Like the Tea Party?"

"Ah, you do keep up on what counts. But yes, something like that."

"Good to know." She uncrossed her legs, preparing to go.

"Would you care to enjoy the pool? I'm sure I have something that can fit you. Did you know I was a buyer for the Broadway Department store chain at one point?"

She knew this from Durkin. "I'd like that Mrs. Horsley, but some of us have to punch a clock."

"Did you also know I'm a partial owner in Grantha Motors?"

"I did not."

She lifted a hand holding a cell phone which Novienez hadn't noticed before. She speed dialed a number then spoke into it when the line connected. "Edmund, Fay. How are you? The lovely Ms. Novienez is over here and helping me with some car matters for my nephews. She may not be back for a few hours. But know she is hard at work, not playing hooky. Okay?...Good ." She severed the call with the sales manager. "Done and done I think you young people say. Now if you wouldn't mind indulging an old lady, I'd like to watch you swim. Mind you, I never had a body like yours but I hope you don't find me too voyeuristic."

"Maybe not too much," she smiled.

"There you go. You see it's all about expanding one's vistas."

And so they had expanded their vistas with each successive encounter at Horsley's mansion. Novienez didn't feel pressured to succumb to the older woman's wishes as she wasn't sucking up to her for her money. It didn't seem to her she was suddenly batting for the other team so much as enjoying a certain shared fantasy with Horsley. Back in the day when she was a gangbanger, forced to sex down vatos in the set, she'd learned to disassociate herself from her body when necessary. For her part, the widow admitted she was exploring desires she'd repressed for decades but was unsure of how far she wanted to take matters.

Novienez bent closer to the enthralled Horsley on her divan. She'd abandoned the feather for the sureness of her finger on the right spot down there. She spoke close to the other woman's lips.

"I have a favor I need to ask, Fay. It involves some risk."

"Ask away, Mona, you know I'll do whatever you want," the other woman whispered.

They kissed and tongued and Horsley shuddered as she had an orgasm.

* * *

Brad Casin was wearing an Hawaiian shirt and had the bottom of a foot propped against the edge of his desk as he talked on the phone. "Look, you're asking me for the impossible. I've given you plenty of leeway here, more than most in fact. Yet you're continually tardy on your payments. Yes, I know, but it's every two weeks for everybody else too. I tell you what, if you didn't waste your money bailing that do-nothing husband of yours out of jail, you'd be able to manage your money better and meet your responsibilities."

He was barely listening to his aunt's response. Casin gazed out at his lot through his sliding glass door. He idly calculated the money he'd made on the 2001 Volvo parked there which had logged more than 130, 000 miles on its odometer. He'd bought the car at auction for seven grand and put another thousand in it to make it road ready. He'd sold and reposed the vehicle three times since then. What with him carrying his own paper and interest at twenty-two percent, that beat machine had earned more than double. This fact made him smile even as his mother's younger sister reeled off her series of woes on the other end of the line.

His aunt whined on and his smile faded. Not because he had a sudden stab of empathy, but a Buick LeSabre suddenly tolled onto his lot, its top on fire. Now he had a look of shock.

"Gotta go," he stammered, bolting out of his seat, tossing the handset aside as he did so. He ran outside.

"Hey," he yelled, "get a fire extinguisher somebody." A salesman was talking to a couple and they stared as Casin gesticulated at the LeSabre which had crashed into a Nissan pick-up, a marked down special. Two mechanics hurried onto the lot, one of them carrying a fire extinguisher. Casin grabbed the thing and laying down cascades of foam, put the fire out. He threw the canister to the macadam in disgust.

"What the fuck?" he screamed, pointing at the ruined LeSabre, pacing to and fro. "Who the hell did this?"

The mechanics gave him a collective blank look.

Casin addressed his salesman. "Didn't you see anything?

The salesman hunched. "I kind'a noticed this flatbed tow truck out on the street hauling the Buick. But I was chatting with these nice people who want to buy a Jeep, Brad." He said it like maybe Casin had suddenly forgotten a salesman isn't supposed to let anything interfere with him and a closing. If your mother called with a heart attack, dial 911 for her, and get back to getting that contract John Hancocked.

Casin blinked hard as he turned to gaze at the area beyond the Carmatage lot. He was about to walk over to the liquor store across the way, where a couple of usuals were out front, when he heard then saw two police cars and a fire truck arrive. Three firefighters jogged to the LeSabre with their equipment making sure it wasn't smoldering. The uniforms got out, the sergeant taking command.

"Dissatisfied customer?" he quipped, indicating the toasted car. The sergeant was a good-sized man who looked like he'd played football in school. The uniforms, two men and a woman, got busy interviewing the others.

"Yeah, I guess so," Casin said. "Crazy, huh?"

The officer remained implacable as he began questioning Casin. He'd about finished getting his statement when the female cop came over.

"Can I see you a second?" she said to the sergeant.

"Excuse me a moment, Mr. Casin." He walked away to confer with his officer.

Casin studied the LeSabre. Using a shop rag he wiped soot from the blackened windshield. He could see the VIN, the vehicle Identification Number, tag had been removed from the crevice of the dashboard. No doubt the license plates were stolen from another vehicle but there were several ways to ID a car, including a serial number stamped on the engine block. Whoever did this, he was going to put his foot deep in their ass.

"Sir?" the sergeant said to him.

"Yes?"

"Follow me, would you?"

Casin walked beside him to where his lot curved. There amid the used vehicles was parked a pristine classic Jaguar XKE. Violently purple it was.

"We ran the plate," the sergeant began.

Casin didn't need him to continue as he and anybody else who watched TV knew the car belonged to a certain famous singer-songwriter. This individual had recently been interviewed on the airwaves because his precious signature vehicle had been stolen from his compound in Holmby Hills a week ago.

"This is bullshit," Casin blurted. "I'm being set-up. I'm not saying anything else. I'm calling my lawyers."

"That's probably wise, sir," the sergeant said. "Because we're going to have a lot of questions for you to answer."

* * *

Ultimately Brad Casin was forced to sell his ownership of the Carmatage chain. Recovered on his desk computer were deleted e-mails indicating he was responsible for the theft of the purple Jaguar. Of course his lawyers argued even if that were so, and hacking into his computer wasn't hard to do they'd demonstrated, why would he be so obvious and have the well-known car on display. But then the several hundred thousands he'd secreted away from skimming off the cash payments he strong-armed from his customers was uncovered, and thus a investigation by the I.R.S. was launched against him as well. Too, his predatory practices of charging exorbitant interest fees helped fuel a series of investigative articles about the venal practices of the buy-here, pay-here lots and their trade association. Several monetary settlements were reached with Carmatage customers. There was also legislation pending in the state capital designed to reign in this type of used car lot practices.

The proposed bill was of little concern to the three who gathered poolside one sunny afternoon at the chalet. They know the scrutiny would die down and yes, maybe there'd be less profit to be made off of poor people—but there was still plenty in their veins to tap.

"Here's how," Steve Durkin said as he clicked his martini with the glasses held by Francine Albrecht and Fay Horsley.

"Bravo," Mona Novienez said, clapping slowly as she walked onto the decking.

"Darling," Horsley said, a nervous twitch to the side of her mouth.

"*Quidado*," Novienez said. "Did you honestly think I'd let you three just play me? Be your goat to get rid of Casin and let you enjoy the rewards? Figuring you could eight ball the eight-ball chick from East L.A.? I'd be too stupid and wrapped up at getting back at him I wouldn't do my homework?"

"Mona, relax, you won," Durkin said. "We all won."

"Save the fantasy for you and your wife, Steve." She glared at Fay Horsley.

"Well now," the older woman said. She'd remained sitting on her husband's lap, where he in turn reclined on the lounger.

Novienez pointed. "I don't give a shit Francine here gets to run Carmatage that I'm sure you three have bought through fronts, 'cause the greedy know how to be greedy."

"You can have a cut," Albrecht remarked.

"Here's the deal," Novienez continued. "The madam here is going to seed fund a foundation I'll run."

"Uh-huh," Durkin said knowingly, giving Horsley a playful squeeze on her side.

"Fuck you, Steve. This foundation is going to have real people, the screwed, the 99ers, whatever you want to call 'em, that's who will be on this board. "

"What will this foundation of yours do, Mona?" Horsley asked, her tone neutral.

"Affordable housing, job training, economic literacy, whatever the fuck the board decides it should do. And you're kicking in some profits too, Francine."

"If I don't?" she challenged.

"I go to the police and tell them what we did, what we all did to net Brad. Paying off the chop-shop guys, hack into his laptop, and so on and so forth. Don't worry, I got plenty of evidence and plenty of duplicate copies with various friends should I fall down some stairs or choke on a chicken bone, bitches."

"You'll implicate yourself, lover," Horsley pointed out. "Child services would take those wonderful children of yours from you once you were convicted."

Novienez walked over and gripped Horsley's face between her hands "That's right Fay, they damn sure would take my girls. But not before I get a few of my homegirls to come after you three." She released the woman's suddenly cold face.

"I'm tired of you Westside pendejos thinking the world owes you a living off the backs of people like me. You're gonna give back and like it," she growled. "You want to call my bluff, do it."

The three stayed silent.

When Novienez and Horsley were doing the slap and tackle the day they got intimate, while looking for the older woman, she saw her cell phone bill on the desk in her study.. She noted that there were two numbers on her account, one of those she knew belonged to Durkin. Thereafter she bought Kel Ritchie, the former Grantha sales manager, a couple of rounds at a bar and learned Durkin and Horsley had an open marriage—but when all was said and done, they were tight he'd emphasized.

"Enjoy the rest of your day. We get to work tomorrow." Novienez raised a fist, shook it, then left.

The $3,300 Loser
Seth Harwood

On Monday morning Larry Sax stalked into ALD's office just after the early meeting. ALD was highlighting the major strike prices on his sheets, using blue highlighter for the tens strikes and yellow for the fives, as he'd done every morning for years. He always prepared his sheets exactly the same way so he'd be able to situate himself in an instant and give a quick quote when brokers came into the ring asking for markets on the Crude options. ALD barely acknowledged Larry, just glancing up.

"Allen," Larry said. "Allen, I wanted to talk to you about something."

ALD did not look up from his sheets. He went on highlighting the tens strikes with his blue marker. "So talk," he said.

"I took a job at Whitter Peabody this weekend," Larry said. "I start in two weeks." He realized he'd been sitting on the very edge of his chair and now he moved back, but not all the way.

ALD looked up. He narrowed his eyes at Larry. "Whitter?" he said.

"On a trading desk," Larry said.

ALD made a noise that was not quite a snort, but it was close. "Let me see your analyzer," he said.

Larry passed the paper across the desk. He knew his position was respectable, that he was long the back months and short the fronts, that he was bringing in $300 a night from decay and was only open to a little risk from market movement.

ALD folded the analyzer and added it to his sheets. "Today's your last day," he said. "We'll have Chicago work off your position starting tomorrow. Just don't put on anything new." He went back to his highlighting. As Larry opened the door, ALD said, "And congratulations."

Larry stopped in the outer office only to put on his trading jacket and badge. He nodded at JCBS, MEH and ROC, all of them sitting on the couch, bullshitting about their positions. They would find out soon enough that he quit and he didn't need to be there when that happened. He stopped in the clerks' office and printed out a new analyzer. Usually his clerk would do this kind of thing for him, but Ben was late again. Larry took the back steps down to the floor and snuck a smoke in the stairway.

Nobody else was there when Larry got to the pit. A few ring clerks were talking about the Yankees in the futures and a few of the brokers were on their phones—those who had booths on the floor—scribbling down orders. Larry sat and rested his head on his hands. He put his sheets down on the riser beside him and stretched his feet into the ring. The carpet was thick enough that sitting on the ring was not uncomfortable. He'd done it enough over the first two months of the summer to know what positions were most comfortable, and with no one around there was enough extra room that he could accommodate himself nicely.

The closest Reuters board ticked off the morning's news above him: Japanese trading had been light in the overnight session and the Fed was expected to put out numbers at 11, among them June housing starts, but Larry knew that these would have little effect on the market and the day would be another slow one. The gold and silver big boards on either side of the Reuters' hung empty, ready to print the day's market trades after the open. Above Larry's head display screens were supported by black columns and tickers waited to show the day's data. Some of these were clocks, correct to the second, letting him know that he still had fifteen minutes.

Larry saw DOC climb up onto the top of the futures ring about twenty feet away. He nodded in Larry's direction and waved. DOC worked for Larry in a sense, carrying out Larry's futures trades, but because Larry was in options and DOC was in futures, DOC held the position of respect. It all came down to the money and there was always more money in futures than options, but trading futures came with more risk. Larry was a local, he made trades not because he thought they were a good idea, but because some jerkoff somewhere else wanted to trade the other side and needed someone to make the trade with. Larry used his sheets and the futures to determine a trade's value and then made his markets above and below that price to take in value.

Larry fingered the silver dollar his mother had given him. She'd thought he'd need a luck charm going into this world, and when he ended up trading silver the dollar was a natural choice. He kept it in his pocket, rubbed it only when he most needed the luck. The three ounces it weighed changed in value constantly, as Larry was always aware of, but as of Friday's close, $5.33 an ounce for August silver, the dollar was worth $15.99. In Joplin, Missouri, where Larry grew up and his mother still lived, you could buy a good steak dinner for that price.

As the open got closer there were enough people around that Larry had to stand to see the futures. The brokers started waving their pads and calling out bids and offers for the pre-open. Guys on the other side of the futures pit waved back. With less than a minute to go before silver started trading, Ben jumped to his spot. Technically he was 19 minutes late, by Weintraub standards. Larry walked out of his pit and approached his clerk.

"Your market's about to open," Ben said.

"You're late."

"I'm sorry. The train was—"

"Don't," Larry started. "Listen up. You're late and you've been late six times over the last two weeks." He held his finger in front of Ben's face to keep him quiet. "And now it doesn't matter but I need you to know it's bullshit. What if you go to cotton and you're late working for Margaret? You think she'd let your ass come in here late for the open?"

"Why would I be going to cotton?"

Larry caught Ben's shirt in his fist. "Can I trade options without my clerk?"

"Why would—"

"Answer my question!"

"You can't," Ben said. "You can't because you need me to put in trades in the futures that hedge your risk."

"Right," Larry said. "Better." He released Ben's shirt and gave him a light slap on the cheek. "Now can you shut the fuck up and get in here on time from now on?"

"Yes. Why could I be going to cotton?"

"Today's my last day," Larry said. "See? For all I care you can come in as late as you want for the rest of your fucking life. You'll last a long time with Margaret and Candace."

"Where are you going?"

Larry didn't wait to hear what else Ben would say as he walked back to his spot between RGB and EGON in the options. Ben would go through a tough period if he ended up with MAR and CND, but it wasn't clear that's where he would go, it was just one possible destination, and definitely the worst. These two women approached every day as a chance to get back at the world and their clerk as the main avenue to doing it.

Ben stood with his hands by his sides, staring at Larry. How's the market? Larry signed.

Ben showed two fingers pointed up with the back of his hand and bent them over, then showed his palm and held up three straight fingers—silver was 2½ bid at 3; the ring would buy August silver for $5.32½ and sell it at $5.33.

How are the spreads?

Ben asked DOC for the quotes and DOC pushed him back, then called for the spreads. He leaned back and showed his pad to Ben. Ben signaled in the Augie/Sep and the Sep/Dec. Just to make extra work, Larry called for the Augie/Dec and the Sep/July. When Ben asked for these, DOC looked around, then pushed Ben completely off the risers. He took his time asking for these quotes and though he knew exactly what was happening, Larry asked Ben a second time for the Augie/Dec and the Sep/July. Ben asked again and got yelled at by DOC, who called for the quotes and then yelled them at Ben. Ben signaled in the Augie/Dec and the Sep/July from beside the ring.

Gold was up on the day and silver reacted with a pop up to $5.35, but soon it came back off to $5.33. Options paper brokers came into the pit and asked for markets for their phone customers. It was Larry's job to make these markets using the futures price and the options values he could discern from his price sheets, but he stood quietly, obeying ALD's orders not to do any new trades. It didn't leave any reason for being on the floor at all. Larry looked at his sheets and his watch and decided it was time for a break.

He waved the break sign at Ben and left the ring heading toward the traders' bathroom, the only place on the main level you could get away with smoking. He heard the buzzer and saw the idiots in sugar just starting their day. They were all little guys, mostly from Jersey. Shitheads really. Their four-hour day was as ridiculous as the fact that they still thought they had something to complain about. None of them had the balls to walk off the floor whenever they wanted. Larry was sure of that.

When he was done, Larry rubbed his cigarette out against the door of the stall and pulled up his pants. He would go to Jackie's 5th Amendment after the close, he had decided, because that'd be the best place to start his vacation. He decided he could take Ben out to lunch. It was the least they could do to celebrate, with Ben going to cotton and all. Really Ben wasn't such a bad guy, just not all that together in the mornings.

He went back to the ring and held his sheets up like a good little soldier. Larry listened to the brokers and thought about what his markets would be, heard the others bid and offer and buy and sell. Ben quoted the futures 5.32 bid, offered at 33.

SEAL came into the pit bidding 2.50 for ten 35 calls and no one wanted to sell them. A couple of locals said they'd be at 3, but SEAL held to his bid. "LMS," he called. "LMS! How are you on the 35 calls?"

Larry waved his hand across his neck. "I'm out," he said.

"LMS!" SEAL pointed at him. "35 calls!"

Larry looked at his sheets and then at SEAL. The 35's were a strike he'd needed for his position on Friday, and now it didn't matter. Although Allen had said not to put on anything new, he had not told Larry he shouldn't take off the ugly parts of his position. "Two bid at three," Larry said.

"Two and a half bid," SEAL said. He stared at Larry as if he could see through him, as if he knew about the Whitter Peabody job, and asked for a market on the 30-35 call spread, which Larry had bid up Friday. It fit his position really well and took away some of his volatility risk.

Larry looked at the analyzer again, saw how well the spread still fit, and said, "Three bid at five."

"Two and a half bid on ten calls."

Larry bit his lip. It was too good of a trade. "Sold!" he said. He checked the delta on his sheets and had Ben buy four futures.

Larry double-checked his calculations, refigured the delta, saw that four futures was right, and Ben came back. Filled. Paid 33 for four.

"Wait, wait, wait, wait, wait a minute!" RGB waved his hand at SEAL. "Hold on a second," he said. RGB was size. He traded big paper for sterling, but also traded his own account. Either way he was size up. "What just traded?" he said.

Larry said, "Augie upside calls trade 2½." He showed his pad to RGB.

"I've been offering halfs in the 35's all morning," RGB said. He held up his arms like there was something SEAL and Larry could still do, like they were supposed to know his markets.

When RGB wasn't around, the other locals argued about whether they'd take one thousand dollars or his head filled with nickels if given the choice of the two. He had a big head, but Larry always maintained that the nickels wasn't realistic. He did, however, hold to the belief that dimes was another matter.

SEAL raised his hand. "Since when? Everyone else was at 3."

August futures widened out to 33 bid, offered at 34.

RGB said, "I'm at a half."

SEAL looked at his card. His face got that twisted expression you'd see on a broker who'd gone against size: his choices were to break the rules or to owe the guy something later. Either way it sucked, but RGB was size and you had to keep size happy. "Larry," SEAL said, and now he had a really pathetic expression on his face, like Larry was his long-lost friend. "LMS, five lots?" Now it was a question. He showed Larry his palms.

"OK," Larry said. "You're out." He waved his hand across his neck. "I sold you five lots," he said. But now he was long two futures. August was 3 bid at 4 though, so the worst he could do was break even on the extra two lots by selling 3's back right now. But why not work it? He had nothing to lose. He had nothing to gain either, but maybe if he had a big winner in the futures he'd make enough for his last paycheck to be worth something extra. Not likely. But it was worth a try. He had Ben work two at a half. If his offer got lifted he'd make a hundred bucks, if not, he'd go after the threes. No big deal, just a little risk. Maybe a trade to pay for a nice lunch.

"What the hell," Larry said out loud, to no one in particular.

"Go there," RGB told him.

Check up.

Working two at 3½, Ben signed.

Larry watched the board for prints. A 33 traded and then a half and then another 33. Ben quoted 3 bid at a half. He should probably sell the two lots back at three, just to break even while he could, but he liked the feel of the futures market, the risk. It felt good to be in on something that could go either way. Watching the futures like this made things interesting. It made standing there seem worthwhile. Maybe he could get 34's out of it.

Across the futures pit MAZA hung up his phone and stormed into the ring like it was a bachelor party with free hookers. He started offering halfs. MAZA was from the old school and had never learned to call from his lungs; probably thought a diaphragm was something his wife kept by the bed. He was all throat—scratchy, but loud. He'd have no voice left by fifty.

MAZA represented the worst of the Trading Floor Element. He was from Staten Island, with probable mafia connections that he tried to wear on his sleeve, was one of the few guys who drove to work every morning, and he had the balls to do it in a black, tinted-window Mercedes, over the Verrazano Bridge, wearing work boots like he was a construction man.

Ben was turned around watching MAZA, like everyone else, and he missed Larry's signal to go to the market on the two-lot. The ring quieted down when MAZA started offering. He did paper for J. Aaron: Size. As MAZA got louder, the bids got softer.

MAZA started hitting the 3's, selling off twenty-lot pieces.

Check up.

What? Ben looked confused. Nothing done.

Nothing? Market on the two-lot.

"Damn," Larry said. He clenched his teeth and swore at RGB under his breath.

How is it? MAZA was at 33 now, and there were a few 32 bids around the ring.

2 bid at 3, Ben signed.

Wait on the two-lot, Larry signed.

Ben caught DOC's arm and stopped him from trading the order. If Larry sold 32's he'd have a clean hundred-dollar loser for the account, but that wasn't going to happen. This one drop was not going to come at the time he had to sell back his two-lot of the day. Plus the excitement felt good, like the best of his high school diving meets, when the most of it was on the line. And when would he be able to play the game like this again?

Size on the 2-bid?

Ben turned around and scanned the ring. He came back, Thin.

Now MAZA was at a half and 2's were trading. "Damn," Larry said. Buy me three. Hell with it. If MAZA was selling down, Larry would buy more. He wasn't going to cover right away so he might as well pick up a few lots cheap and then sell off the whole five-lot later, when the market came back up. He fingered the silver dollar, watching Ben hand DOC a ticket and DOC signal across the ring at MAZA.

Check up.

Paid 2½ for 3.

The 2½'s were a definitely shitty fill. They were shit because MAZA started selling 2's right after that and then he was at 2, but DOC was sucking up and Larry wasn't going to say anything about it now. He was long two at 3 and three at 2½ and the market was 1½ bid at 2, which was against him, but it would have to come back soon. He rubbed the silver dollar and let the air out of his cheeks as hard as he could. "Let's go," he said. This thing was starting to feel good.

Larry still felt safe. In three weeks silver hadn't fallen below 30 or broken a five cent range. And MAZA was the only seller in the ring. Larry was not going to lose it all to a gorilla like MAZA on his last day in silver, or let this get to him either. He walked out of the options and crossed to the futures to size up the trading. He pulled on the back of DOC's coat. "Where we going, big guy?"

DOC turned around. He said, "Larry, how's things with the eggheads in options? Good? Good." He clapped Larry on the shoulder, and turned back around.

Larry climbed up to Ben's spot behind DOC and looked into the futures. "Where we going, DOC?"

DOC shook his head and shrugged Larry away from his shoulder. "How the fuck should I know?" he said. "Look around this place, you think any of us knows?"

Larry leaned closer to DOC and whispered, "I'm long, DOC."

DOC elbowed Larry this time to get him away from his space. "You're long? We're all long. Long or short. Pick a position. MAZA is the only seller all day, and who of us knows what's behind him. He's been selling twenty-lot pieces down from three," DOC said. He started bidding 1's, offering 2's.

Larry watched MAZA offering 2's. There was an artery in MAZA's neck that Larry could see from across the ring. He kept barking out, "At two."

The clocks above them all read 9:28.

Larry tore off his card and handed it to Ben, pointed in Ben's face. "Listen to me," he said. "I'm taking a break but I'm long futures so I want you to stay here and watch them. If August trades below 30 come in the back and get me. You know where I'll be."

Larry made sure Ben had the card and then he slapped him lightly on the cheek. He went back into the bathroom, really took a shit this time, and smoked another cigarette while he did.

When Larry walked back out on the floor, the 30-print was the first thing he saw. He broke into a run to get back to silver so he could do something. If he sold 30's right now he'd be out $300 on two lots and $250 on three. $1,350. And no options to hide it against. That'd be hard to camouflage. Larry ran the rest of the way back to silver.

"What the hell's that?" He pointed to the board behind Ben. How is it?

"30 bid at 1."

"Why didn't you come get me?"

"It just hit 30."

"What'd I say?"

Ben shrugged.

"SEALie, what's going on over there?" Larry asked.

SEAL looked up from an order and turned to see where Larry was pointing. "The futures?" he said. "That's trading. It's what they do."

The board printed a 29½.

"Then what's that?"

"Can't be," RGB said. "The 30 bid is for 30. We haven't been through 30 in weeks."

"Take it down then!" Larry pointed at Ben, trying to get him to make the ring clerks take down the print. Ben changed his quote to 9½ big at 0½.

SEAL shook his head. "This is The Range. If we go through here we're fucked."

"Look at the gold, though," RGB said. He pointed to their right. "Look at those guys—down a frigging dollar and trading strong."

He was right. The gold ring looked like a pack of wild dogs going after a downed wildebeest.

Paper came in asking for a quote on the August 30 calls but Larry couldn't even look at his sheets. He watched Ben make markets, showing 0's bid at 1's again.

"That's right," Larry said. "Now that's more like it." No one responded. They were all selling 30 puts and selling futures. "Hell," Larry said. He signaled to buy another five.

"You're doubling up?" The look on Ben's face was enough that Larry didn't even need to read his lips.

"Fuck me!" Larry hit his pad against his chest. Buy five. Total of five. Check up.

Ben leaned toward DOC and DOC carried out the order. Ben punched a ticket in the clock and stuffed it inside his jacket. Filled, he signed.

Check up. Where'd I get filled?

Paid ½ for five.

Good. That was a good level. If he bought lows five times and they bounced back then the whole thing would work out. Even if he broke even on the 2½'s and the 3's, he'd win on the 0½'s really big. 30 had to be The Level.

How is it?

0½ bid at 1½.

Good. 30 was The Level and he was right. He couldn't even see MAZA in the ring anymore and he was right. It took balls but he was right to double up against a thirteen hundred dollar loser. Who said he couldn't be a Big Swinging Dick? Fuck these futures pussies.

Ben came over to get a card but Larry had nothing, no trades done in the options.

"10:30," Ben said. "Time to run one."

"No," Larry said. "No analyzer." if Chicago saw him trading futures, he wouldn't make it to lunchtime.

Ben started to walk away but Larry caught him by the shoulder and spun him around. He pushed his face right up in Ben's. "Did you hear me? You forgot to run the morning analyzer today. Is that right?"

"Whatever you say, boss. As long as you know what you're doing."

Ben needed a shave and it was clear he'd been drinking the night before by the smell on him.

Ben pulled away from Larry and stepped back into the aisle between the two rings. "Right," he said. "No analyzer."

"Good." Larry ripped off his blank card and then slapped Ben on the cheek, not as lightly as before. "Now go up there and tell me how's the market."

Larry went back to his spot and when he turned he saw Ben standing where he was supposed to be, quoting like he was supposed to.

0 bid at 1, he signed.

That was how it was supposed to go: Larry made the decisions, Larry ran the show, Ben quoted the market and relayed Larry's orders to DOC. It was a system. The system did not involve Ben questioning Larry. Larry rolled his neck around his shoulders until he got a good pop.

"Oh, we're going!" SEAL yelled.

Larry could hear the gold ring get louder. He looked over and saw the frenzy the pit had become. The board was printing new lows.

How is it?

0 bid.

"Gold's hitting sell stops," SEAL said. "Here we go!"

Where's the offer?

At 0½.

Larry watched Ben's hand quote the market and tried to shut out all the noise around him, like he'd done as a diver in the Missouri State meet when he was a senior competing for the Nationals. 29 bid at 30.

At 29 now. Ben's hand kept moving. 8 bid with the back of his hand, at 9 with the palm. He flicked his wrist and showed both sides. 7 bid at 9. Then at 8. The sound of the futures was an empty roar without numbers but Larry could see Ben's quotes and the prints on the board. He saw it print 27½. Sell stops were getting elected; people were dumping their longs at their worst-case loss-level and selling out. But Larry wouldn't sell. He alone had faith in his beliefs and the fact that things would go well. He clenched the silver dollar into his palm and closed his eyes.

RGB called for a market in the 32 put and SEAL wanted the 34-37 Butterfly and EGON asked for the 30-35 call spread. There was a 27 print on the board. RGB asked for markets in the 30 put and the 25 call.

DOC's voice stood out above the others and he could hear the man sounding his 6-bid. "At seven," someone yelled.

Someone was poking Larry in the arm. "Sell ten?" Ben said, leaning in between RGB and EGON. He looked worried. "I know this is your last day but what the hell are you doing with the futures? We're hitting sell-stops and you're holding naked longs."

"No," Larry said. "It can't go like this. It'll come back for us. It always does. Then we'll get out of it later."

"I think we need to get out of it now."

Larry grabbed Ben's shirt again and pulled him close.

"You don't think," Larry said, trying to spit as he yelled. "You're the clerk. Now go back and quote me some futures." He pushed Ben back away from the pit and a few of the locals howled, cheered him on for abusing his clerk. Nothing on the floor was lower than an options clerk.

The market had to come back, and it would. If Larry got caught losing this much in the futures on his last day, it'd be grounds for going to mediation with Weintraub and the floor. It'd become his responsibility and he'd start his new job with a nice hefty debt Weintraub and a fine probably as well. That wasn't going to happen. If he could hide the trade until the futures came back up above 30, he'd be fine. He knew it would happen.

The market grew even louder now, and the big board was printing 25's and 26's. Larry had bought 33's, 32½'s, and five 30½'s. If he sold now, it'd make two lots for 16 tics, three for 15, and five for 11, *if he could sell 25's.* At 25 dollars a tic that made it—32 tics and 45 tics and 55 tics were over a hundred ticks: 132 ticks. 132 times $25 dollars was? Larry pulled out his pocket calculator: times $25—$3,300! A thirty-three-hundred dollar loser! Larry closed his eyes.

All around him he heard the roar of the markets, people yelling for their livelihood: making markets and executing trades. He made out DOC's voice and GIL's and, somewhere, MAZA's were apparent. Next to him RGB called for puts and SEAL was still selling his spread.

Larry cupped his hands over his ears. The blood pumped in his body like a metronome beating out his pulse—a steady beat that was so different from the naked mayhem and chaos of the markets. He thought back to Iowa growing up. Waking early in the cold winters to go to school. The cows, his parents' farm. He thought of the swim team and the debate club, how happy he felt when he'd been accepted to Columbia. His heartbeat pounded inside his head, and as he took a deep breath he knew he was alive. He opened his eyes.

The artery bulged in MAZA's neck and another stood out on his forehead. DOC was waving his arms and his hair stood out wet with sweat below his bald spot. It stood out around the circle of skin like a child's drawing of the sun. Next to DOC, Ben was gone.

Larry looked around the futures but he couldn't see his clerk. He waved his hand in the air, calling for a market, but no one answered. The other clerks quoted it 21 bid at 23. Larry called Ben's name out loud. He wondered if anyone could hear him in all the noise. He called again.

Then he saw Ben standing in the middle of the Crude options pit with ALD. Ben was pointing to the silver futures big board and Larry's card of trades for the day. Soon it would all be over. He just hoped that Ben had managed to sell off 25's before he left his post.

Survivor
Kelli Stanley

Gordon Grazier shoved aside the large platter of untouched Eggs Benedict. He caught eyes with a willowy blonde holding three orders of pancakes and crooked his finger, eyebrows lowered. She distributed the dishes, smiling weakly at a family of tourists, and slouched toward Gordon's booth.

"Yes sir? What can I do for you?"

She sounded Russian or Polish...some Slavic intonation. Gordon looked her up and down. Tits weren't big enough to bother with.

"These eggs aren't cooked."

"I'm so sorry, sir, I'll tell your waitress—"

"My shit-faced waitress disappeared. You fix the fucking eggs."

"Sir, there's no need to use profanity, I'd be happy—"

"You want profanity? These eggs are the fucking profanity. You know who I am?"

She nodded, already tired of the fight, scanning the room for the brunette who belonged to the section, the one who'd suffered the misfortune of taking his order. Gordon dug his back against the seat, pointing a long, hairy finger at his empty coffee cup.

"This over-priced dump's got the worst service in New York. Get me some cooked eggs and coffee if you want to keep your miserable fucking job."

The blonde woman stared at him, pale blue eyes unemotional. She lifted up the platter, walked back to the kitchen. A middle-aged Latino, thick around the middle, appeared at the booth and refilled the coffee, steam rising from the white stoneware mug.

Gordon licked the dry skin on his lips, tasting salt. Pulled out his Blackberry.

8:18. The fucker said he'd be here at 8:00.

He glanced at the brown leather briefcase beside him. His practiced fingers ran over the phone. Email, voice mail, market ticker.

A whiny text from his ex-wife about the fucking Swiss boarding school. News from Roger on another interest rate hike. Sylvia, she of the tits worth bothering about, though the bitch wouldn't give him the time of day—Sylvia and the report on the grace period lobby effort in California. Fucking Barbara Boxer and her fucking consumer protection shit. And then there were those unwashed moron losers dogging his path to work in the morning...he closed his eyes, envisioning himself holding an assault rifle and mowing them down in front of the bank. Occupy dirt, assholes.

Gordon sighed and sipped the coffee, ran a hand over the monogrammed briefcase as if to make sure it was still there.

In this world lived morons and smart people, the leaders and the led, those who ate and those who starved. Science, simple science, Darwin in action, just like those Darwin awards they gave every year. Did the deer get fucking protection from the wolves? Did anyone hold a gun on the morons in middle America to open up a credit card account with 30% interest?

He pocketed the smart phone, picked up the mug again. Opened his briefcase, shook out a Vicodin and an Ativan, popped the pills with another swig of coffee. The blonde waitress was finally threading through the crowded floor with a new order of eggs.

He grunted at her, picked up a fork.

"Get the spic back over here with coffee."

She straightened her back, marched away like a Russian soldier-woman.

Gordon mopped the pieces of poached egg and English muffin in the Hollandaise sauce and shoved them in his mouth, eyes on the door, endless stream of mid-town Manhattan traffic pouring from Grand Central Terminal.

So he was nervous. So he'd never been blackmailed before. That Josh bastard at Club Marquis had bent over for him like a fucking queer, no worries, she's a snatch and grab, fresh meat, saved just for him.

Gordon closed his eyes, retracing the night, five, no six weeks ago. No fucking Viagra, not then, and this one lasted until the next morning, until he grew tired, spent, and Josh had promised to dump her in the park. No worries, Mr. Grazier, he'd smiled, clutching an extra five Gs for the trouble.

Trouble. Josh had run scared, away from the Club, but Gordon would trace him, take care of him. Goddamn meth head.

Because someone found out. Someone found him.

Gordon ran his hands over his briefcase again. The blackmailer didn't know who he was dealing with. Gordon Grazier, top dog, number one man, wunderkind of the new economy.

He'd worked his way up from the fucking mail room, passing Series 7 and his first job on the floor, earning his M.B.A. at night school, then finally his J.D. and the move to the top floor, the center of the bank.

Center of the fucking world.

He'd taken them down, one by one. Bill, Andy, Margot, Taylor—whoever stood in his way, until his way was clear, and he was where he was born to be.

Top floor center.

Survivor.

A skinny man in a faded blue jean jacket and Lee jeans slid into the seat across from Gordon. He was wearing sunglasses, even though the early morning autumn light was pale and weak, filtered through glass canyons and the red-orange shadows of ancient brick. His hair was dark gray, skin a deep, almost yellow tan, gray stubble carpeting his chin and neck. He smiled like a Sunday School teacher.

The thin man kept both hands in the pockets of the jacket. He murmured: "You've got the cash, Mr. Grazier?"

Gordon stared at him. It excited him in a way, excited him more than the sex he'd been buying. Even the underage whores usually lasted only a few seconds, novelty fading along with his hard-on. But this...this was danger, the kind he hadn't felt in a long time. A challenge.

The Latino with the coffee appeared and refilled his mug. Gordon glanced up at him.

"Get me my check."

The man with the glasses moved one of the hands in his pockets. His voice was soft.

"Couple of things, Mr. Grazier. My finger is resting on the trigger of a gun. I know how to use it. If you do or say anything I haven't told you to do or say, I'll kill you. I don't care if I die. I fully expect to go violently, in fact, most likely at the hands of law enforcement." He bent forward over the table, elbows akimbo, hands in his pocket, right hand moving slightly.

"Please remember, Mr. Grazier. I'm not bluffing."

Gordon shivered, the thick hair on his arms standing up and rubbing against the pale pink cotton blend of his Tom Ford shirt. Life in high-definition, slow motion action, that sensation of excitement he hadn't felt since his first big killing on the market, the insider tip he never told Bill about, the killing he made and Bill's face when the securities commission agents knocked on his door.

Bye-bye, Bill.

He'd bought his first Porsche with the money. He remembered the smell of Bill's old office, cigarettes and aftershave, putting his feet up on the desk. He remembered how the blonde with big tits sucked his cock like a lollipop, until he tired of her and palmed her off on Tony on the 15th floor.

Life was good then.

He tried to find the eyes behind the glasses. Too dark. The thin blonde arrived with the check. He ignored it. Opened his wallet, threw a twenty on the table, stood up.

The man with the glasses stood up, too, and said in a low voice: "Walk out with me, just a little ahead. Turn left toward 40th."

Gordon stretched, smirked at the man in glasses. Some bozo with a complex, one of the morons he'd spent a lifetime taking down. For now, he'd play along, enjoy the thrill. And when the time was right, he'd trip the fucker or even get his knuckles dirty and punch him in the face. Then he'd grab the gun and get the evidence, and then he'd make a couple of phone calls and make the prick disappear.

Too bad he couldn't get his own reality TV show.

Sometimes he really resented his anonymity.

He pushed past the other patrons in the crowded restaurant, swinging the briefcase, the man in the sunglasses on his elbow. Shoved open the thick door and hit the wall of New York noise, a man from the Ivory Coast trying to sell tour tickets, an Indian hawking the *Times*. Shoe-shine stand full of middle-aged men smoking cigars, sidewalk cigarette smoke thicker than Chanel No. Five.

Gordon turned left. The man in the jean jacket was taller but not in the kind of shape he was in. He'd kept himself fit, plenty of racquetball and tennis and golf. Some of his best tips came through the racquetball courts at the club.

The man in the jacket nudged him. "Go inside the Quik Park. Seventh floor."

They entered the low, dark building, following the faded "pedestrians only" lines on the cement floor. Gordon punched the elevator button, waiting beside a redhead drenched in gold and a 60ish businessman in Brooks Brothers. Everyone stepped into the elevator, smell of piss rising up like steam from the grates outside.

The blackmailer nudged him again, and his finger snaked out and hit seven. Gordon was glad he'd taken the Ativan. No panic attacks, not for him. He didn't need a fucking pill to control any situation, but he liked how it helped drown out nagging voices. Too bad it couldn't drown Jill and her fucking whiney-ass pleas for more money. Swiss fucking Boarding School...

He shook his head. First things first. Get the moron monkey off his back.

The brunette and the businessman got out on four. Gordon tried not to breathe in the acrid smell of piss, mulling over which mafia connection he'd call to dispose of the nuisance at his elbow. The smell was making the thrill wear off.

They stepped out. The taller man pressed behind him.

"White commercial truck, five rows to the left, fifteen cars down the middle."

Gordon walked slowly, pulse racing, body tensed, sound of their footsteps echoing around the cement pillars and quietly waiting cars. He ran a hand over his thinning brown hair. Jumped slightly when the lights flickered on in a truck ahead and the horn made a 'beep-beep' sound. It was a cutaway van cab, commercial class. Green graffiti scrawled over the white container.

The man behind him said: "Go to the back and open it."

Gordon hesitated, stepped to the rear of the truck, balancing the briefcase in his hand. No fucking way was he going to get in the back of a truck with some fucking nutcase. Blackmail was one thing, kidnapping something else. He turned around.

"Take the fucking money."

The man with the sunglasses shook his head. "We've got to get someplace safe, Mr. Grazier. You need to get inside. Don't worry, there's water in there."

Gordon tried to see the eyes again, see past the straight-lipped, stoic line on the other man's face. He grimaced, the words hissing between his teeth.

"I'm not getting in the fucking truck. Take your money now or forget it."

They were on a row with a wall to their backs and empty cars to the right. Women's voices raised in greeting from the other side of the floor, no one nearby. The blackmailer sighed and withdrew a Glock 17 and showed it to Gordon, holding it in his right hand. His left hand stayed inside the pocket.

"Don't make me use this on you, Mr. Grazier. You'll be sorry later."

Gordon looked back and forth between the pistol and his adversary.

"Go ahead and shoot—somebody'll hear and call the cops. You already said you want to take me to some safe place which means you won't kill me. Your game's over. You're fucked, bozo. Fucked."

The man with the sunglasses nodded. His left hand jerked suddenly, and a loud siren shrieked from the truck, echo exploding through the garage.

Gordon grabbed at his ears and dropped the briefcase, mouth open, dizzy from the sound and shock. The gray haired man in blue jeans lowered the pistol and pulled the trigger. Gordon felt himself flopping backwards, spine hitting the steel bumper of the truck. He crumpled to the floor, clutching at his leg, blood between his fingers, mouth still open and mewing, saliva dripping from the corners.

The siren hit the walls of his brain, around and around, and he thought he heard sobbing and the sound of a truck door scraping open.

The last thing he remembered was being hoisted up and shoved inside a dark, warm place. Then the scraping again and finally the siren stopped, and it was dark and warm and he fell asleep.

* * *

Daniel pulled off I-80 at 153, heading for the Moshannon State Forest. He could circle back down and refill in DuBois, white truck and green graffiti invisible in the east and west bound traffic rushing through Pennsylvania, searching for a job, a home, a safe place to raise kids.

Like the Joads, he thought.

Rebecca would have quoted from the book. All he could remember was the movie with Henry Fonda.

He hit the accelerator, careful to keep just under the speed limit, and rolled down the car windows a few inches, enough to catch the smell of sun on hickory and beech. Dappled green, warm, mild day for October.

Cherry trees, birch trees, chestnuts, all rushing past the window, small byways winding toward Parker Dam State Park, white-tailed deer and wild turkey, beavers gnawing the conifers. Fresh cool scent of water from Parker Lake, kids digging in the beach, chasing each other while the blonde lady watched, smiling, her husband at the grill.

Daniel turned off on Mud Run Road. Exactly three cars had passed him going south, and one car was behind him. It continued on 153, and he breathed out, wiping his forehead with the back of his hand. He eased the truck into a pull-out and sat staring out the window, hands still on the wheel.

A year's worth of work, finally over. The execution took nearly a month by itself.

Last one, last one.

Rebecca would be mad at him, he knew, for going underground, for disappearing, for stopping the treatments, for doing what he did. But he had no choice. They'd never had kids, and this was his legacy. To her. To America.

Daniel took off his sunglasses and stared ahead, eyes unfocused, windshield dusty and stained with the crushed bodies of insects. He sat unblinking in the sharp light of the autumn sun, his skin creased and wrinkled, his cheeks sunken and prematurely old.

Her face shimmered with the light in the trees, blonde hair sun-yellow, blue dress sky-blue.

"Soon," he whispered. "Soon."

* * *

Gordon woke to the smell of a Big Mac and an intense, throbbing ache in his right thigh. He opened an eye.

A dim fluorescent light from the ceiling made him blink rapidly. He was still in the back of the truck, a brown sleeping bag beside him along with a paper bag from McDonald's. He twisted his neck to the left. The man in the jean jacket was shooting him up with something.

Gordon watched, eyes wide, as the blackmailer slid the hypo into his arm. He tried to scream, to shout, but the gag in his mouth choked him, and his legs and wrists were bound with nylon rope.

"Don't worry, Mr. Grazier. This is just a painkiller and a sedative. I gave you a flesh wound."

Gordon tried to yell, to call him names, to shout, but the white cotton handkerchief in his mouth made him sound like the fucking Elephant Man, he, Gordon Grazier, King of the Put-down, Count of Profanity.

Top floor center...survivor.

Gordon closed his eyes and thought about surviving. About what he'd do to the fuckwad that shot him. About the pain the fucker would feel, and the pleasure, the intense pleasure, inflicting it would give him.

The thin man in the jacket spoke again. His eyes were watery blue.

"I'm going to slide the gag off so you can eat. I'll also untie the knot on your right arm. Your phone is back in the parking garage in New York, Mr. Grazier, so please don't try anything and make me shoot you again. It'll spoil everything."

Gordon twisted his neck around, checking his surroundings. His briefcase wasn't in the truck either. The bastard had both him and the money. He'd better act now, before the sedative kicked back in. He'd probably been doped since this morning, which was...how long ago?

The blackmailer crouched over him to untie the gag. Gordon eyed him, timing it, then suddenly shot upright with as much force as he could muster, his head slamming the thinner man in the lower jaw. A pair of false teeth and spit sprayed out, and the man in blue jeans fell backward, blood spewing from his mouth and nose.

Adrenalin kicked in for Gordon now, and he inched his way down the bed of the truck toward his kidnapper, thigh and buttocks muscles tensing despite the pain, heels digging into the truck floor and propelling him forward. The shoe rubber made a repetitious, high-pitched squeal against the truck bed.

Squeel-lunk. Sqeel-lunk.

The crazy fucker was dazed, blood drenching half his face, eyeglasses dangling off one ear. Gordon was sweating. He wriggled toward the pocket with the gun and heaved himself into a sitting position with a groan. His long fingers inched closer toward the goal.

Then the other man moaned and slid away from him, the soft cotton fibers just out of his grasp along with the Glock. Gordon froze. The other man was breathing hard, coughing.

"Why—why'd you have to do that, Mr. Grazier? Now we're going to be late, and that's not fair to the others."

Others?

Gordon's pulse pounded against his skull, still throbbing from the head-butt. What the fuck kind of crazy was he dealing with?

The kidnapper sighed, breath rattling. Small groans peppered his movements as he groped for the false teeth and found them, inserting them with a couple of clacks.

"All right, Mr. Grazier. I'll still take off the gag, because the truck is soundproofed. But you'll have to eat the hamburger off the floor, because I obviously can't trust you to follow my instructions."

Gordon felt the man's warm breath on the back of his head. The gag loosened, and he started to spit it out. The kidnapper reached an arm around to the front of Gordon's face and pulled down the rolled up white cotton to his neck. Gordon gulped the stale air, still humid with sweat and blood.

"I'll leave this Big Mac unwrapped. You'll have to scoot yourself backward and eat it on the floor. There's blood on it, but that can't be helped."

Gordon started to hunch himself backward like a worm. Maybe if he ate something, he'd figure out what to do. Figure out how to kill the motherfucker and get out.

Squeel-lunk. Sqeel-lunk.

The blackmailer pulled himself up to his feet.

"I can't give you water, either. You really messed things up."

Gordon blinked repeatedly, licking his paper-dry lips. His voice was a croak.

"You got the money. Why're you doing this? You want more?"

There was blood on the bastard's boots. Maybe he'd overlook it, and someone would ask questions. Fuck, Gordon thought, I'm depending on other people. Strangers. His body was starting to shut down, the sedative kicking in. He struggled to keep his eyes open.

The blackmailer's voice sounded like sand paper rubbing wood, far away on a carpenter's bench.

"You wouldn't understand, Mr. Grazier. You didn't know Rebecca."

He bent down to pick up a first aid kit. Gordon tried again, the truck dimensions bending and curling around him.

"Maybe I did. Maybe I did know her. Maybe I know you. What's your name?"

The blackmailer stared down at him in silence. His voice, when he finally used it, heavy and sad.

"My name is Daniel. Go to sleep, Mr. Grazier. We have another few hours ahead."

* * *

Daniel pulled over after Ann Arbor, gas tank full from a fill-up at a Phillips 66. Took the 9 Mile Road road off 23 and drove around Whitmore Lake, finally coming to a rest at Lakeview cemetery. It was dark, and the moths danced hysterically in the truck beams until he felt sorry for them and shut off the headlights.

Frogs from the water, a couple of dogs barking in the distance.

Too late for fireflies.

He opened another McDonald's bag and bit into a cold Big Mac. Twisted the cap off the bottle of water and washed down the meat and bread. Leaned over Gordon's briefcase to reach the glove compartment and flopped down the lid, plucking out an orange prescription bottle. Straightened up with a wince, read the label under the cab light.

His hands shook as he pushed and twisted the cap, pouring out two of the pills. He threw both of them to the back of his throat, washing them down with the rest of the Dasani water.

Daniel breathed in and out, in and out, while the tears pooled under his eyes and ran in rivulets down his cheek. He curled forward, prying out the wallet in his back pocket. Caressed the worn, faded leather, and opened it to the center.

Photo of a blonde woman in her fifties, plump but fit, wearing fishing gear.

Rebecca.

The thought came in a stuttered sob, washing him in tears that never subsided, a misery never broken, and they dripped down the jean jacket and blue works shirt while his narrow shoulders hunched and he cried and he cried.

And remembered.

Remembered when she told him the news, remembered the shock and despair and anger, then the determination to fight.

Remembered the insurance letter cutting off her coverage, and the doctor with kind eyes who helped them apply for Medicare.

But it wasn't enough. It was never enough. And he remembered how the jobs had been sent to China and Korea and India, and how everyone was leaving home, and he'd had faith, then, he'd believed in America, believed in the American Dream. He was a good man, Daniel, and a good worker, his wife was the smart one, fifth grade teacher, thank God for their union coverage.

He remembered how they fought and how it wasn't enough. Because then he got sick and ran out of benefits.

That's when they turned to the credit cards.

How proud they'd been of their credit. Gold American Express cards and Platinum Visas and Rebecca was smart, she never fell into the game of big screen televisions and new lawnmowers.

No. The credit was saved, and they used it for him. And still it wasn't enough, but she was hanging on, Rebecca was, a tough Michigan lady. He'd sing "Saginaw, Michigan" for her and make her laugh, even when she wasn't strong enough.

But then the downturn happened, what all the news people called a recession. Hell, they'd lived with recession for years in Freeland, Michigan.

This was different, though. The interest rates went way up, and all the grace periods were gone.

They changed the rules.

It was their game.

He traced the lines of his wife's face with a bent finger.

The medicine was starting to work now, and he felt strong enough to go on, to finish the job.

He hoped she wouldn't be too angry with him.

* * *

The light hurt Gordon's eyes. He blinked rapidly, tried to speak but felt the gag in his mouth again. The crazy fucker was standing over him with a flashlight.

"Try to stand up, Mr. Grazier. I've cut the ropes. I warn you again, and please believe me: if you try anything, I'll shoot you, and this time I will kill you."

The dope made Gordon too sluggish for fear, but he believed the man in the thick eyeglasses and jeans. He rolled over on his face and grunted, pulled himself up slowly, his right leg stiff and painful and swollen. Beads of sweat poured from his forehead, neck and scalp.

The blackmailer's voice sounded encouraging. "You need to get your circulation going. Stand up when you can. There's a ladder down the back. I want you to climb it and wait."

The words were muffled and strange, but Gordon managed to stand, and he tottered toward the open darkness. The light from the bed carried to the edge of the bumper, and he saw a two-step ladder propped against the edge.

A dark, wet smell blew into the truck, like fresh-churned soil. The cool air hit the sweat on his skin, and Gordon shivered, shaking off some of the drug. He opened his eyes wide and craned his stiff neck back toward his assailant. As if in reply, the kidnapper said: "We're by Skidway Lake, in Michigan."

Michigan? No fucking wonder. Yankee fucking hillbillies, crying over the car companies and the layoffs. Bile rose in Gordon's throat. Shot or not, no assembly line moron sobbing about the fucking rust belt was going to take him out. No Occupy Wall Street hippie, no fucking moron from Middle America.

He was a survivor.

He stretched, the pain helping him focus, and he hobbled down the ladder until his feet touched soil, securely under him. The kidnapper climbed down facing Gordon, the Glock in his right hand, the flashlight in his left.

Gordon made guttural noises through the gag. The thin man spoke quietly. "I'll remove your gag in a few minutes."

He pointed the flashlight ahead to a small cabin. Gordon could hear the sound of lapping water, the croak and hum of frogs and insects. Daniel spoke again, voice soft.

"Walk up to the door of the cabin."

Gordon's deerskin Prada loafers slid on the damp soil, but he righted himself, making a strangled noise in his chest. He groped in the thick, humid air for support, his hands finally hitting the rough wood of building.

Daniel gestured with the light. "Go ahead. I already unlocked it."

Gotta play for time, Gordon thought. Crazy fucking bastard. His head was on fire, and he stopped to wipe the sweat out of his eyes. Daniel waited patiently. Gordon finally turned the old steel knob.

Daniel pushed him forward a few more feet, Gordon almost falling, and pulled the door shut behind him.

Clack.

Gordon lowered his head and charged the other man, knocking him down on the dirty wooden floor, felt his bladder empty at the rush, urine running down his leg. The flashlight fell out of Daniel's hands and rolled away with a grinding sound. Gordon grunted and grappled with his kidnapper, his forty pounds of extra fat and muscle finally paying off against the older, thinner, kidnapper.

Fucking Michigan fucking hillbilly, thought Gordon, he's gonna pay, he's gonna pay, 'cause I'll do him myself...

Daniel couldn't see, couldn't breathe, the heavier man on top of him, groping for the gun.

Then Rebecca's face, and a soft breeze caressed his cheek, a soft touch guiding his hand to the wound in Gordon's leg.

Daniel reached up with three extended fingers and dug them in as far as he could.

Gordon screamed through the gag, grabbing for his leg with his right hand, lifting weight off Daniel and allowing him to slide away and pull out the Glock.

He heard Daniel ready the pistol, breath coming in gasps. Gordon rolled over on his back, rocking back and forth, wound bleeding again, sweat pouring down his face, the piss cold and wet and sticky against his skin.

The flashlight fell on his contorted face. Daniel stood in front of him, blood flowing again from his mouth. He reached toward the back of Gordon's head and untied the gag.

On the floor, and quieter now, Gordon felt thumping through the wood, heard a dim, distant noise. He yanked the gag down, still breathing hard. Looked up at Daniel, voice a rasp and for the first time...fearful.

"What the fuck do you want from me?"

"Justice, Mr. Grazier."

Gordon shook his head. "You one of those bank haters blocking traffic? You think Wall Street's fucked you in the ass? What have I ever done to you?"

The flashlight shone steadily on Gordon's face, until he had to raise an arm to shield his eyes.

Daniel's voice was low and resonant. "You killed my wife."

Gordon tried to stand up, tried to reason. He wasn't used to reasoning with people.

"Listen, uh, whatever you said your name was—"

"Daniel."

"Yeah, OK, whatever. Daniel. I don't know who you are and I never met your wife, but whatever your, uh, your problem is, I'm sure we can work it out, you know what I mean? I mean I got a lot more money, got some in Swiss accounts. Name your price, OK? I just want to walk away. That's all I want, to walk away—"

"It's time, Mr. Grazier. I told you we were going to be late."

"Late for what? Listen, maybe you got me mixed up with somebody else, and I don't know anything about your wife and I sure as hell don't know how you found out about the Club Marquis, but I mean it—I'll give you the numbers, you let me walk. OK?"

Daniel waved the gun in the air. "It was easy to find out about, Mr. Grazier. You don't feel guilty, so you don't try to hide. A young girl, a child. She lived, just barely, but she's alive. She'll need your money, and I'll make sure she gets it. But it's time, like I said. Walk toward the middle of the floor." This time he waved the flashlight.

The room felt large, a little dusty, and as close and shut tight as a tank. Gordon limped into the dark space, caught glimpses of windows boarded up from the inside, two by fours and sheet metal.

"Go sit against the wall—over there. Face me and keep your hands up." The flashlight illuminated one of the boarded up casements.

Gordon slowly turned toward Daniel, who stood in the middle of the floor. He grimaced, a moan escaping his lips, as he slid down into a sitting position.

"Hands up, Mr. Grazier."

Gordon raised his hands above his head.

Daniel knelt down by the edge of a thick, dirty rug, the gray industrial type. He flipped up the mat to reveal a thin open line in the scarred wood, with a padlock and bolt in place on a trap door. He reached into a pocket and pulled out a set of keys on a Ford keychain, then placed the flashlight on the floor, aiming it at Gordon's legs. With two hands, he jerked open the padlock. Gordon didn't move.

Daniel lifted the door up with a handle, and walked it backwards, lowering it to the rug. His eyes flicked toward Gordon every other second.

Finally, he picked up the flashlight and gestured with it toward the dark hole in the middle of the floor.

"Climb down, Mr. Grazier."

Gordon was getting dizzy. Sweat dripped in his eyes, and he blinked. Fever from the fucking bullet in his leg. He'd have to see where the crazy one was going. Fight him one more time, last stand.

"You got any water?"

Daniel shook his head. "I told you, we're late. There's water downstairs."

Gordon limped toward the trap door as Daniel backed away. "I can't see anything."

"A light will come on automatically."

Gordon started to walk down the ladder, facing the room and Daniel. He led with his left leg, but once his right leg slipped and he yelped until he steadied himself with his arms. As if in response, he heard the same muffled noise from earlier, a little louder. He descended five more steps and a light clicked on from below.

He reached the bottom and turned around. The basement was damp and larger than the shack on top, about 1,000 square feet. It was divided in half by a wall with a scratched metal door in the middle. It looked like some kind of building, riveted together with layers of sheet metal and thick pieces of wood over a concrete foundation. An odor of excrement and urine rose on damp air.

There were sounds coming from behind the wall.

Gordon turned wide eyes toward Daniel, who was stepping down the stair-ladder facing him. The portable flashlight was upstairs, and Daniel gripped the back of the ladder with his left hand, the Glock in his right.

"Move aside, Mr. Grazier. Toward the door. That's it."

Gordon felt a growing, crawling horror as he limped toward the metal door and heavy wall, the basement spinning, sweat drip-drop, drip-drop in his eyes.

"That's it, Mr. Grazier. Stand in place. You can brace yourself if you're too dizzy. I told you I didn't want to shoot you, that it wouldn't be fair, but you left me with no choice."

Blood was still dripping above Daniel's right eyebrow. He wiped it away with the arm of his jacket and pulled out his keys again. The metal door was scratched and orange with rust, covered with two heavy padlocks and a chain.

Daniel unlocked each one, checking afterward to make sure that Gordon was resting against the sheet metal of the wall and not tensed and ready. He'd been hurt far too much collecting him, but Gordon was the last, the final piece. The jewel in the crown, Rebecca would say. She always liked the British stuff.

Daniel slid off the locks and opened the door. A fetid smell, wet earth mixed with algae, sweat, piss and excrement, rushed into the basement, nearly gagging Gordon. He coughed.

Daniel flicked a light switch and a blurry, pale yellow slice cut into the darkness. There was a scurrying sound, then a shout and a hoarse yell.

"Police? Police?"

"It's not the police. They'd have identified themselves."

The answering voice was low and thick, the rumble of a fat man.

Daniel stepped back and hurriedly gestured toward Gordon to step through the opening. Gordon's feet obeyed, his fever playing mind tricks. That's what this is, he thought, Bill finally getting even, the stupid fuck. Gordon blinked, stumbled over concrete, choking on the bile in his throat. He was in.

Daniel pulled the door shut and leaned against it. The room was long, rectangular, with two bulbs hung on an electrical cord at each end of the room. A wooden barrel stood in one corner next to a nearly empty plastic gallon water jug, and torn McDonald's bags littered the concrete floor. On the opposite end was a portable toilet, spilling over with human waste, a couple of half-dead flies buzzing around the seat.

Gordon rubbed the sweat out of his eyes, still getting used to the dim light. The sheet metal walls were covered with that gray eggshell soundproofing stuff he'd seen in recording studios...all except one side. On it hung a large board, with a framed photo of a fat blonde and newspapers and other paperwork tacked up beside it. All the tacks were yellow.

He turned toward his left. Two men were staring at him. A forty-odd year old blond with matted hair, wearing a torn Dolce and

Gabbana suit, and a fat silver-haired man around sixty in dirty golfing clothes. They were sitting on the cement floor.

Daniel spoke to the two men on the floor, nodded toward Gordon.

"This is Mr. Gordon Grazier."

The blond wrinkled his forehead. "The banker? Used to be a big-time stock broker, right? I read about you in *Forbes*."

Gordon felt oddly gratified. If only the world would fucking stop spinning.

"Who are you?"

"His name is Scott Towson. He canceled our health insurance."

The blond was thin, twitchy, pale, scratches on his hands, fingernails bloody. Gordon became conscious of the piss on his legs again, blinked and tried to wake himself up.

Towson was pleading, voice raised to a scratch high-pitch. "I told you, Daniel, that was not my doing, I'm really, really sorry about your wife, but it's not my fault—"

The fat silver haired man wheezed, spoke tiredly. "Save your breath, Towson. Won't do you any good. I've been here longer than you have."

Daniel turned toward Gordon, spoke conversationally. Gestured with the gun at the fat man.

"Robert Wheedleton. He moved my job to China. Lots of jobs."

Wheedleton ignored Gordon, peered up at Daniel.

"What's this one supposed to have done to you?"

Daniel was silent for a moment. Then his voice cracked, and he met the eyes of the fat man on the floor.

"He killed Rebecca."

Towson glanced at Wheedleton, his fingers and hands twitching and shaking. He hoisted himself up using the wall behind him. Wheedleton remained sprawled on the concrete, the mass of his body spread out like soft cheese.

The blond man bit his lip, tried again. "We've been reading about her, Daniel, while you were gone, until we ran out of matches and lighter fluid. I can help you. I know I can't bring her back, but if this man murdered her, why not just deal with him? Why not let us go? I told you I can get you all the money..."

Daniel's voice was quiet, the gun trembling but aimed at the man.

"Shut up, Mr. Towson."

The thin man sank down to sit next to Wheedleton. Their eyes followed Gordon, who was reading the cork board on the wall.

Obituary in newspaper. "Rebecca Atkins, 56, was found dead of a self-inflicted wound on October 7th. Mrs. Atkins was suffering from breast cancer, and it is believed that depression over this and the financial strain caused by her illness were responsible for her suicide. She is survived by her husband Daniel, who is currently undergoing treatments for prostate cancer…"

Letter. "We regret to inform you that your coverage will not extend to the drug recommended…"

Photograph. A man in a hard hat, smiling, rows of sheet metal behind him…

A small form, small type, barely legible, lots and lots of words. Something about Notice of Rate Change and Payment Information.

Gordon took a few halting steps toward Daniel. His mind felt surprisingly clear.

"You're going to kill us, aren't you?"

Daniel shook his head. "I'm not a killer. You three are, that's a fact. You killed my job, you killed my wife. You, Mr. Grazier, were the last hope we had. You're a bank. You're supposed to be like Jimmy Stewart at Bailey's Savings and Loan, you're supposed to help people get on their feet. You hold the money and you make a fair profit. But after the bailout, you kept changing the rules. You took the money and didn't pass it on. You just wanted more."

His voice broke, but the gun was steady in his hand.

"Rebecca couldn't handle it. Couldn't keep fighting."

He gestured toward the barrel in the corner, addressed it to Wheedleton.

"You still got water?"

Towson spoke eagerly. "We've got water, yes, thank you, Daniel, but we need food, we ran out of the hamburgers about two days ago, and I'm sure you don't really want to kill us, so if you just tell me how much money you need—"

"I don't want money, Mr. Towson. I told you that already."

Daniel began backing toward the ladder. He spoke to Gordon but didn't look at him.

"Join the others, Mr. Grazier. Sorry about the gunshot, I told you it wouldn't be as fair as I wanted it."

The metal room was spinning again, lines of motion blending with the photo of the blonde woman and the two men huddled in the corner. Sweat poured down Gordon's cheeks, and he stumbled into the wall.

"What's your game, Atkins?" Wheedleton's voice was slow and furred. "Starve us to death?"

Daniel reached the edge of the door and turned to look at the men, at the photographs and paper and letters and pamphlets and promises on the wall.

His tone was soft and measured.

"You know, I got to thinking about what you've been doing. To me, to Rebecca. To a lot of people. You all believe it's a dog-eat-dog world, and top dog wins the race. Top dog lives. So you devour people like me and Rebecca."

The blond Towson, breathing heavily, chattered again, desperation making his voice higher. "Anything you want, Daniel, anything at all, just please remember, I tried to help your wife, I tried—"

Wheedleton smacked him with a heavy arm. "Shut up." The silver-haired man looked up at Daniel, asked again: "What's your game?"

Daniel studied each of them in turn, the fat Wheedleton in golf shoes and dirty Polo shirt, the thin, red-nosed Towson, the feverish, balding Grazier.

"I figure I'll leave the lights on, should make it easier for you. You got plenty of water, and somewhere in this room is a hunting knife. You could last, maybe, until somebody catches up with me. At least one of you could last that long."

He glanced at Gordon. "Sorry again, Mr. Grazier. I thought you'd have the best chance of anybody."

Daniel's hand was on the door. He crossed himself and said: "Let justice be done." Then he swung it shut.

The others heard the sounds of the locks clicking into place.

Gordon felt the others' eyes fall upon his leg.

Him, top center, top dog.

Survivor.

He screamed.

* * *

Daniel burned the jean jacket in an outdoor campground off I-80. He'd cleaned the boots, no sense in getting rid of them.

Daniel wiped the sweat off his head, and turned on the FM music station. "Take Me Home, Country Road" was playing. He'd always liked John Denver. Rebecca used to love him.

He smiled at the photo in his wallet, laying open on the seat beside him, and picked up the map. The money in Gordon's suitcase would last awhile, even after he took care of the girl. Long enough to find another place, maybe, build another bunker.

Washington, D.C. was only ten hours away.
Take Me Home, Country Roads...

CONTRIBUTORS

David Corbett
David Corbett is the author of four novels: The Devil's Redhead, Done for a Dime (a New York Times Notable Book), Blood of Paradise (nominated for numerous awards, including the Edgar), and Do They Know I'm Running (Spinetingler Award, Best Novel—Rising Star Category 2011). David's short fiction and poetry have appeared in numerous magazines and anthologies, with two stories selected for Best American Mystery Stories (2009 and 2011). Mysterious Press/Open Road Media will re-issue his first two novels plus a story collection in May 2012, and Penguin will publish his book on the craft of characterization in early 2013. http://www.davidcorbett.com

Tyler Dilts
Tyler Dilts received his MFA from California State University, Long Beach, where he now teaches. His writing has appeared in The Los Angeles Times, The Chronicle of Higher Education, The Best American Mystery Stories, and in numerous other publications. He is the author of the novels *A King of Infinite Space* and *The Pain Scale*, both featuring Long Beach Homicide detective Danny Beckett.

Travis Richardson
Travis Richardson was born in Germany, raised in Oklahoma, and currently lives in Los Angeles. He has worked over 20 jobs in fields ranging from hot dog vending to television post production to university fundraising. He is editing his first mystery novel, *The Prodigal Detective*, and has signed a contract for a novella and will have a short story coming out in May 2012 in the anthology *A House With Many Rooms*. He also writes screenplays and directs short movies. Find out more at http://tsrichardson.com.

Reed Farrel Coleman

Called a hard-boiled poet by NPR's Maureen Corrigan and the noir poet laureate in the Huffington Post, Reed Farrel Coleman has published fourteen novels. He is the three-time recipient of the Shamus Award for Best PI Novel of the Year and is also a two-time Edgar Award nominee. He has also won the Macavity, Barry, and Anthony Awards. Reed is an adjunct professor at Hofstra University, and lives with his family on Long Island. http://www.reedcoleman.com/

Eric Stone

Eric Stone worked for many years as a writer, reporter, photographer, editor and publisher in the U.S. and Asia, covering everything from economics to crime; politics to sex, drugs and rock & roll. He has traveled the world for both work and play, and lives in Los Angeles. He wrote the four Ray Sharp novels: *Shanghaied*, *Flight of the Hornbill*, *Grave Imports* and *The Living Room of the Dead*. They are set in Asia and based on stories that he covered as a journalist. He is also the author of the true crime/sports biography, *Wrong Side of the Wall.*

SJ Rozan

SJ Rozan, a life-long New Yorker, is the author of thirteen novels and three dozen short stories. She's an Edgar, Shamus, Anthony, Nero and Macavity winner, as well as a recipient of the Japanese Maltese Falcon award. SJ has been Guest of Honor at a number of fan conventions and in 2003 was an invited speaker at the World Economic Forum in Davos. She's served on the boards of Mystery Writers of America and Sisters in Crime, and as President of Private Eye Writers of America. She leads writing workshops and lectures widely. Her latest book is Ghost Hero. http://sjrozan.net/

Bob Truluck

Suspected pop-noirist and crime fiction writer Bob Truluck resides in Orlando, Florida where he writes and lives life to the fullest with his wife and ardent supporter, Leslie. Truluck has been nominated for some good stuff and has actually garnered a couple of nice looking awards. His *Street Level* and *Saw Red* in the Duncan Sloan series are considered, by some dubious authorities, to be modern cult-classics. His influences would include Raymond Chandler, Elmore Leonard, Charles Willeford, Nathan Heard and James Crumley, but not necessarily in that order. Bob has no favorite color or lucky number and will eat most anything but rutabaga.

Pamela Samuels Young

Pamela Samuels Young is a practicing attorney and the author of several award-winning legal thrillers. Pamela loves a good mystery and started writing because of a desire to see women and people of color depicted as savvy, hot shot attorneys in the legal thrillers she read. Her fast-paced legal dramas are known for their unexpected twists and their strong female characters, which earned her the label "John Grisham with a sister's twist." The Compton, California, native is a former television news writer who lives in the Los Angeles area. To read an excerpt of Pamela's legal thrillers, visit www.pamelasamuelsyoung.com.

Darrell James

Darrell James is a fiction writer living in Tucson, AZ. His short stories have appeared in numerous book anthologies and have garnered a number of awards, to include finalist in the 2009 Derringer Awards. His debut novel, *Nazareth Child* was recently published by Midnight Ink/Llewellyn Worldwide. His personal odyssey to publication appears in the Writer's Digest Book *How I Got Published*, with J.A. Jance, David Morrell, Clive Cussler, and other notable authors.

Brendan DuBois

Brendan DuBois is the award-winning author of more than 100 short stories and twelve novels, including his latest, Deadly Cove. His short fiction has appeared in Playboy, Ellery Queen's Mystery Magazine, Alfred Hitchcock's Mystery Magazine, The Magazine of Fantasy & Science Fiction, and numerous anthologies including The Best American Mystery Stories of the Century, published in 2000 by Houghton-Mifflin. His stories have twice won him the Shamus Award from the Private Eye Writers of America, and have also earned him three Edgar Allan Poe Award nominations from the Mystery Writers of America. One of his stories has recently been optioned by CBS for development as a television series. Visit his website at www.BrendanDuBois.com.

Lono Waiwaiole

The world's leading half-Hawaiian writer of crime fiction (read: only), Waiwaiole has published four noir novels, beginning with a finalist for an Anthony award for best first novel of 2003 for *Wiley's Lament*. He now lives in Portland, Oregon, where he teaches occasionally, coaches high-school basketball and writes sporadically. "Leverage" is his first short story.

Gary Phillips

Son of a mechanic and a librarian, *Scoundrels* editor Gary Phillips draws on his experiences as an inner city activist, union organizer to delivering dog cages in writing his tales of chicanery and malfeasance. Other current work includes on the 20th anniversary of the '92 L.A. riots, a re-issue of *Violent Spring* in e-book form, and "The Silencer Strikes," a retro '70s vigilante short story for bloodandtacos.com. He has won the Chester Himes award for his fiction and his website is: www.gdphillips.com.

Seth Harwood

Seth Harwood is the author of *This is Life* (Oct, 2011), *Young Junius* and *Jack Wakes Up*. His novels and short stories are available at iTunes, and http://sethharwood.com/, where readers can find his blog, contact him and buy special editions of his work. He lives in San Francisco and once worked on the commodities exchange in New York.

Kelli Stanley

Kelli Stanley lives in Hammett's San Francisco, where she pens noir thrillers, including the Miranda Corbie series, the first of which, City of Dragons, was nominated for a Los Angeles Times Book Award and a Shamus Award and won the Macavity for best historical mystery of the year. City of Secrets, the sequel, is nominated for an RT Book Reviews Reviewers Choice Award and the Golden Nugget Award. She's written two short stories featuring Miranda: "Children's Day", which was published in the International Thriller Writers best seller First Thrills, and "Memory Book", which is available as a stand-alone e-story. She writes a second series set in ancient Rome, the latest of which is The Curse-Maker. Nox Dormienda, her debut novel, won the Bruce Alexander Award, while her first short story, "Convivium" was shortlisted for a Spinetingler Award. She contributed to Shaken, the first e-book charity anthology, with a short story called "Coolie." "Survivor" marks her first contemporary-set work.

OTHER TITLES FROM DOWN AND OUT BOOKS

See www.DownAndOutBooks.com for complete list

By J.L. Abramo
Catching Water in a Net
Clutching at Straws
Counting to Infinity
Gravesend
Chasing Charlie Chan
Circling the Runway (*)

By Trey R. Barker
2,000 Miles to Open Road
Road Gig: A Novella
Exit Blood

By Richard Barre
The Innocents
Bearing Secrets
Christmas Stories
The Ghosts of Morning
Blackheart Highway
Burning Moon
Echo Bay
Lost (*)

By Milton T. Burton
Texas Noir

By Reed Farrel Coleman
The Brooklyn Rules

By Tom Crowley
Vipers Tail
Murder in the Slaughterhouse (*)

By Frank De Blase
Pine Box for a Pin-Up
Busted Valentines & Other Dark Delights (*)

By A.C. Frieden
Tranquility Denied
The Serpent's Game

By Jack Getze
Big Numbers
Big Money
Big Mojo (*)

By Keith Gilman
Bad Habits

By Jon & Ruth Jordan
Murder and Mayhem in Muskego (Editors)

By Bill Moody
Czechmate
The Man in Red Square

By Gary Phillips
The Perpetrators
Scoundrels (Editor)

By Lono Waiwaiole
Wiley's Lament
Wiley's Shuffle
Wiley's Refrain
Dark Paradise

(*) - Coming Soon